HERO WORSHIP

DARK URBAN RISING BOOK 2

S M HENLEY

HERO WORSHIP

Billy just wants to fit in. So, why does he insist he can fly?

For rich technomancer, Billy Nadig, life's a game: he lives in a cool East London penthouse, has a bedroom stocked with blond-haired lovelies, and an unhealthy obsession with women's shoes. But when Billy is told he's a Sleeper, awoken by Heaven to stop his best friend, Tazia—a half-vampire girl—make a decision that could destroy the world, even he realizes it's time to get serious.

Billy's agonizing transformation couldn't come at a worse time: demons are rising, evil angels take centre stage, and an indomitable mercenary continues to dog his every step. Saving the Earth will take both hard fighting and hard choices, maybe even the ultimate sacrifice —to kill his best friend. But if she dies, who will save Billy?

With his perfect hair and a slick line in chat, Billy says he's just trying to fit in. But in the second of the *Dark Urban Rising* trilogy, "fitting in" takes him to another level entirely. *Hero Worship* is a supernatural thriller set on the streets of modern-day London, Las Vegas, and Boston. It digs into the darkness, with not a small amount of blood and gritty humour.

Another book I'd like to dedicate to my mother but, hey, would you dedicate a book to your mum that starts with a butt-spanking scene? So, this one goes to my sister who has lived with these characters almost as long as I have, and who I know can cope with a little colourful description. Hers has been a continual voice of encouragement.

Soon, mum, soon.

THE IMPOSSIBLE GIRL

THE STEADY SLAP of polished wood against bare skin should've been doing the trick. It wasn't. Bloody hell, he was even boring himself. Billy picked up the pace—*thwack, thwack, thwack*—more for curiosity than pleasure.

Momentarily, the flesh tensed before settling again into softness. Knees and hands remained rigidly planted on the bed, and a toss of long blonde hair indicated he should continue.

Under the action of the paddle, a vivid red splotch had bloomed, the same colour as the high-heeled shoes that protruded over the end of the bed. Billy peered more closely. The mark looked familiar, like something off a map. France? *Nah*—not square enough. Spain—*nope*. Another slap, and a triangular extension burst onto the skin. *Africa!* Christ, he was paddling geography lessons onto her arse. It made him sort of proud.

The last slap also finally earned him a slight "*ahh!*" from the woman straddled on his slickly wrapped bed. The black silk sheets were a recent purchase made from boredom and a brief desire to be Hugh Hefner. Too slippery. One unfortunate bunny had already shot across the bed and landed in a twisted heap on the floor.

He wouldn't keep them; not the sheets or the blonde.

Regardless of the cartographic potential, she seemed preoccupied. Her sighs all sounded the same, like she was phoning it in. *Brilliant.* He was so dull even his lovers ran on autopilot. That stung more than he wanted to admit.

The last few months had really put a crimp in his performance and, truth be told, left a cramp in his thigh muscles.

Thwack!

With one last energetic slap, which took the bottom quite by surprise, he said, "Time to bugger off, love." The look she shot him back? Pure bloody gratitude. *Shit! She is bored.*

Without waiting for the woman to get up from the bed, Billy pulled on his designer underwear and the shirt he'd removed earlier, and made his way into the living area of his East London Docklands penthouse, a pristine tea warehouse conversion of exposed brick and cast iron.

The stiff black leather sofa still dominated the room, its only saving grace the flat arms, perfect for balancing bottles of European lager on footy nights. Flanked by its two matching armchairs, the arrangement pleased his need for order, at least. Opposite, the wall was covered in parallel rows of his shoe photography of stilettos and steampunk-inspired thigh-highs. Truth was, he barely got a kick out of them anymore.

Only one photograph got his attention: a study of well-used workman's boots back-lit and placed attractively, one leaning its heel against a satin-covered box, and the other resting at a sideways angle against its companion. Placed at eye-level, dead centre.

He clocked the picture now, on his way to the kitchen, and gave a lazy salute.

After retrieving a beer from the fridge, Billy pried off the metal bottle top with an opener styled as Dracula's open mouth. It released with a pop. He took a quick swig, then studied the gadget. The vampire grimaced at him, its flat central teeth providing just enough space to grip a top tightly while the two sharp canine fangs added no function.

He smiled, thinking back to the day he'd received the opener as a gift and the accompanying lecture. *Vampires only use their fangs for the 'grrr' factor, Billy!* She'd said, dead serious. Then, without missing a beat, up went her hands like claws and she gave him her best, *grrr!* He hadn't resisted, not for a second, and gone full camp vamp, stalking across the flat like a Hammer Horror extra: *Dahling, I want to drink your blood!* They'd both collapsed in tears of laughter.

That was the day his best friend, a tough and often impossible half-demon girl, had chosen to give him a lesson about the supernatural world. When he'd dropped her at a South London psychiatric unit four months ago, those conversations had stopped.

The sound of high heels clipping sharply over his polished wood floor brought him up short. He winced and, without looking up, said, "Shoes!"

"I know!"

He felt her eye-roll.

The footsteps paused by the front door, and the offending heels clattered to the floor.

Looking up, he noted the mid-length, brown, wrap-around dress tied at the waist, not a hint of cleavage. A strangely sedate outfit for the woman's chosen lifestyle. She pulled on low wedge-heeled canvas sandals, kissed the air vaguely in his direction, and was gone.

Billy's shoulders sagged in relief. Even his heartbeat steadied.

He pulled the kitchen drawer open to return the bottle opener, but hovered instead, his fingers running over the sharp little teeth. Dracula's wide, staring eyes looked back at him. The memory of Tazia's laughter ringing out, had brought his empty flat alive. With a sigh he dropped the opener to the drawer with a clatter.

Crossing to his desk, Billy switched the window on the PC to his calendar. Boring meeting after boring meeting. But today a big red TAZ. The only one this week. Scrolling back, the last twelve weeks had been littered with them: daily visits. A haze of shared pots of flavoured yoghurt (*guess the berry, Taz!*), mindless board games (*Snakes & Ladders or Cluedo?*), and tales of his latest plaything to make her smile.

Four bloody months, and she was still curled up in the corners of her room, shut down. Like someone had switched her off. He was supposed to get her through it, but he was bollocksing that up too.

He switched to his email. A new one from Thomas, just a question mark in the subject line. *Nope.* Billy dragged it to the *Trash* folder. *Fuck it!* Love could wait.

The alarm from the Mac cut through his contemplation.

Video call. His stomach fluttered. Maybe news about that red-haired bitch? His fingers hovered. Did he want to know?

2

———————

FAIRY DUST

THE ALARM SOUNDED A SECOND TIME. The little B-flat scale had seemed such a good idea, but now it set his teeth on edge. Billy accepted the call. On screen, a man talked to an out-of-sight companion. He looked like he was in an open topped vehicle, occasional blasts of dust blew past, most of the screen bleached out from the sun.

"Hey, Hux!"

Soren Huxford had cut his long, blond hair slightly shorter than usual; it was a little above his chin and pushed roughly behind his ears. A decision based on the inability to purchase his favourite body-enhancing shampoo in the African desert, no doubt.

He turned back, and his face filled the screen, blocking out the sun. Tiny specks of sand had gathered in the roots of his hair and in the slight crow's feet in the corners of his light blue eyes. Dark shadows traced tiredness, and a week-old stubble studded his chin.

"Wow, Hux, this connection is fantastic, mate." Billy squirmed slightly, distracting himself from Hux's good looks by admiring the Wi-Fi.

"Not my end—you're breaking up." Hux drew his hand through his hair, disrupting the sand. A little cascade caught the light and sprinkled across the screen like fairy dust. "How's Anastasia?" The first question he always asked.

"Same," Billy said, the lie sliding out easier than it should have. The truth—that she was slipping further away each visit—wouldn't help either of them.

For a moment, Hux gazed past the screen, apparently lost in his own thoughts about the young woman they both loved.

Billy sighed, irritated. *Byronic bullshit.*

He was still dead certain Tazia belonged with him, not some emotionally stunted assassin who'd already got her lover killed. But since Turin, he had grudgingly accepted that Hux did indeed care about her. Besides, if using Hux's guilt and resources kept Tazia safe from the Advocate, he'd swallow his pride. Anything to get her out of that hospital and back to smiling.

But it grated. He was running around the world, doing the Romantic Hero act. Leaving him to pick up the bloody pieces.

"Do you have news? Or were you just calling me to stare at my well-developed abs?" Billy's shirt was still wide open.

For all his quippy efforts, his reward was the usual field report. "I tracked the Advocate to Africa. She appeared in Southern Sudan. I followed her up to the north, over to Morocco, then down the west coast. The usual pattern: she's collecting acolytes. I've spoken to some of them. She's full of promises to end the Risings. Swings her arguments according to local religion or customs."

He paused and looked with meaning into the camera. "She's talking about the *Saviour* again."

Billy steadily held his eyes, seeing for a moment a flash of something there. Regret? Fear?

"She's not backing down." Hux shifted a little. "These guys

she leaves behind are convincing. They talk others around once she's gone."

He squinted at the screen and moved his head. The glare from the sun bleached the picture again. "You still there? Damn bright out here."

"Yeah, I'm here."

Hux readjusted to block the sun and gave a slight nod before continuing in a less soldierly style. "Her argument is working, Billy. People are frightened."

"Well, they're quite right to be scared, bruv. They see demons everywhere—see humanity slipping away. *She* turns up, quoting scripture, flashing her wings, preaching soul-saving shit about the coming Saviour. Seriously, who is going to say no to that when they feel so desperate?" Billy leaned his head on his open hand, feeling at least a thousand years old. His wrist painfully cracked, the after effects of all the paddling earlier. He circled it gingerly to make it crack again, but it brought no relief.

"But Tazia's not their Saviour." Hux's voice was flat.

"*We* know that. But the angel's weaving a good tale, telling them she's someone who's fought against her own demon self —and won. She got her soul back! That's irresistible spin."

"We can't let her get to Anastasia." Hux looked away.

Billy could see pain on his face. Wow! Real emotion. Was his energy starting to fade? He'd been charging after the High Advocate ever since she'd tricked him into murdering Tazia's lover in Turin. He'd thought killing Conn O'Cuinn would save her, but by doing so he'd actually put Tazia into the angel's grasp.

Until now, his energy and determination had never weakened.

"Hux, you okay, bruv?"

"Yeah, frustrated. I'm always one step behind."

"I know."

Hux leaned back and stretched, his elbows shifting out of the screen and his khaki tee tightening. The light cotton clung to his broad chest, and the armholes were snug around his biceps.

Billy took in the view with only vague appreciation this time. "Any good news?"

"I've met a guy—"

"Didn't think you swung that way…" *I'm tired, not dead.*

"—the son of an elder. Village south of St. Louis in Senegal. Name of Jacob. He listened to the angel, let her speak her piece. Wasn't convinced by her. Former military and smart too. Didn't challenge her until every villager was out of earshot. Only then said no. He already knew the fire was inevitable. A Precog. Seems powerful. I got there as the smoke was dying away."

"This 'Jacob,' will he help us?"

"I explained all we knew. He's been fighting the Risings, too. Not just here. Cairo, Lagos, Boston, cities all on the brink. He has allies. People who believe in him. I said we were determined to track that bitch down and finish it." The vitriol in his voice faded as quickly as it had sparked. When he spoke again, it was only a whisper. "Said we needed to guard a woman. It all hinged on her."

He looked at Billy squarely, and for a moment a brief hopeful smile hovered. "He's going to help."

"How?" Billy was pleased they had someone else on the team, but couldn't imagine what a human could do.

"He's already anticipating her movements using his sight. We only missed her by a couple of hours this time. Next time we may just get there."

Billy leaned back but caught the flicker across Hux's face, as if something unsaid scraped at him. "What aren't you telling me? You're twitchy."

"Nothing." Hux's glance slid sideways. "Well, he said he… saw me before we met."

"What, like in a dream or on your OnlyFans account?"

"In a vision." His tone flattened. "And he said *I was at the beginning and the end.*"

Billy sat forward, grinning despite the fatigue. "Dramatic much. Bet you loved that."

Hux ignored him, face hard, professional again.

"We still don't know how to kill her." Billy's research into how they could kill the Advocate had led him to nothing helpful. Lore said, only an angel could kill an angel; they didn't know any more of those.

"We should stop thinking of killing. Instead, consider control." Hux said.

Would controlling the angel save the world? Was she even connected to the Risings or just taking advantage of them? He held back a sigh. Hux was finally looking a little positive, and he didn't want to dampen his enthusiasm. "Maybe. Are you coming back?"

"Yes. We've got no leads and I want to… see her." He glanced away and shifted a little in his seat. "I'm bringing Jacob with me, too. He may pick up something from around her."

As they said goodbye, Billy did a mock salute. He didn't receive one in return.

"Bye. And by the way, Billy?"

"Yep?"

"Your abs aren't anything special, man. Eat more protein."

Before he could reply, Hux closed the connection, and he was left frowning at a blank screen. He glanced at his stomach. *Was that a joke? His abs were golden.*

He walked back to the kitchen and picked up the beer he'd abandoned earlier—now warm piss. He drank it anyway, pacing the flat for a while before settling at one of the floor-to-ceiling picture windows and considering a cigarette. Despite the oncoming demon apocalypse and almost certain death, he'd been trying to cut down.

After struggling for a full thirty seconds, he pushed the terrace door open and went outside to light up.

With his elbows resting on the railing and smoke easing from his mouth with every gentle exhale, he looked down at the River Thames. The water was grey and sluggish as always, but the tide line was lower than he'd ever seen it. No rain for months. Dying vegetation dotted the river banks, too.

He flicked the ash over the balcony, where it got caught on the tiny breeze and floated gently back through the railings onto his bare feet.

The demons were getting more of a hold on London. So far, the city had escaped the worst, and overall England was doing well. Though, the songbirds had all gone.

Billy rubbed the ash from his foot onto the back of his opposite calf and wondered how long he'd get before he'd have to move away from his East London home. Would he become a victim of the violence like thousands of others? Would he lose his soul too?

A notification pinged on his smartwatch and interrupted his musings. An appointment: Dr. McKenzie. He sighed. Time to go pay a man to listen to his lies.

3

———————————

ARGYLE SOCKS

OF THE MANY doctors practicing in Harley Street, Billy had chosen the only one still wearing argyle socks when off the golf course. They covered the space between his scuffed brogues and the folded cuffs of his over-short trouser legs.

He also jiggled his bloody foot as they spoke—constantly.

The office looked like old rental accommodation: little furniture, few comforts, and grubby in the corners. For Billy, this last point gave it a high creep factor. He perched at the front of the easy chair opposite the doctor's and tried not to look at the layers of dust and grime.

The sessions always went the same way. They started with warm up questions like: *And how have you been, Billy?* To which Billy always replied. *Fine.* Regardless of whether that was the case or not, and then moved on to: *Any dreams?*

This one was no different.

"How have you been, Billy?" said Dr. McKenzie. Bone-thin, his mop of coarse grey hair sprouted at odd angles from his head and ears. His gold wire-rimmed spectacles jiggled on his nose in time with his bouncing foot.

"Not bad!" Billy decided to buck the trend and was

rewarded by a sharp look and a scribble on the doctor's notepad. He glanced out of the window, hoping for a distraction to suppress the sudden giggle forming around his diaphragm.

The sun glared off a parked car, momentarily blinding him and killing the laugh in his throat. "Have you noticed how hot it's getting, Doc?"

"Hmm?" The doctor was still scribbling.

"The heat. It's very hot."

"Yes, it's beautiful weather." He made eye contact with Billy again and gave him a big, genuine smile, obviously pleased that the sun was always shining these days. He crossed his legs the other way, revealing his patterned ankles. Golf, of course! Mustn't let the demon-created climate change interfere with your handicap, Doc.

"Any dreams, Billy?"

Billy nodded.

"Do you want to tell me about them?"

Not particularly. "Sure."

He left three, four, five beats of silence. "The usual."

"Yes. Which is?"

Billy wriggled in his seat. The edge had no stuffing left and it cut into his arse.

"Come now, Billy. We've talked about this. The dreams hold the key, we *must* explore them."

Bloody hell.

"Shapes moving around the bed, shouting at me to wake up. Trying to slap me awake. Blinding light." He shifted again. "Then last night one stabbed me with a sword."

He looked apologetically at the doctor. This last detail was new. No doubt, it would send him into paroxysms of delight. A new image he could dissect and classify, and blame either on his mother's prescription drug habit, his father's death, or his early puberty.

Instead, Dr. McKenzie scribbled on the notepad balanced on his knee with his right hand, his left was busy pulling invisible strands out of the thread-bare arm of the chair. "Anything else?"

"No." Billy frowned. "That not enough?"

The doctor shrugged. "I assumed the violence would intensify at some point. Actually, I'm surprised that it's taken… What is it? Four months since the dreams started?" He flicked back through the pages and pages of notes that were an intimate summary of Billy's last two years. All the obsessions, sexual exploits, confessions of unrequited love for Tazia, even bathroom habits.

"Yes. About that, but—"

"Yes, they started when your friend went into hospital. That's right, isn't it?" He was still flicking through the notebook and ignored Billy's response.

"Yeah, and—"

"And that's also the time when you started to see a drop in your libido?" The doctor stopped flicking and looked straight at him with a little tight-lipped smile on his face.

Billy raised his eyebrows, saying dryly, "There's been no drop in anything. It just doesn't live up to expectations anymore."

"Your partners? Or your performance?" The doctor leaned forward and opened his eyes a bit wider.

"Both… I guess."

"Tell me about that." Dr. McKenzie turned to a fresh page in his notepad and raised his pen, poised to scratch away at the paper.

Billy gazed through the glass door into the waiting area, where Julie, the receptionist, tapped at her computer. He suspected it was just a pretence at busyness. He was hoping for a glimpse of her ankles, but they were hidden under her desk.

He struggled to give his attention back to the doctor. "What was the question?"

"Tell me about why you now find your sex life unfulfilling." The doctor swiped a quick finger at the corner of his mouth and wiped it on his trousers. *Is he dribbling?*

"I think I always have." Billy sat up straight in his chair, trying to find his focus. "It's like this. Sex has always been about discovering something. Different gender. Different positions. Pain and pleasure. Always about seeing—and feeling—a reaction, innit?"

He added the colloquialism to try to dissipate the tension he felt in revealing so much of his thought process. But the doctor hadn't finished with him.

"A reaction for you or… for them?" He panted a little, and the tip of his tongue peeked wetly between his lips for a moment.

"Both." Billy sounded very sure, but his eyes desperately explored the back of Julie's head again, trying to find something as attractive about it as her ankles. He couldn't, so he said, "We're just people trying to figure it all out." Meaningless, but it filled the silence.

"Through sex?"

"Sometimes." *Always.*

"Does love figure, Billy?" There it was. The question he'd waited for, the one that made him so uncomfortable. His reaction always the same: a simple shrug. Love had nothing to do with it.

Today, he tried for more. "I don't associate the two, Doc."

Dr. McKenzie caressed the arm of the chair with his left thumb with what looked like genuine affection. A little white spittle had collected at the corner of his mouth again. Billy risked a quick look at his groin. *Is the fucker getting off on this?*

"You don't associate sex with love?" The doctor urged him on, pushing ever harder on the frayed fabric.

"Yeah… I guess." *Jesus, give it up, mate!*

The doctor was going down a completely wrong path. Billy's obsessions weren't about keeping love or commitment at bay. They were all about discovery. The reactions of his lovers helped him figure out where he fitted into the world. He'd never understood that, even as a little kid. But the more he tried, the more lost he felt. Love didn't figure.

"It's just…"

"Yes?" The doctor was on the edge of his chair rocking forward and back.

Feeling queasy, Billy ended the series of questions with: "You know, Doc, I'm just a freak, right?"

Dr. McKenzie sighed, his excitement subsiding. "Let's talk about your mother."

Billy silently groaned. Another rabbit hole he didn't want to explore. Not today. What the hell was wrong with him, anyway? He was so impatient and… and… itchy! Like his skin needed a good scrub. He wasn't normally like this. The fake tick of his smartwatch sounded loud in the room.

Another thirty minutes of questions droned on before he jumped up from his seat and paced back and forth across the low-pile rug, mumbling monosyllabic answers in response to the doctor's questions. There were large brown stains on the rug. Rather than stepping on them, he shuffled around or over them.

For five more minutes, the doctor gamely continued with question after question, but eventually, he said, "I think we'll leave it there today, Billy. I feel we've made… progress."

That was fine by Billy. He already felt rather more vulnerable than he usually did after a bout of questioning, and even though he didn't believe Dr. McKenzie had made any great breakthroughs, he was tired, irritable, and imagining a cool beer and a smoke.

After saying goodbye, he walked back into the reception

area, ready to flash Julie a suggestive smile. She really was a masterpiece of female creation.

Instead of returning the smile, though, Julie said something that stopped him short. It wasn't even so much the words she repeated, but the way she did it, slow and steady, each one pronounced emphatically. "Is. It. Time. To. Wake. Up. Billy?"

He turned to face her. "What did you say?"

"Is. It. Time. To. Wake. Up. Billy?" she repeated.

The ticking of his watch grew louder. It entered his right ear, crashing around his skull. Louder and faster. Merging into a long, loud drawn-out hum.

Abruptly, his mind wiped clean. His brain, ice. No thoughts. No memories. He couldn't move a muscle. Was he breathing? Did his heart stop?

Then all the synapses triggered at once.

In front of his wide eyes, a bombardment of vibrant images. Tragic, terrifying, sexual, beautiful, nonsensical pictures whizzed past.

An impossible flood. A world's worth of pain. A lifetime of joy in a single, searing instant. Despair and confusion and ecstasy slammed into him, a tidal wave of raw humanity. Rushing forward, on and on. The hum became louder, screaming at him. Deafening him. Above it all, violent vibrations deep in his throat, his chest.

Julie grabbed his arm, and this time shouted above the noise, "Is—it—time—to—wake—up—Billy?" There was a flash of light so intense, Billy closed his eyes against it. The room shrank back to stillness and silence.

4

————

SLEEPER

WOOD SMACKED HIS CHEEK. A bat? Did someone… ? No—floorboards. Splintered oak dug into his skin. Then scents. Bleach—*good*—polish, and last week's dirty mop—*yuck*. Each smell distinct. *Since when?*

He chose to lay there longer. The room rocked back and forth. *Christ, gonna—*

The first spew of vomit surprised him, shooting from his mouth, a decorative orange spray across the boards. Juice box from earlier.

He groaned. *Stop swaying!*

Another spew. Samosa. *Ugh!* The lumpy mess stuck in his throat and on the back of his teeth. He gagged and spat in an effort not to swallow the bitter mixture back down.

"Do you need a hand up?"

The voice came from above and to his right, echoing in and out with the sway. He didn't answer.

"I know it's tough, the shift. We expected that."

The voice sounded again, but this time he recognized it as belonging to receptionist, Julie. She of the long, flippy hair, the ample boobs, and shapely ankles. *Not the time, bruv!*

"When you're ready, let me know and I'll pull you up."

"I-don-nee-ya-help!" His tongue was suddenly far too big.

With a huge effort, Billy pushed onto both hands and twisted into a seated position. His right palm slipped in the pool of orange vomit that now trickled back toward him along the grooves between the planks. He was both disgusted and indifferent; all his focus went into forcing the see-sawing to stop.

The clip-clop of Julie's heels faded and returned. A small white hand towel dropped in his lap. He wiped his mouth and right cheek before cleaning up his hands. *Thank God.*

"That's better. All clean." He could hear the smile in her voice, imagined her talking to a small child instead of a man in his late twenties. The humiliation was motivation enough to get to his feet, so he heaved himself up using the edge of the reception desk.

Julie had repositioned herself behind it and waited for him to focus. "Do you need a chair?" She rushed out from behind the desk wheeling her office chair in front of her, nudged the back of his legs with it until he carefully sat down.

"The dizziness should pass in a minute or two. I'll get you some water."

Again with the mothering.

He squeezed the thin plastic cup she offered so hard, most of its contents landed in his lap before he could get it to his mouth. After a refill, the cold water settled his head a little. He looked around.

The room was still. As in, absolutely static.

A waiting patient sat in the corner like a statue. Her mouth slightly open, stretched pink gum caught mid-chew. She'd pulled her right ear-bud away from her ear as though she was readjusting it and now the tinny sounds of Avril Lavigne leached into the room. So, sound still works?

Billy turned back to Julie. "What the fuck is going on?"

"What do you remember?" Julie perched on the desk and crossed her legs to reveal some pasty white thigh. Her foot jiggled.

"I remember leaving the doctor's office, saying goodbye to you, then… nothing!"

"Think again, Billy. Think hard."

He wanted to pace, but the tremble in his legs still persisted. He wouldn't make it. Instead, he clutched even more tightly to his chair. Digging at memories, he hissed, "You said something to me, didn't you?"

"Yes. I told you to wake up."

It flashed back, her strange statement. "There was a bright light!"

"Yes." She nodded and smiled encouragement.

"Then I was on the floor—throwing up." Billy scowled at the memory and glanced at the putrid mess that still gave off an obnoxious odour. "Did you hit me with something?" He glared at her and automatically put his hand up to the back of his head, looking for bumps or blood.

"No, but you're right about the light." She paused, then leaned forward a little more eagerly. "I want you to think back further now, Billy. Much further. To a time when you could remember everything." Julie looked at him like he was the long shot she'd bet everything on.

Billy, on the other hand, was not seeing a finish line, or playing ball, or any other sporting analogy. "For fucksakes, girl, just tell me! What am I supposed to remember?"

She shook her head. "I can't tell you, hun. It doesn't work that way. You have to remember. But you have time. I can keep the stasis going for a while longer."

"This?" Billy pointed at the still-as-a-statue girl. "You're doing this?"

"Yes."

The room snapped sharply into focus for the first time

since he'd woken up. Colours brightened and the lines around objects jumped out as though he was watching a three-dimensional movie. It felt like he could even—almost—see through things. *What the fuck? Too much!*

"I'm out!" He pushed himself up from the chair, found unsteady balance, and took a few steps toward the door.

Julie called after him. "Not to be negative, love, but you won't get far. I've created this little snapshot in time and space that we're both trapped in right now. It's a bit like treacle, sticky and thick. But try if you want."

He did. He pulled hard on the outside door, but couldn't shift it. "Is this a spell?"

"Sort of. Strictly speaking, I don't cast spells. It's more a dimensional shift, if you like." She shrugged, as though stopping time was the easiest thing in the world.

Billy backed up against the door. "Are you Jegudiel?" He knew the angel could take the form of inanimate objects, but could she take the form of a living breathing woman?

The skin puckered around Julie's eyes and mouth, instantly adding ten years to her appearance. "I am not that bitch." She crossed her arms over her chest. "How could you even suggest such a thing, Billy?"

A low rumble threaded the air and the room gave a slight jump, blurring in and out of focus. He wasn't a physicist, but if the room suddenly shifted at the wrong time, couldn't they all end up in a different universe? Would he be lost forever in a doctor's waiting room, spinning through time and space like the TARDIS, but with no one at the controls? He didn't fancy Dr. McKenzie's chances at being the next Time Lord.

"Okay, okay. I'm sorry. Calm down. I'm just confused."

Julie flipped her hair and grinned, her annoyance apparently forgotten.

"Can you really not tell me who you are?"

She shook her head. "Sorry, love. *You* have to remember.

But I *can* say you've known me for a really long time. I know it's hard, but focus."

Out of nowhere, a terrible sadness gripped him. Billy let out a sob and returned to the office chair. He covered his face with his hands. Focus on what?

Then *she* popped into his mind.

Tazia.

His friend of six years. His would-be lover. The young woman who'd never scoffed or criticized him. Her gentle teasing. Her bad jokes. Her hugs. Her beautiful smell.

And then it happened. The air hummed, like a power line overload, and the reception bled away. Tazia wasn't just a memory. She was in front of him, sitting on her hospital bed gazing across the room.

Or at least he felt she was. *Not real. Not there.* But he stretched out his hand to check and it grasped empty air.

She still hovered. Red waves of energy reaching for him. *She's scared!*

He looked to where she was staring. Reflected in the window was the face of a thin pale woman with pointed features. A cascade of red hair streaked with silver-grey fell against the purple material of her clothing. Her face was pinched and her lips formed a thin smile.

Jegudiel!

"I have to save Taz," Billy whispered. He'd told himself a thousand times before. But in this place, apparently spinning in space, it meant so much more. "I have to save Taz!"

He looked at Julie. "Right?"

"Yes! What else?" Julie dragged a chair in front of Billy so they sat knee to knee, both leaning forward, concentrating hard.

He could feel her willing him on. He ignored his wet cheeks. "The angel has her. And if that ever happened, I needed to… wake up?"

Julie smiled broadly at him. "Keep going, hun, keep going!"

As he grasped at snatches of memory, his tears ran harder and faster. *But I do know it!* There was something right at the back of his mind, data he just needed to locate.

It jumped at him.

A conversation with Tazia not five months earlier, while they'd prepared for her trip to Detroit to track down the Irish demon, Conn O'Cuinn. He'd wanted to go with her, and they'd argued animatedly back and forth for a while. He'd said he could help if he travelled with her—protect her. But she wouldn't hear of it.

His heart lurched. *Something else…*

Tazia had wished she could be fully human. Just so she could truly feel the gratitude for him she knew was inside her. "You've always been there for me, Billy," she'd said. "My very own guardian angel. With balls, though. You're my guardian angel with balls!" And she'd laughed long enough her stomach hurt.

His world crashed in—

He wasn't human; he was an angel. Tazia's angel. Not a guardian with a halo and fluffy white wings, but a bodyguard with a battle-ready body and a lion heart, sent here ready to protect her. To be here when she needed him. To love her and fight for her and, if need be, kill those who threatened her.

I'm here to save her.

The shock of his awakening vibrated through the earth, and at that instant, he felt part of something incredible. Eyes turning towards him. A surge of smiles. Wings whispering in the air.

An old one—a Sleeper—was reborn.

5

―――――

SILENCE

HIS LIPS ON HERS. His hand on her cheek. The smell of blood and smoke. Conn O'Cuinn's final moments were the only reality Tazia had left. The rest was a muffled replay: Soren Huxford's knife, the dark, airless panic, the weight of a body growing still in her arms. Hux's broken face. Proof that her newly-sparking soul was working just fine, thank you very much. It could scream, over and over.

She never let herself forget that two men died that day—

A faint shimmer in her peripheral vision. The window. No, the plastic sheen of the visitor's chair. *If I don't look—*

Don't be a fool, Anastasia. You know I'm here.

Jegudiel's voice cut into her skin, a disembodied hiss that made the sterile room feel crowded. Tazia didn't need to see the reflection in the mirror or the floor. The angel was a constant pressure behind her eyes, a parasite feeding on her grief. *My pet. My little saviour. All this pain has a purpose. Don't let it be in vain.*

Tazia squeezed her eyes closed. *Shut. The. Fuck. Up.*

The quiet of the room pressed in. But she never rested. Always scanning for the voice.

The faint hum of the lights. The distant squeak of the food cart. Other patients in the hallway…

Someone cleared their throat. "Eat up, Tazia, huh? Custard for dessert!" *Thanks, Pete. I'll eat it after I've saved the world.*

The orderly's cheerfulness was an absurdity. He smiled at her silence and dull eyes, and left the meal on the sideboard beside the ornament a church visitor had sworn would bring her comfort. As he left, the cheap Mary figurine winked in the light. *Of course it did.*

Tazia rolled to her side on the bed, pulling the sheet over her head.

Still there. Always there. *Stop!*

The angel's argument never changed: Tazia was living proof that a human soul could tame a demon. She must show the world how to do it. How to resist the darkness and end the Risings.

At first, Tazia had laughed. *A half-breed assassin turned messiah? Right!*

But the words kept circling, wearing her down until they made sense in a hollow, exhausted way.

She clenched her fists beneath the sheet and breathed through her teeth, just loud enough to cover the chatter. Her tattoos, now gone, still clenched her spine. She'd screamed enough with that pain.

Up to you, my pet. All free will. As she circled from mirror to window.

Tazia wouldn't answer. Not yet. Her silence was her power.

Outside, the orderly's cart clattered down the corridor, metal wheels scraping the tile. Three beats and a squeak. She counted until it faded. Far away, the opening bars of *that* song on someone's sound system—"Uprising." *Huh!*

Rhythm was all she had: meal breaks, counselling sessions,

doctors with soft voices, and the endless spotlight of Jegudiel's attention.

And Billy. *My Billy.*

He used to stay all day, talking nonsense just to make her laugh. Now the visits were short and stiff. He'd sit by the window, body coiled, eyes searching her for the girl he used to know. She couldn't give him that. Not with the angel listening to every word.

Once, she almost told him. Her mouth opened, the truth rising… then Jegudiel's whisper crept through her mind. *Tell him, and he dies, pet.*

So she shut up. Watched him search for how he could save her. Watched his face fall and pack away the banter. After that, he stopped coming altogether.

Good. Safer. He was just human after all. She didn't need him.

She glanced at the empty chair he usually occupied. *Liar.*

Tazia pressed a hand to her eyes for the black. She'd learned a lot since the seals on her soul burned open: pain, loss, fading hope. But mostly guilt. Billy's, Hux's, her own—solid in her heart. Permanent, gauging pain.

Of all the people she'd lost, Billy was the one she wanted back.

———

"I'm an angel?" Billy blinked. "Truly?"

Julie nodded, her wide smile drooping a little, no doubt dampened by his disbelief.

"Bloody hell." He slumped back in his chair, drawing away from her.

She frowned, deep lines carving between her brows, and eyes pinning his. Was she looking into his soul? Did he even have a soul?

Every nerve screamed for him to run. To turn the clock back half an hour to when he was just Billy. His obsession-filled, freak-self. Life had been simple then.

Too late now. There was a reason why he'd "woken up" like this.

"And my role is to save Tazia, Julie?" *Do I serve… God? Jesus, does that fucker really exist?*

"Oh, shit, sorry!" he blurted.

"For what?" Julie tilted her head.

"I think I just blasphemed… in my head. Not that I really know what blaspheming is."

Religion had never been Billy's thing. There was more sense in the heat shared between lovers than in the archaic words of an old manuscript.

Julie laughed. "I can't read your mind, Billy. Stay on point. And the answer is, 'if necessary'."

"What?"

She leaned back in her chair and crossed her legs, flashing her thighs again, bringing him back from his brief reflections. She suddenly seemed a lot more relaxed. "It's always been the plan that you save Tazia—if necessary. That's why we woke you up."

"We?"

"The angels. They call us The Watch. Dramatic, if you ask me." She sighed and straightened her skirt, pulling it back down to just above her knees.

"Go on!"

"We're a small band of angels observing how world crises play out. Show-stopping events like wars, revolutions, all that. We can't intervene, but we can give humanity a nudge if things are about to go belly up. Provide other alternatives. Do you remember yet?" She squinted at him. "This ringing any bells?"

Something flickered. "I'm trying. Sounds familiar. Like something I learned at school."

Billy pushed to his feet and paced, words spilling faster as he walked. "Do I have any super powers? Or some sort of time-shifting shit like you? Can I fly?"

"Not right now, but no doubt when you're fully yourself again."

He paused his pacing. "How long will that take?"

"Depends. You'll gradually get the whole picture clear."

Julie's head followed the backward and forward movements he'd started up again. "The most important thing for you to remember now is how you can help Tazia—help the human race. And the best way for you to do that is to remember your Faith, Billy. Angels are driven by it. It's why you volunteered in the first place."

"I volunteered?" He stopped again, eyes wide. He'd never volunteered for anything in his life. "You're shitting me!"

"Erm. No, I assure you, I am not 'shitting' you. You *did* volunteer."

"Seriously, I put my hand up and said: *Here Miss, pick me?*"

"Well, it was more like, you stepped forward from a battalion of soldiers with your sword held high, and shot a piercing laser of light into the air... But yes, I suppose that would count as, 'pick me'."

"Fuck me."

"We're getting off point a little, Billy. Try to remember. We needed someone who would be human for a while to get close to Tazia, monitor her decisions. Report in when Jegudiel made contact. We hoped—"

"And, did I?" he interrupted.

"What?"

"Report in? I don't remember..."

Julie smiled. "Of course. You were programmed to. That night when Tazia came to London. When she first told you about Jegudiel. Your angelic essence travelled to us through a dimensional shift and told us all about it. Reported direct to Ezequiel, you did." She sniffed.

"Wow!" He dragged a hand through his hair. It was a little worse for wear after his earlier collapse, but the knowledge only vaguely concerned him.

"Yes, wow! Everyone was pleased to see you. Though not the news, of course—"

"You *programmed* me?"

"Yes. Something like that."

"Right. Brilliant. And I gave you permission to mess with me like that? Or am I coded? Am I a robot, Julie?" He raced to her, getting nose to nose again.

Julie lurched back in her seat. "No! Of course not. You are an angel. A light-being. An emissary of God. Not a bloody rob—"

"Who is Ezequiel?"

"Our superior. Are you okay, Billy?"

He'd plonked himself back down on the office chair and was absently turning slow circles. Eyes staring forward, and sweat pricking again on his brow. Red lights flashed in his vision. Breath gone. *This feels dangerous.*

"Billy?"

"Overloaded!" He wheezed the word out.

"You'll be fine, love." Julie put a hand on the chair to stop him spinning. She patted his shoulder a little awkwardly, for such a hot older woman. *Nice perfume.*

The red lights faded to tiny silver sparkles at the edge of his vision. "You said that if I warned you Jegudiel had made contact, you hoped something… What?"

"We hoped it would be enough to stop her, but…" Julie scuffed her heels on the floor. "She managed to get to Tazia, anyway. And now things are looking a tad critical. That's why we had to wake you and get you back to full power."

Billy frowned. Had he failed his first day on the job?

Julie faced him, gripped his shoulders, eyes fierce. "You're a soldier, Billy. Remember that. You will fight for her, and if you can't, you'll take whatever action you need to save this beautiful world. You—"

"Oh, yuck, who the hell spewed on the floor?"

A courier stood in the doorway, helmet dangling, spongy soles of his expensive high tops suctioned into the puddle Billy had created earlier.

Billy blinked. He stood in the middle of the room. Julie had reverted to her spot behind the desk, apologizing to the kid who was still whining about his trainers.

Julie winked at him. "Have a nice day Mr. Nadig. Take care, though. That sun's only going to get hotter out there."

Message received. Billy needed to take action. Apocalypse pending. He felt like throwing up again.

6

THIS FIGHT IS JUST STARTING

THINGS FINALLY STARTED MAKING sense as Billy took the long route home, sticking to the Underground until he had to switch to the overland train for the last few stops into East London.

The descent into London's guts always thrilled him. Maybe it was a Freudian thing—back to Mother Earth and all that—but more likely it was the grime. Down here, among the sweat, dust, and stale air, he had no control. He felt released.

And everyone had a purpose. Get home. Get through. Get somewhere. They pushed and muttered *sorry*, even while elbowing past each other—English manners. They put up with the plastic seats, moaned about delays and graffiti, eyes pinned to the clacking time clock. It made him grin because he got it. They all shared the same bloody purpose.

He'd thought his love of the Tube was about being normal. Like everyone else, he'd get through the journey and get back to his life.

But today was different. The smells clawed at him; the lights cut sharper. He felt every heartbeat, every desperate wish in that packed carriage. And for the first time, he saw what they were: beautiful, messy, determined humanity.

Maybe that's why you never fit, mate. You weren't less. Just other.

The nature of his relationship with Tazia was clearer. He was her protector—always had been. The only one there for her when the shit hit the fan.

He gave her a place to hide when the crazy got too close, came up with schemes to save her from whacked-out arms dealers or over-enthusiastic demon suitors. Once or twice, he'd even called an unsuspecting meal or two from his little black book when she'd been too lazy to hunt. Feeding, not killing, she'd promised.

One thing hadn't changed: he'd always love her. No matter what each of them became.

The train slid into another tunnel; his face flickered on the darkened windowpane. For a second he watched it hover there—a ghost overlaying the glass. Same dark eyes, same sharp bones, same hair threatening rebellion the second the gel gave up. Still Billy.

Only now, something behind the reflection hummed differently, like the power running through the rails. He wasn't sure what it was.

The train rolled to the end of the line, and Billy climbed the steep stairs to the surface platform for the final leg home. The overland turned up early—small miracle—and he dropped into a window seat, same spot as before.

He stretched out, Chelsea boots on the seat opposite, jeans still too skinny for current fashion, but they made his arse look good.

Outside, the last of the industrial brick blurred past: platforms, warehouses, scattered silhouettes hurrying home. The tracks lifted over the Thames, lights smearing across dark water.

The train clattered into its steady rhythm. *Click-clack, click-clack.* Soothing, relentless. His head tipped against the window, eyes tracing the lights until the motion began to pull him under. His lids began to close.

"So, angel, you've finally decided to step out of the shadows?"

Billy's eyes flicked open. Like he'd known it was coming. The hum deep inside him intensified.

The voice was right beside his ear—sharp, female, with that high-brow English clip he couldn't stand. Her image bled slowly into the window glass beside his own reflection. For a moment the light outside bleached her face and hair to grey, but his mind filled in the truth: bone-white skin, that shock of long red hair.

How did I forget?

"Jegudiel." Billy mouthed her name.

"Pet, you *do* remember me!" Her tinkling laugh set the compartment light flickering, and the ceiling creaked ominously. She shook her head as though she was a slightly impatient horse, and her fingernails drummed against a surface somewhere he was not.

One passenger glanced up at the light and caught Billy's eye. He gave her his sweetest smile, which did its usual job, and she dropped her eyes back to her book with a shy smile, tucking hair behind her ear.

"Still got the charm, Billy." Her eyes narrowed. "Always the favourite, weren't you?"

They pulled into the station before his own. Passengers filed out, the girl among them. Not his type, he reflected. Not blonde and Crocs? Seriously, love.

The doors beeped shut. The carriage was now empty but for Billy and the Advocate.

Billy faced her. "I wasn't the favourite. I was just a soldier."

"Just a soldier?" She snorted. "You were a paragon of virtue. You served without question and did anything Ezequiel asked of you, just like the rest of his flock—"

Her voice raised to a level a tad below shrill. The carriage rattled loudly.

"—*You* were the perfect example of stupid subservience to a cause you never thought to question. *You* were a robotic half-wit. *You*—"

"God, you still love to hear your own voice, don't you?"

But puzzle pieces were fitting together as she spoke.

"Ezequiel was—is—braver than you'll ever be. He outranked you, and you hated him for it. That's the truth, Jegudiel. He blocked your attempt at saving that animal of an Abbot you loved so much, and your enormous ego couldn't take being told no."

As memories rushed back energy surged through him, his voice boomed through the carriage. It felt so bloody good!

He wasn't finished either. "You couldn't stand it, could you? Instead of respecting his command, you abandoned your post. And your *Faith*, Jegudiel, your *Faith*." With the memory, the taste of sour vomit returned to his mouth. "You chose all that's rotten in this world—all that the demons have created. You chose them over your own kind."

Exhausted, Billy stopped.

She looked strangely calm, with a serene, twisted smile. "And now, Billy, you have your own demon lover."

He dropped his eyes.

"Anastasia never loved you. So you whinged and whined —" she imitated a crying baby "—*poor* Billy, oh so *lost*, so *different*. Living a life of debauchery, just to fill the space you wanted her to have. A pathetic mess of a man. You're not a soldier anymore, William" She spat the last words.

"No," he said quietly. "That's not why I've lived the way I have." He looked up at her reflection. "All this time, I was an angel fighting for space inside my human self. Confused, scared, weak. No wonder I couldn't make sense of it."

The train slid into his station. He felt energy rush into him again. Time slowed. He rose, leaned in, levelled his gaze with hers. "But I know who I am now, Advocate. And you're not taking her. This fight's just starting, bitch."

7

GOOD ANKLES

WITH EVERY STEP away from the train, Billy felt his energy grow—along with his grin. He was indomitable. He could free the princess from the grasp of the evil witch, kill all the dragons, and set fire to the prison tower. Was that a bright red cape flashing behind him? And a gorgeous bevy of blond-haired beauties falling at his feet? *Bloody right, it was!*

He felt strong and focused and determined. Until he entered his penthouse.

As soon as the door shut behind him, his smile hit the floor and his body followed suit. The enormity of the changes he'd gone through thumped him in the gut. He collapsed to the ground, breathless and gagging.

A smear like black ink leaked into his field of vision, spreading inwards, leaving just a tiny spot of clear, distortion-free light. He clung to it, breathing shallowly until, finally, it began to expand again and his sight cleared.

Flat on the ground, Billy's confidence oozed from him. Not a superhero or dragon slayer. Now, he was the prisoner chained in the dungeon, with long unkempt hair and a straggling beard, sitting in a pool of his own piss. *Fuck. Fuck. Fucking-fuck!*

He covered his eyes and let out a groan that filled the room long and low; a last-ditch attempt to scare off the churn in his stomach. It helped.

Pushing up from the floor, he got to his desk, sank onto the chair, and stabbed each character of his password into the keyboard with one finger. He had one thought: Joshua.

Josh's face flashed onto the screen, glinting with piercings, dirty blond hair falling over his eyes. "Whatsup, dude?"

"Not much, bruv. Been a while. Sorry."

Billy hadn't spoken with the spirit of the necromancer for weeks. The kid's relentlessly hopeful cheeriness about Tazia was way too much. His hope grew as Billy's faded.

They'd got closer since the events in Detroit and Turin. Joshua was free but had chosen to stay in Billy's various hardware, gaming with "little dudes" across the globe. He hosted *Dark Souls* tournaments on weekends and made bank on online poker the rest of the time. His two thousand years gave him a certain edge.

"You're sucking up all the energy in the room, man!" Even as a collection of ones and zeros, Joshua could read the aura around people as clearly as words on a page.

"I feel like shit!" Billy said.

Joshua peered more closely. "What the hell's going on with you? Like you're on a different plane. Sorta there in front of me and then… not."

"I've had a bit of an… awakening, I'd guess you'd call it." Billy hunched over, eyes fixed on nothing. "I'm a fucking angel, Josh," he whispered.

Joshua glitched from one surprised look to another, nominally different one.

"No shit! So, you're actually transforming? Or you've been an angel all along, just squashed inside that human form?"

"Squashed."

"No shit!"

Billy nodded hard. "Had no memory until today. Julie woke me up, said a few words, and it seemed like the world stopped turning for a minute. Then *bam!* Angel."

"Who the fuck is Julie, dude?"

"Dr. McKenzie's receptionist. Nice girl. Good ankles."

They both nodded. Silent, brotherly agreement.

"So, why, exactly, have you been an angel moonlighting as a sex-crazed pervert?"

Usually, Billy would argue about the "pervert" label, but this time he shrugged and uttered one small word: "Tazia."

"*Ahh!*" Joshua nodded again.

"They needed someone to watch her."

"In case?"

"In case the High Advocate got her hands on her."

"And then?"

"Be activated if needed."

"Activated? Like a robot?"

"That's what I said! But no. More like a sleeper soldier." He paused, pulled himself a little more upright. "I am a Warrior of Heaven." The look faded. He slouched back down again. "Apparently, I'm really good at it."

Joshua's eyebrow glitched. "Bro, you don't look like a warrior of anything right now."

"So tired. Energy wiping me out."

"Yeah. It'll do that. Go get some sleep." Mild concern cycled onto his face.

"Can you do something while I sleep, Josh?"

"Sure."

"Go back into the old lore—pre-Biblical stuff—and see if you can find references to The Watch. That's my old, erm, unit, apparently. I've still not got the whole story in my head." His voice faded to a whisper. "Need to know what to expect next."

He got up and shuffled toward his bedroom, heard Joshua's

agreement vaguely in the background before face-diving onto the bed and burying his head into the cold black sheets.

8

____

HIS GIRL

SITTING ON THE FLOOR, arms wrapped tightly around his girl, Billy felt the aftermath of panic ebb from her. Her trembling eased, the rigid set of her spine softening against his chest. The attack had started the moment he'd entered the room that evening.

After he woke, he'd rushed to the hospital before evening visiting hours finished. She was shocked to see him. A smile lit her face briefly. Then she collapsed, arms wrapped around her body, like she was trying to comfort herself. Her breath hitched in wheezes and gasps, never really catching air.

He had no idea why. Could she sense the change within him? Or had she thought he'd abandoned her? *I could never, love.*

"You're here?" She said, when her breath was in control again.

He was slumped against the wall in the corner of the room; Tazia curled between his open legs and tightly wrapped arms.

"I'm here."

He felt her relax against him. Head to toe sweat had soaked her clothes and started to leach into his. He didn't care.

Billy kissed the top of her damp head, tasting a mixture of

salt and shampoo. To distract her, he talked about what he'd been up to. Made it silly. Included the tale of paddling the backside of his latest conquest and creating the image of Africa on her arse. That made her giggle.

He didn't mention his recent transformation to an angel.

Finally, Tazia stretched out her legs, releasing the almost fetal position she'd held for the forty minutes or so since he'd arrived, and twisted to face him. "I wasn't sure you were coming back." Her tone was shy and not a little desperate. Not the Taz he knew. No fire.

"I wasn't sure either, babe." Not yet willing to let go, his arms still circled her back. "You've been so hard to reach. Just blank when I spoke to you."

"I was gone," she said, her voice barely a whisper. "Couldn't find my way back."

"And now?" Billy was almost too frightened to ask.

Tazia's eyes hardened. "I know what to do now."

His grip around her tightened. "What?"

"What she wants."

He closed his eyes for a second. His heart pumped faster. "She?"

"The angel."

He stopped hugging her and, instead, squeezed her shoulders in such a way that a normal girl would be loudly protesting. "What does she want, Taz?"

"She wants me to show the people how they can win against the demons. I'm a perfect example of defeating evil with good. My soul crushed my demon side. It's true. I hardly know I'm bad anymore."

Her sudden wide smile sapped Billy's strength. These weren't her words. They were Jegudiel's. "She's been here a lot, then? Talking with you?"

"She's here all the time." A slight tremor in her voice. Her smile faded, and her eyes shifted to review the room.

Billy followed her gaze. There were reflective surfaces everywhere: the window, mirrors on the wall and wardrobe door, the faucets at the sink. The picture of the surly child on a swing. All things Jegudiel could use to appear or possess.

He remembered how, when Tazia had first arrived, she'd smashed the mirror on the wall and broken the head from the Mary ornament. The hospital staff was used to such behaviour. They replaced the mirror and stuck the head back onto the ornament without fuss. "She's been here since you arrived, hasn't she?"

Tazia nodded.

"Why didn't you tell me, love?"

She shrugged. "You were being so strong, so hopeful. And with Hux trying so hard to find her… I didn't want to tell you it was all a waste of time." She paused. "I guess I was hoping one of you would find a way."

Billy's heart dropped. Had they already failed her? Was the tiny spark left in her eyes accusing him. Not wanting to see it. He pulled her back against his chest.

How much should he tell her? The odds were better now. Angel against angel. Would it change anything? Was she already too far under Jegudiel's influence? He'd have to tread carefully.

"So you think becoming the people's saviour would help, babe?"

"I'm not sure. I don't even fucking know who I am anymore, Billy. I need out."

"We can get you out. Come to my place, make a proper plan with me and Hux."

"Isn't that what we've been doing all this time—planning? And planning what? A battle? Who are we even fighting?"

She had a point. Fighting the Advocate was one thing. But was she facilitating the Risings or just taking advantage of them? It was something he'd discussed with Hux repeatedly. Even if they killed Jegudiel, would it actually stop anything?

"We're fighting the enemy we know right now, Taz. The Advocate." He shrugged, at a loss. How could he convince her? "She talks a good game, I'll give her that. But what's the endpoint, eh? You really think she gives a toss about freeing humans? For fucksakes, love, she chose Hell. Your own dad told you that."

Tazia's eyes glazed over. There was no reaching her. What lies had the Advocate promised? In her disturbed state, if the Advocate had offered her freedom, safety, and purpose, could he convince her otherwise? He needed to up his game.

"It's time to come home with me, okay?"

"Today?" She twisted around to look at him, eyes hopeful.

"Well, not tonight. I'll have to talk to the doctor in the morning and find out what we need to do to get you out of here."

The flicker in her eyes died.

He lifted her chin. "Don't get down, girl. I'll be back first thing to sign the forms and shit. Then home. I'll get you fresh blood, a comfy duvet, hot bath, and hours and hours of soap opera to catch up on."

She winced. "I'm not that desperate!"

"Hey, don't knock it. Jessica's sleeping with three guys in *Mayfield High*. It's gonna be explosive."

The eye roll was a glimpse of the Tazia he loved.

After covering the mirrors with towels, turning the pictures around, and stuffing the ornaments in a drawer, Billy returned to his car. Maybe it would at least buy him the night.

9

———

JACKED

BACK AT HIS PENTHOUSE, Billy was greeted with a sight that put a little patter in his angel heart: Soren Huxford.

He sat splayed on the hallway floor, blond hair flopped over closed eyes, one long leg wedged against the bottom of the door frame, and the other knee bent, resting on the floor. His denim shirt had fallen open, revealing a well-muscled and lightly tanned chest. It was like looking at a cross between a denim-clad cowboy and a tall Viking warrior.

Sitting at a ninety-degree angle from him was an equally sensational-looking man. Billy guessed he was around the same height, six two or three, but in contrast to Hux's Nordic features, this guy was an African god. Close-shaved head, darkest of dark skin gently catching the moonlight coming in from the floor to ceiling windows, pronounced muscles, and a beautiful set of lips that pouted as he slept.

"Wow!"

The men opened their eyes at the exclamation and regarded Billy with a lot less interest than he looked at them.

Hux stretched and exhaled at the same time, the sides of

his open shirt flapping even further apart, and hauled himself up from the ground. "Coffee?"

"Sure. Come in, I'll put some on. By the way, *hi!*" Billy emphasized the greeting with not a little sarcasm.

"Stop staring at my chest." Hux pulled his shirt together, revealing what looked like a large fresh coffee stain leaching its way across damp material.

"Accident?"

"Yeah."

Billy nodded sagely. He turned to the other man. "And, hello!" *God, you're jacked!*

The man held out his hand to Billy, who took it and shook over firmly. But still, the man had the edge. His grin followed, easy and gleaming. "I am Jacob, Billy. It is a pleasure to meet you." His English was impeccable despite the strong African French accent.

Billy found himself bowing slightly in response. *God knows why.* Then he turned to Hux. "Did you hear that? That's what being polite sounds like." He turned back to Jacob. "Very pleased to meet you too, bruv."

Hux made a sound like "pffft" before pushing past him to enter the apartment.

Billy interpreted the sound as "whatevs" and followed him in. "No need to be rude, Hux. Just sayin' that our boy, Jacob here, seems to understand the basic rules of hospitality a little more than whoever dragged you up."

Hux glowered. "My mother and father dragged me up, Billy. Along with several nannies and the help of four private schools." He paused. "I know about manners, don't you worry."

Okay! Billy had just found out more about Hux than he'd learned in the previous two-and-a-half years they'd been acquainted.

"Where were you anyway?" Hux was already in the kitchen

looking for the Moka pot. He found it and rummaged in the fridge for the fine roast espresso.

Jacob followed them both in and stood in the middle of the room, holding his beige designer jacket like he was waiting for a butler to take it from him. His gaze lingered on the footwear photographs systematically. Billy felt oddly like one of his walls had been catalogued and filed away.

"Please sit down, Jacob—" Billy held out his hand for the jacket, then turned back to Hux "—with Taz, innit."

Hux paused for a moment as he screwed the two pieces of the coffeepot back together. He put it on the gas hob. "How is she?" He didn't look up.

"Same. Confirmed the bitch has been visiting with her. Seems like she's been there all along."

Hux stopped dead. He and Jacob exchanged a look before he addressed Billy again. "She there now?"

"Probably not. I covered all the reflective surfaces, hid anything that could act as a channel." He'd made Tazia promise not to touch a thing. A game. A kiss. *Bloody stupid now.*

"It's not going to stop her forever, though." Billy flopped onto one of the bar stools by the kitchen counter. "It's worse than I thought. The angel's been with her the whole time. Insidious little shit's been filling her head with promises of saving the world. Whispering to her day and night." He looked warily at Hux, who was standing poker straight, waiting for his next words. "I think Taz is going to say… yes."

Hux dropped onto another bar stool. He gripped Billy's arm. "That can't happen. It'll destroy Anastasia and—"

"—the world! Yeah, I remember!" Billy shook off the other man's hand too roughly, and it smashed into the countertop. "What do you think I've been trying to do all this time?"

He sucked on the sore spot. It was all right for him, swanning off around the world to catch an angel that would never be caught. He hadn't been here butting heads with a semi-mad half-demon.

He left the stool to stand by the window. Lights shone from the buildings on the far side of the river. They bobbed and danced on the surface of the water itself. Tazia had stood there the last time he'd seen her in the flat, telling him she'd be just fine in Detroit without him. He should have never let her go.

Jacob's voice sounded low but steady. "Fear makes people say yes to many things. We must help her find her strength again, so she has the courage to say no."

"I told her I'd bring her home tomorrow." Billy said softly. "Going first thing to see the doctor, sign the papers and whatever."

"Understood. We'll come with you." Hux's voice had softened. He poured small cups of coffee for each of them and then began to repeat the whole process.

"Whoa bruv. We won't sleep if we drink too much of that stuff."

"We won't be sleeping, Billy." He looked up from his activity at the stove. "Plans to make… bruv!"

10

CAFFEINE

BILLY FELT he was knocking his head against a brick wall; the wall being the solid and stubborn shape of Soren Huxford. Three pots of coffee down, the conversation was going in circles, and the plan had yet to materialize.

"Let's review the intel." Hux said from his position on the centre sofa, or *command central* as Billy had flippantly referenced it an hour ago.

"Again?" Billy's whole body simmered. Not with anger, but vibrations. They centred in his chest, radiating outward, uncontrollably infecting his whole body. Like chattering teeth —but on the inside. Trying to follow Hux's train of thought was bloody impossible. He seemed to be speaking in slow motion; Jacob was the same. Slow as Hell. *How come the caffeine has only worked for me?*

"Yes, Billy, again." Hux turned to face him. "For Anastasia's sake, we have to get this right."

Billy forced a nod and paced toward the window, shoving his hands in his pockets to stop the shakes.

"We know the Advocate is being tracked. We've seen as much—in Detroit and Turin. She's a traitor to Heaven, right?

The pursuit force—whoever they are—come for her when she's corporeal. That's when you see her too." Hux looked to Jacob, "Correct?"

"Yes. I can feel her presence. She reveals herself like lightning on a dark plain—a blinding flash of presence. Then she is gone, and my sight is blind to her."

He pushed out his lower lip in a manner that made Billy—despite his high vibratory state—want to take a little nibble.

"So, if we force her to be solid, the angels will find her, Jacob can track her, and we can get Tazia to safety. End of." For a moment, Billy felt hopeful.

"Not quite." Hux returned the pot from the latest round of coffee to the kitchen counter.

"What? Why?" Billy felt tingling building in his hands, and he fingered the packet of cigarettes in his pocket to distract himself.

"First. It's too random. Sure, Jacob will track her, but we don't know where or when she'll pop up. We have no control. Second, to gain control we'll need to know how to make her solid. We don't."

As a distraction, Billy pulled open the door to the terrace and fiddled with his cigarettes. Couldn't he call the angels? Couldn't he blow a fucking trumpet or something?

Hux continued, voice dropping. "If she feels under threat she'll go dark, maybe take Anastasia wherever it is she goes when Jacob loses track of her. I'm betting that's a place we can't follow. It's too risky just to chase her down. We have to control the field of engagement."

Billy lit a cigarette and held it out the door at arm's length. The smoke hung languidly in the air outside before finding a light breeze and flowing back into the apartment.

Hux looked daggers at him. "Really?"

"My bloody place, Hux. You don't like it, don't breathe in!" Billy took another drag, and blew the smoke out of the door.

Hux turned a slightly deeper shade of pink and coughed dramatically.

Faker.

"So, how do we bring her to us?"

"We draw her into the open."

"How?"

"By providing something she needs more than her safety."

"She needs Tazia."

"I know." Hux spoke softly. They stared at each other. Sharing love for this girl had given them an unlikely connection. Sometimes, like now, it was too hard.

"No. I'm not giving her up to the Advocate. Never." Billy sucked on his cigarette again and blew the smoke out with force.

"We don't *give her up*. We use her as... bait." Hux didn't quite look him in the eye.

"Are you serious?"

Hux flicked his eyes to Billy's. He nodded.

Billy charged straight up to the bigger man and shoved the cigarette in his face, stabbing it just an inch from his nose with each word. "You talk about loving her, but you really don't give a shit about her do you! Do you even know what the word means, Hux? After everything she's been through. You're a fucking monster!"

Hux stepped an inch closer. With his eyes wide, jaw clenched, and chest pushed out, it would have looked like posturing to an observer, especially when Billy matched it, pushing back at him—a wrestlers' face off.

But it wasn't pretence, it was desperation.

Instead of fighting, Hux exhaled and gently took the cigarette from Billy and threw it outside, then held him by the shoulders. "I *do* care, man."

He dropped his arms and returned to the sofa, where he sat down heavily. It slid backward, drilling a scratch into the antique floorboards. "Don't forget, Tazia is mission trained. She's fought beside me. Years before that on her own. I know what she's capable of. She can do this."

Billy shook his head. "And she's my friend. I've seen her after your 'missions' with her. Seen the confusion between her demon half and human self battling out what the rights and wrongs were. Seen her polishing her fucking guns rather than sitting on the couch watching crappy reality TV without a care in the world."

He stepped onto the terrace to retrieve the cigarette and stubbed it roughly into the ashtray, still shaking his head and muttering. "She's only a girl. Just a girl."

"No, Billy. She's a fighter. She's strong. She can do this. She doesn't need a babysitter, man. She needs someone to help her fight back."

Billy simmered at Hux's words. He was wrong. Tazia needed love, protection, freedom; nothing else would do. He charged back from the terrace and settled on his desk chair, arms crossed. "You scratched my fucking floor!"

Jacob had stayed out of the discussion. Now, he finally spoke—voice low, unhurried. "You are the same, the two of you. One speaks of love as protection, the other of love as strength. But love is not either. It is both. And it is never safe."

Billy ignored the wisdom. "Who are you? Bloody Ghandi?"

Jacob didn't argue, just lifted one shoulder in the barest shrug.

When he sat, Billy had nudged his computer mouse, and the Mac had come to life. Joshua woke up along with it. "Wait, whoa—hold up. New guy alert. Did you guys hire a Marvel extra without telling me?"

Noticing the new voice in the room, and the face staring at him from the PC, Jacob inclined his head once, polite but not playing. "Jacob."

Joshua grinned from the screen, flickering lights catching

the edge of his skater boy face. "Bro, your handshake probably cracks walnuts."

Jacob's mouth flickered—not quite a smile. "Only when I mean it."

Billy groaned and flopped back onto the sofa cushions. Great. One existential necromancer in his hardware and one African god throwing deadpan shade in his living room. He needed more coffee.

"Hey, bros? I heard some of your chat from the depths of the circuits. Forget using Taz as bait. You're thinking about it all wrong."

Catching their attention, Joshua continued. "Jacob said it— if the Advocate is disappearing from his radar, she's most probably leaving this dimension. Dudes, she's not doing it for a vacation, she's doing it cos she needs to! Staying here takes up too much energy. Right?"

He stopped as though he'd said enough. The three men waited for him to continue.

He caught their looks. "Okay, look, it's like this. When I'm out of this box, I'm just a soul, right? Just like all the other balls of energy whizzing around the Earth caught here before they move on, you know, like ghosts and shit. But, I don't wanna move on, do I? I don't wanna go off to Heaven or Hell or wherever. So, to stay a viable soul, I jump into a warm body. It's the only way I can live, to be physical on Earth. I've got to MacGyver myself into blood and bone. Without it, I'm nothing, just a blob of energy to be maintained somehow— and that takes juice, dudes." He stopped again. "See?"

The others shared blank looks before Billy spoke up. "Not exactly, Josh."

Joshua glitched to an expression of brief frustration before trying again. "The angel's just a ball of energy, like me. She can't jump into a body like I do—that's not her thing. Instead, she's like a reflection in the mirror or a statue or whatever, but what she does doesn't matter. How she does it is the thing—it still takes juice. Juice is key!"

"So, it's like she has to go rev up somehow?" Billy was catching on.

"Yeah, just like that monkey-bro eating all those bananas, except she's likely doing it when she disappears. That's why she keeps falling off the radar."

From the confused looks, neither Jacob nor Hux seemed to understand the reference to *Donkey Kong*, but Billy did. He nodded in ardent agreement.

"How does this help us?" Hux pushed.

"We wait til she's gone off the Earth plane, then put up a wall to stop her getting back. Tech-head can do his magick-shit, right?"

Billy nodded. "Yeah, I can create a boundary. I did something similar that time with the demon who—"

"Whatever, dude. The point is, we don't have to use Taz as bait, we just trap the angel someplace else. Grab the girl and run." Joshua's image flickered dramatically on screen.

"And would your magick delay or trap her, Billy?" Hux asked. He'd gotten up again and was pacing as he spoke, his heavy footsteps flexing the solid planks of wood that ran the length of the floor.

"Delay. I'm pretty sure she'll have some tricks to bring down the wall. But it would hopefully give us enough time to alert the angels somehow. Or get Tazia safely with us. Why? What are you thinking, Big Guy?"

"Don't call me that—"

"All right, Ice Man." He smirked at the look he received back, his sense of humour returning. "It's a good plan, Hux," he added.

"It's a partial plan." Hux turned to him. "There's still too much we don't know."

"Like?"

"Like we don't know how to draw the other angels' attention when Jegudiel is not on Earth. And, if they're so good at finding her, why haven't they already chased her down?"

Billy addressed his shoes. "But we don't have the luxury of waiting until we know everything before striking. Surely it's worth a try if it means we could save Taz?"

Hux stopped pacing and leaned against the wall between two of the big windows, arms crossed in front of him. "What do you think, Jacob?"

Jacob shrugged. "I think we should try. I do not know your girl, Hux, but it is obvious she has many friends here who think we should not put any more of a target on her back than she has already." He shrugged again. "It is worth it, yes?"

Despite smarting at Jacob's words describing Tazia as "Hux's girl," Billy was pleased with the support. "You need to give the magick a chance, bruv. With my coding and Jacob's senses, we might just have enough."

"And alerting the angels?" Hux asked, his eyes pinning Billy in place.

Billy's stomach tightened. It was a million-dollar question, and he had the answer. He could just tell them. *I'm an angel. I can call them.* But the words caught in his throat. It felt fake. He couldn't say it. Not yet.

He looked at Joshua with a frown. *Say nothing.* "Uh… Praying has been known to work…"

Hux still stared, then nodded tersely.

He knows I'm lying. He cleared his throat. "Looks like it's down to me, then."

Billy crossed to his computer, cracked his knuckles, and rubbed his hands through his already immaculate hair a few times. Then he got to work entering the encoded magick that was his second language.

11

———————

WARD 14

BILLY PULLED INTO ST. Bartholomew's Psychiatric Hospital under another cloudless sky. The early morning sun made London feel tired, dusty, and hot. Rain made it sparkle. *God knows when it'll rain again.*

Getting three large guys into his three door Volkswagen Golf was like a game of *Twister*. As the driver, Billy occupied the front. Hux sat as his front passenger. Even with his seat pushed far back, he still had his knees rammed against the dash. That left the back seat for Jacob.

He sat sideways, legs stretched out into the adjacent footwell, looking every inch like a relaxed puma surveying the landscape from a low tree branch. Warnings to use the seat belt were ignored politely, something Billy couldn't bring himself to admonish after he caught sight of the man's deep brown eyes staring back at him from the driver's side mirror. *Beautiful. Soulful. For fucksakes, stop it!*

The red-brick bulk of St. Bart's loomed ahead. Victorian poorhouse, then school, before the NHS got their hands on it. Now it was clean and up to date with well-trained staff and decent food. Though it still had more than a few ghosts, he reckoned. The sort of place paranormal investigators would love to hang out.

As Billy drove into the hospital car park, he automatically looked up to the window that marked Tazia's room. Miles of identical metal-framed units rammed into the brickwork, but he knew hers by the tightly drawn curtains with their childish bunny print.

As they walked into the building and up to the first floor, Billy's plan was a simple one: to sign the discharge papers and bring her home. From his flat, they could wait for Jacob to sense that the Advocate had jumped to another plane, or wherever the bloody hell she went, and Billy would run the spell he'd generated in the early hours. Thousands of lines of precise magickal code just waiting. *Beautiful.*

On the instructions of the reception desk, they strode through the hallways looking for Ward 14 and the doctor on call. Flickering strip lights sparked off the maze of yellow painted walls. Billy had once called the effect sporadic jaundice, and Tazia had cracked up. One of the few times her laugh sounded like it used to. Now the lights just gave him a headache.

Hux and Jacob charged along like they knew where they were going. Maybe Jacob's sixth sense? Patients and orderlies pressed flat against the walls to let them pass, or scattered like bowling pins. Billy chased behind: "Sorry, bruv… You're okay, love… Thanks, mate!"

As they turned the corner into the narrow first floor hallway, a weedy-looking doctor in an oversized white coat leapt in front of them, palms held forward as though he was stopping traffic. Five foot two, specs sliding down his nose, clipboard shoved under his right armpit, and the strands from his white comb-over in disarray, he said, "Gentlemen, one moment, please." It seemed the receptionist had paged him. "Ms. Savoy will not be going home with you today.

You do not have the authority to remove her from our care."

Billy talked fast. Hux just got loud. The doctor stood his ground, his white coat and clipboard used like the weapons of a matador. After waving the board in Billy's face several times, Hux lost his cool and grabbed it.

The subsequent scuffle was inevitable, with the doctor desperately reaching for the clipboard while Hux held it out of the small man's reach. Billy continued to talk fast, arguing for their desire to bring Tazia back home to family.

Jacob left the wall he'd been leaning against to put a gentle hand on Billy's shoulder. His calm voice cut across the scuffle. "Doctor. I'm sure you believe she is safer here. You are wrong, Sir. She will heal with friends."

Silence.

The doctor met the gaze of each man in turn. "I agree she may make better progress with *family*. The only one listed is her father, an Italian Abbot whose whereabouts is—" he glanced at the clipboard which he'd snatched back from Hux at Jacob's interjection "—*not known*. Do you know where he is?"

"He's dead." Hux filled in the doctor abruptly.

"I see. Well, that complicates the paperwork considerably," the doctor replied. The strong prescription in his lenses made his already wide eyes huge.

"Why?" Hux and Billy spoke in unison.

"If she doesn't have a living relative—"

"I can sign. I'm her… partner," Hux interrupted with a quick sidelong look at Billy, who raised his eyebrows and made a little trilling noise with his teeth. "Partner" could be interpreted in a number of ways, especially when the main partnership was targeting which demons to shoot and secretly plotting each other's death. Some sex, also.

"We lived together in Turin," Hux added, as though this would make it a truth that the doctor could not debate.

"Are you married? Do you have proof of your cohabiting status?" the doctor asked, taking a little step back.

"Not married, no. Proof? Like what?"

"A joint tax return, perhaps?"

Despite the seriousness of the issue they faced, Billy couldn't help but smirk. Perhaps the most renowned demon assassin of all time and his half-demon lover also went to church on Sundays and had cribbage nights with their neighbours!

Hux glared at him, but addressed the doctor. "No."

Billy tried again. "Look, Doc, we brought her in didn't we —the two of us—four months ago? We handed her over to you. Asked you to get her well. And you have. She's fine now. She wants to go home, and we want to take her. What's the problem, bruv?"

He was smiling, but already aware the usual magick that happened when he flashed his remarkably white teeth was not sparking with this sixty-something doctor.

"Without a relative, we can only let her go if she passes a board assessment. The last one was two weeks ago. She did not pass. She appeared to be holding discussions with her Virgin Mary ornament." As he spoke, he edged away, and had already got a way down the corridor before he called back, "I'm sorry, gentleman. There will be another assessment in four weeks and she can try again then. In the meantime, we will continue to monitor her and let you know of any changes. You are welcome to visit her, of course."

He rushed the remaining few feet before rounding the corner and disappearing out of sight.

"We just take her," Hux said, and strode off down the corridor in the other direction to the doctor. Jacob shrugged and followed him.

Billy stuffed his hands in his pockets and exhaled hard enough to rattle the light fixtures. *Fuck it.*

———

Hux was already inside her room when Billy reached the doorway. He'd come to a dead stop just inside the door. This was the first time he'd visited since bringing her back from Turin four months ago.

He stood. She sat on the bed, both silently staring at each other. His jaw flexed as he stared. Her eyes flicked between his and the blanket on the bed, which she clutched in her fist. Billy felt a pang of sympathy for both of them. This was the young woman Hux, just a few hours earlier, had been claiming as a strong, determined fighter. Now he saw the truth of what Billy had told him.

"Okay, guys, you should at least say hi," he said. They needed to focus.

"Hello," Tazia spoke first. Her chin went up, and she gave both a brief smile. "I kept everything covered, Billy. I've earned that kiss!"

"Here's another one, love." Billy circled the bed and kissed her briefly on the lips and grinned. "You did amazing, girl!"

"Was Jegudiel here?" Hux side-stepped the greeting.

"No. I don't think so, anyway." Tazia glanced at the tall, broad form of Jacob now standing in the doorway. "Who are you?"

"My name is Jacob. How are you, Tazia? It is an honour to meet you." He stepped forward, hand outstretched, wearing the beautiful smile that had so disarmed Billy earlier.

She returned the smile, taking his hand, which he continued to hold. *"Vous êtes une âme forte."* His words sounded like prophecy.

Great. Gorgeous French accent beats nerdy best friend's kiss. "Okay. Okay. Introductions done. Let's all sit down," Billy urged.

Jacob sat by the door in the easy chair. Billy sat on a metal dining chair he'd pushed back against the low window, the curtains parting a little as he did so, and a blade of sunshine cut across the end of the bed.

Only the bed was left. Hux hesitated and then sat beside Tazia. He took her hand.

"We've got a bit of bad news, Taz." Billy prickled as he spoke, but refused to let the hand-holding wind him up. He focused instead on her release. Making a run for it would be difficult, but leaving her there could push her into the arms of the Advocate. He needed to play for more time.

"What is it?" Her body stiffened slightly. Hux put his other hand on hers to hold it completely in his grasp, and her shoulders relaxed again.

"We can't sign you out the way I hoped, love. I thought because we brought you here, we could take you away. But they're looking for a signature of a relative or else you have to pass some sort of board assessment."

She stared at him, eyes blank, forehead furrowed.

"It'll take a little more time than we thought. But we've kicked off all the paperwork now so we just have to hold on a bit longer, okay?" He was being forcefully cheery. How she reacted now could decide their next course of action.

"But I *am* getting out?"

"Yes, of course." She'd addressed Billy, but it was Hux who replied. He pushed her hair a little away from her face. It was a lot longer than it usually was; she'd not had access to her knife to chop it back. The bangs sprang straight back. He repeated the movement.

He wants to see her eyes.

Billy battled with his desire to launch across the room and smash his fist into Hux's face. Behind him, he heard a loud creak, but ignored it. Jacob, though, shifted in his chair, muscles taut, eyes flaring in warning as he scanned the area. Billy clocked his look, felt a flicker of unease, but pushed ahead anyway: "It's just going to take a little longer, Taz—"

"He means it'll take a *lot* longer, pet." The female voice came from the window. The three on the other side of the room stopped short and looked in his direction. Billy himself leapt up off the chair and turned to face the sound.

The curtains hung a shoulder's width apart and revealed the profiled torso and head of the High Advocate. She was not her usual translucent self, but in full technicolour glory, just bleached slightly at the edges in the strength of the sunlight outside. Her long, straight, red hair fell in a single heavy curtain reaching to her lower back and clashed violently with her purple dress. Ice-white skin and sharp features highlighted her Pre-Raphaelite resemblance.

She also looked like she was filing her nails.

Billy was not impressed with her apparent ability to kill two birds with one stone, and a low rumble emanated from the area around the window.

"Oh, Billy. You're making me vibrate!" She batted eyelashes over wide eyes at him.

He battled to regain control of his energy, clenching his fists, and repositioning himself to face her more solidly.

"Morning, boys." She ran a quick, dismissive look over Hux and Jacob. "Didn't see me coming, huh? Is that radar of yours not working so well at the moment, Seer?"

"I see what I am supposed to see, witch." He said calmly.

"Not a witch, pet. An *angel*. Is my halo not on today? Did I forget it again?" Her laughter echoed around the room.

Jacob, still calm: "And I do not waste sight on what does not matter."

A small flock of magpies rose from the trees bordering the parking lot. In one movement, they settled in the arms of the large willow tree that overlooked Tazia's room. *Vying for a better view. Little buggers.*

Billy glanced at Hux who held Tazia's hand tightly, as if he expected the Advocate to jump out of the window and grab her any moment.

For her part, Tazia stared ahead, her face relaxed. *She's used to her turning up like this.* The thought disturbed him even more than the image on the windowpane.

"Why are you here?" He sounded more confident than he felt.

"Billy, careful." Hux's voice. He would be wondering where this newfound strength came from. Maybe it was time to let his freak angel flag fly for the world to see?

"I just wanted to give Anastasia the truth, pet."

"Which is?" Billy said.

"That you three numpties won't be able to get her out of here unless you *blow the joint.*" She mimicked the American accent of an old noir detective movie.

Tazia looked at Billy. "Is that true?"

"No!" He took two steps and squatted in front of her, resting his hands on her knees. His voice softened. "Don't listen to her. It'll take a bit longer like I said, but it'll happen soon. You've got to trust us, Taz."

She nodded.

"Pet, you're still so naïve where these young men are concerned. They signed you into this God-forsaken hole and won't be able to get you out until you are deemed 'fit.' That means no more talking to the walls or windows or hiding those kitsch little ornaments. No more scratching at your legs or pulling out your hair. No more smashing the mirrors. In effect, my dear, it means that you will need to spend time with me. Every. Single. Day. Goodness, the fun times we'll have! Chatting all day, singing those songs you love, braiding each other's hair…"

Her smile blazed for a moment and then fizzled to ice. "We could even talk about daddy, Anastasia. Now, won't that be fun?"

"You won't have her, Jegudiel. She's stronger than—"

"I *will* have her, Soren Huxford. She will be my plaything just as she was yours when I allowed it. I will have her because she has no option, boy." The lights in the hallway flickered, casting short, dramatic shadows through the open doorway and across the room. "I will have her because your ridiculous plan to trap me in another dimension will not work."

The breath each man took was audible.

"Yes, boys, *so* many shiny surfaces in your flat, Billy. *Tsk. Tsk.* You missed a few!"

The vibrations in Billy's hands heated his palms even as he balled them into fists, never once removing his eyes from the Advocate's.

"I was working magick before you could even breathe, Billy. That code you created last night is missing a little something, and without it, you can't trap me anywhere. And anyway—" She swished the skirt of her dress and looked like she did a little jig "—even if you did, I'm too fast for those angelic Dick Tracys to find me. And by the way, they don't answer prayers, just so you know." She winked at Hux.

Billy rose from his place in front of Tazia and stalked to the window. A magickal glimmer formed behind him, disguising his actions from the rest of the room. "You will not have her, Jegudiel. It is against all laws. It is against our plan. And you will be defeated even if it takes another three thousand years." The words, their tone, felt like many were speaking through him. Like the energy of the past. It felt… natural. He wasn't alone in this.

Flashes of energy flew from his fingers into the room, traversing even the window glass. The magpies rose from the tree squawking, feathers tinged.

For a moment, Jegudiel reached out a solid arm and poked at his chest. "You are brave for an angel who cannot yet freeze time, Billy. This smokescreen you've created between us and them—" she gestured at the other occupants in the room "—this is magick a five-year-old can perform."

"I'm getting stronger."

"Yes, but will it be too late? You won't be strong enough to defeat me, pet. Not before I have the girl under my wing. She just has to agree to take on the role of Saviour. And she *will* agree, Billy, because she has no choice. She cannot leave this place alone. The drugs keep her so compliant, she does not have the sense to even try."

She waved her hand in the direction of Hux and Jacob. "The Hunter and the Seer cannot protect her, either. I will take them both, and she will be alone. With her soul in place now, she is nothing. Its power triumphs over her demon-self—until I decide different. She is clay."

Billy's shadow grew huge on the walls. A thousand wings lined up behind him. The room darkened. "We will defeat you. we—"

"There's only one way, pet. Are you strong enough for that, William? Really?" The Advocate drew back her hand into the pane of glass with such force it cracked from top to bottom.

The sound broke his focus, and the room was back to normal. Sun streamed through the window.

"She is gone." Jacob searched the space, eyes tight shut.

Tazia shrugged. "She does that." She shuffled down the bed, out of reach of the sunlight.

The High Advocate had scuppered their plan before they even had a chance to put it into operation. Billy stood with his back to the room. Fists clenched. Still as stone, apart from the tremors racking his taut body. He saw nothing but tiny dots of light in his rapidly shrinking vision. So much energy still coursed through him. *Need to let it go.*

He felt Hux grip his shoulder. "Easy."

His low voice and his touch had an effect. Billy turned his head. "She needs to die."

"She will, man. We just need a new—"

"You say plan, Hux, and I fucking swear…"

He could feel the energy again. Inside him. His cells shifting. He saw it in his mind's eye. Like a moving X-ray. Not just bone, but flesh. Flesh made of light, expanding, heating up. He knew the feeling. He was part of something else. Not this world.

Bloody hell. This is the power of Faith.

The feeling, no, the *knowing* was urging him to pick up a sword and chase Jegudiel down, killing anyone who stood between him and his goal. It ordered him to merge dimensions to pull her closer to him if need be. To destroy whatever was in his path. On and on until he had her.

No, too much!

The familiarity—the comfort—vanished. Now just buzzing in his head, vision fading to pinpricks. Pain behind his eyelids. Muscles tight, taut strings.

Fucking stop!

Blind, Billy flailed. Found the metal chair he'd been sitting on earlier, and hurled it at the window.

Propelled by overflowing power, it became a missile, shattering the glass where Jegudiel's image had appeared just a moment or two earlier and bursting into the air outside. The impact pulled the window frame from the brick surround. Twisted, jagged pieces of metal and glass rained down on the pavement below.

Thank god!

He could finally breathe again. His vision had cleared. Just flesh and bone again.

Hux gripped the top of his arms and guided him to the bed. Tazia was beside him, too, with an arm around his shoulders and repeating, "It's okay" over and over again. The line he fed her when she was in panic.

In contrast, Jacob stood by the door, unmoving. His eyes

open, and flitting back and forth, tracking something. "She jumped from place to place, but has now gone. Off this plane. I do not know what happened, but she was affected by it, Billy. She was weakened."

"Not enough!" Billy glanced at him. "Stop, Taz." He pushed her away from him. Seeing her face fall, he instantly pulled her close again and kissed her head. "Sorry, babe. I'm not… myself."

Hux still held one of his arms tightly.

"It's all right, Hux. You can let go of me, bruv. I'm in control."

"Sure? You seem… different."

"Anger got the better of me, okay? It's fine." He pulled away. "Look, guys. She's not coming back yet, not if Jacob is right. I'm gonna get going. I need some time to calm down properly. Go through the code, maybe. She said there was something missing? Well, I'm gonna bloody well find it."

Hux stood too. "We'll come with—"

"No!" Too abrupt. He smiled. "Bruv, you stay with Taz. She needs someone to watch over her, right? And I need some time."

"Billy?" Tazia said.

"Yeah, love?"

"I'm going to stop all this."

"How?"

"I'll go with her."

This time, he didn't attempt to dissuade her. In fact, he didn't answer her at all. He held her look for a few seconds, then walked purposefully toward the door.

Sounds of running feet echoed down the corridor. Billy peered out. "Someone better think of a bloody good reason why that window got broken." Two muscle-bound blue-clad orderlies tried to intercept him. He side-stepped them and pointed at Hux. "It was him."

12

ROUGH DAY FOR A SUPERHERO

NOW HE WAS HOME, the helplessness Billy had felt in Tazia's room curdled into a rage so hot his blood felt like it scalded him. He wanted a target, a battlefield. He wanted Jegudiel's throat in his hands. The hatred burned, a foreign poison flooding his muscles, turning his own body against him. *What the hell is happening to me?*

The Mac on the desk was still active. Joshua's face peered at him, cycling into a variety of expressions.

"I'm n-not... c-c-oping... t-too well... Josh," Billy stuttered, and dragging himself to the sofa facing the desk, he lay stiffly on his side. The action of touching limb to cushion lit fires in each and every nerve. His skin glistened with perspiration in the sunlight that flooded in through the windows.

"I can see that."

Billy's pain increased. Sweat erupted from his skin as tremors again took hold.

"It's the transformation, dude. I read up like you asked. That outfit you used to belong to, back in your angel days, it was created by angelic magick. Taking ordinary humans who demonstrated total Faith and devotion to God and instilling them with angelic power. It forced their bodies to change on a molecular level. You're a fucking butterfly, dude!"

"And… wh-when… I'm… trans… f-formed?" Billy shook so violently he was finding it a struggle to stay on the slippery leather sofa, and it passed through his mind once more what a stupid purchase both it and the black silk sheets had been. *Hugh Hefner, my arse!*

"I dunno—I couldn't find anything that really spelled out what the changes would be when they're done. Wings? Lightning bolts from your eyes? The power to strip a woman from thirty feet? Who fuckin' knows, bro!"

Joshua's voice faded.

Images pulled Billy away. Was he sleeping? No. A memory.

One moment he was on the couch; the next he stood on a mountainside.

He was with Julie and several other angels, but his attention was on the tall, indistinct figure standing in the centre of the group, Ezequiel. He asked one of them to step forward, to volunteer.

Below them, far below, Billy could see an army of demons marching across the battered remains of a fallen city. The tower blocks had toppled, smoke rose from hundreds of fires burning across the landscape, and everything was scorched and broken.

Abandoned cars lay on their sides in the streets. Their paint blistering in the relentless sun that seemed to have doubled in size. There were no humans to be seen. Billy instinctively knew that the last of them had been chewed on and torn up years ago.

In front of the group was a young woman. Her long, dark blond hair swept behind her as she marched energetically forward. She wore full combat gear with a leather breastplate and old black army boots. She carried a rifle on her back and a hunting knife on her thigh.

Now and then, she lifted a handgun and shot at dark shapes that peered from behind the remaining walls of half-demolished buildings. These were the humans that evil had twisted into deformed, mindless beings and then discarded. Ready now to be put down.

He looked closer at her. She laughed as she shot them, and was almost dancing along the street. This was Tazia, the Saviour. This was what she would become.

Back on the mountain, he stepped forward, and Ezequiel smiled and nodded at him. Her bodyguard had been appointed.

Billy sat up abruptly, the vision seared behind his eyes. The pain was gone, replaced by a cold, horrifying clarity.

That laughing, killing thing on the street—that wasn't Tazia. Not his Taz. Not his girl. But it was what she would become. And he... he was meant to stand by and guard that monster? To protect it? She would hate him if he let her become that.

No.

For fucksakes, no.

The path was laid out, a straight line from this moment to that hellscape. There was only one way to save her soul, to keep her from becoming that thing. Only one way to break the path.

The thought appalled him, a betrayal so profound it felt like dying. But it was also the only answer that made any sense. The only way to truly protect her was to stop her from ever getting there.

Only minutes had passed since he'd crawled to the sofa, but now he knew what to do.

He addressed Joshua. "We can't beat the High Advocate. Not yet. She has too much strength and influence. I need time to catch up."

"Okay…"

"And we can't save Tazia. It's too late."

"Erm, well…" A flash of concern cycled over Joshua's face.

"She has to die, Josh."

Joshua stared at him.

"I have to kill her."

———

HE'S COMING TO KILL TAZ.

Joshua had entered the hospital via the intercom system, zipped through the cabling, and jumped from one electrical circuit to the next until he found them.

Locating Hux's phone had been the easy part, but getting him to understand the text was proving troublesome.

Joshua manipulated the phone's display again, this time also making it beep urgently. HE'S COMING TO KILL TAZ!

Hux picked the phone up and stared at the message, his blank expression turning to a frown, but he did nothing.

Fuck! In his frustration, Joshua couldn't manipulate the code fast enough and just managed to make a series of unintelligible letters and emojis appear on the screen.

"What the hell?" Hux inspected the screen more closely, but still… nothing.

Joshua silently screamed.

He'd tried to make Billy see sense, reminded him that there was absolutely no way Hux would let him simply walk up to Tazia and kill her. "He'll fight you tooth and nail, dude. You ready for that?"

Billy had shrugged. But with a face painted with such fierce determination that Joshua truly believed he had the power to pull it off—taking down ten of Hux if he had to.

"It's my sworn duty, Josh," he'd said. "I have to save the world." In that moment, Billy was every ounce a superhero—sans cape, wings, or indeed, rockets shooting from his backside.

So, Joshua had changed tack. "Looks like you'll need help, though, dude." He blinked as innocently as possible from the computer screen. "If you let me out again, I can be your eyes and ears. Go places. See things. Report back."

He cycled his expression into what he hoped was a wheedling smile. "Let me out, bro."

To his surprise, it was as easy as that.

Billy was so focused that he didn't seem to care and quickly ran the code that gave Joshua free rein to use the Wi-Fi and electricity cabling. As soon as he was done, Billy disappeared in a flash of light that blew out the glass fronts of the pictures on the walls.

He'd just learned how to fly.

Joshua, hot on his tail, scooted through the wires so fast he'd got to the hospital a fraction before him.

Luckily, the staff had moved Tazia to a new room. He'd watched from the security cameras as Billy strode into her old one only to find it empty. He stopped, took a breath and, for a moment, he looked his old self again, young and lost. But it didn't last.

Joshua dove back into the wiring in search of Tazia.

Now, here she was—with the two man gods—in the opposite wing of the hospital where they were sharing a breakfast of toast, orange juice, and coffee. When he got there, they were even laughing about the look on the orderlies' faces when they'd heard Hux's rather weak explanation about having a pigeon phobia, prompting him to launch a chair through the window at the birds outside.

He beeped the phone again, hoping that Hux's blank expression would change sometime soon.

IT'S JOSH. BILLY IS COMING TO KILL TAZIA. HE'S AN ANGEL! GET OUT!

Still looking perplexed, Hux just prodded at the screen, and Joshua became exasperated.

ICE MAN! GET THE FUCK OUT! HE'S NEARLY HERE!

"Josh?"

YES! NOW GO!

Jacob stopped mid bite and looked up, eyes wide and staring—"We have to leave. Now!"

Hux stood up and grabbed Tazia. "Come on."

Confused, Tazia nodded automatically, and the three of them ran from the room, leaving the phone where it sat on the bed. Joshua mentally listed a string of expletives; Jacob had gotten the reaction he'd tried so hard for and now, to add insult to injury, he'd been entirely forgotten in the rush.

Seconds later, Billy strode into the hallway. He systematically opened doors looking for his best friend, the girl he was about to murder.

Jumping into the electricity wires again, Joshua did some quick manipulation to the circuit, then waited.

When Billy reached the door to the room, it was dark inside. The orderlies had given Tazia a room without a window this time.

He reached for the switch. The light flashed. Electricity surged from the socket where Billy still had his fingers. He had no time to scream. He flew backward out of the door and into the hallway, his head slamming into the solid wall. Blood smeared the painted brick as he fell sideways, out cold.

The sound of feet rounded the corner, and two orderlies rushed to Billy's aid, while Joshua jumped once again into the nearest live cable and zipped after the others.

13

FRENCH FRIES

SOREN CHOSE LAS VEGAS for their escape. The city reeked of instant gratification and sin—the perfect place to hide. At least until he could forge a more solid plan. Billy wouldn't think to look for them here.

Seventy-two hours since London. He'd pushed them through a circuitous route—Florida, Dallas, then a plane to LA before hiring a car for the final drive to Vegas. Joshua had scrubbed their digital trail, a trick learned from his time in Billy's computer. It might buy them a day. Two, if they were lucky.

Jacob flew with them to Florida, then headed to Boston. His focus was to set up a second line of defence. Friends there were fighting the Risings with all they had. They might have a lead on how to defeat the Advocate, too. Their weapon was magick, of course. Lots of it—ancient, strong, and primal—according to Jacob.

He'd left managing Billy to Soren.

And Soren was left with Anastasia. It wasn't going well.

In the seedy motel room they'd rented off the Strip, sitting opposite one another in the semi-darkness, he'd accepted she would never forgive him. Hurting her in Detroit. Then murdering Cuinn. It was too much to expect.

He'd had plenty of time to mull it over, but just came up with questions. Why had he chosen that path? Why was violence always his go to solution? How could he have hurt her when he'd just realized he loved her? Jesus, he was so broken. *Pathetic.*

With his confidence low, his planning skills had also gone to shit. They couldn't just sit there and wait for Billy to bash the door down. But his mind spun with rejected options.

If she could just give him something… anything.

After fetching some takeout food, he'd sat for an hour, nursing cold French fries and trying to read the copy of *Sons and Lovers* he'd picked up from the bookstore in Heathrow. But even the details of Paul Morel's torturous relationship with his mother couldn't distract him. He grew more frustrated with every page.

How could he keep her safe when she wouldn't even engage with him?

He roughly pushed a few stray locks back behind his ear. The grease from his fries transferred from his fingers to his hair, and the smell of cooking oil brought him up short. "*Shit!*" He swiped the fries roughly off the dresser and into the trash can. The book also went flying. Cursing under his breath, he fished it out of the garbage and wiped the worst of the grease from the cover with his forearm.

Anastasia hadn't reacted or moved a muscle. She sat on the end of the bed staring unblinkingly at the television, her own food lying untouched beside her.

Despite turning the brightness right down, the screen lit up one side of the room and flickered against her face. She'd complained the light hurt her eyes. She'd complained a lot. Nevada was too bright, too hot, too loud. She was bored, exhausted, overwhelmed. Now she'd subsided into silence.

"Are you hungry?" He'd asked regularly. It was a safe, necessary question.

"No." She didn't look up.

He couldn't blame her. The last few days reflected badly on him. He'd come back into her life, and all hell had broken loose. He'd forced her to travel thousands of miles away from London and away from Billy, the person she'd relied on before he'd pushed his way back into her life. He couldn't compete. Her love for Billy was natural. He had to fight for every soft glance.

It brought a knot of pain to his chest. It was always there, twisting. Even before Detroit. Even before he'd recognized it as love.

He'd tried to explain. Billy was the enemy too, now. *Jesus, the hate in her eyes.* They'd pulsed to pure demonic amber. A reminder that she was still dangerous. The knot grew claws and ripped at his insides.

Joshua, too, explained that, right now, Billy was not "Billy." He was an angel, a warrior, coming into enormous celestial power that he couldn't yet control. His priority was no longer Anastasia, but the bigger picture—whatever that meant to a newly awakened angel. Certainly, a newfound faith was telling him that killing her was the answer.

Then there was the Advocate.

Soren knew her better than the others. Right now, though, that didn't matter. His usual ability to think clearly, to get into the skin of his enemy, was lost.

He had no damn plan.

The pain in his chest threatened to still his breath. *Move, Huxford.*

He threw the remains of his burger in the garbage can with force.

Keep it simple. Process the threat.

Billy's new mission was at odds with his own. His was to

keep Anastasia alive; Billy's was to kill her. It made no sense, but at least black and white gave him something to fight for.

So, for the first time since they'd arrived that morning, Soren took charge.

He got up from his seat, crossed to the bed where her plate of food lay untouched, picked it up, and held it under her nose. "Eat!"

———

Billy had made it to America a few hours earlier. He followed the trail to Florida, then Los Angeles. It took a while. He'd searched for their usual pseudonyms, "Sahara Dune" and "Richard Hunter" but found nothing. It stank of a cover up. No doubt Joshua's doing. *The little shit!*

He dug deeper, with magick this time, and found a trail of deletions which led him to LA. Now he was here. Where the fuck were they?

More data sweeps, magick, even wishful thinking, all came up empty. Perhaps they'd moved on. Another plane? Bus? Hire car? He needed to wait until they made a mistake. A credit card transaction was unlikely; with more financial institutions collapsing each day, a cash-only culture was emerging worldwide.

Frustrated, he'd hoped that by now the angelic energy would have settled and he'd have some way of feeling out Tazia's location. Instead it just kept building—like the thermostat was broken. If he didn't regularly let the energy fly, he didn't just overheat, it battered him from the inside, blazing scalding trails of pain through his nerves leaving him bent double.

And the thing that really pissed him off? He still couldn't fly.

It turned out the flit from his flat to the hospital was a fluke.

To him, flying through the air on fluffy wings should have been the easiest of his new skills, but no. He'd still had to hack a ticket, travel to the airport, and sit on a plane for ten hours to get to the USA.

It had been intolerable. Each shudder of turbulence set his head pounding and his seat vibrating from his barely contained energy. And there'd been too much time to think about Tazia.

If he did, he had an image of her sitting in paralyzed confusion while Joshua filled in the details of his desire to wipe her from this world. It would be tearing apart every loving memory they'd shared together to be replaced only by loss and betrayal.

She would never turn against him, the way he was doing to her.

He picked up the coffee cup from the table in front of him, abandoned since his thoughts had started to flow more than an hour ago. Getting perspective through a caffeine injection in the airport diner had backfired. The semi-warm liquid had just made him feel queasy.

The stylized all American diner didn't seem to know whether it wanted to be a little bit country, rock and roll, or unrelenting metal. Country was currently winning, with Johnny Cash crooning the opening bars of "Ring of Fire" from the jukebox in the corner that ran the same short list of recordings over and over. He already knew Korn would be on next; it had looped half a dozen times already.

Tazia liked Korn. *Fuck!*

He didn't want to kill her. Just the idea cut him in two. No! That would be painless. Killing her would pull out his still-human heart, wring the blood from it, and stomp it to pulp. In the corner of his mind, Tazia rolled her eyes and scoffed, *dramatic much!*

He'd known her for the last seven years, since he was barely out of his teens. Adored her from the moment that stupid panda bear avatar she'd used online had appeared on screen to take a pot-shot with a little gun it carried on its back. A splash of bright blue blotting out his comments on the discussion forum.

She'd used it with abandon on everyone else, but only a couple of times on him, before he'd been switched to a private list where the panda threw love hearts instead of shooting blue splats. From there, they talked more, and she asked for a little hacking help. He took the job instantly.

The first time he saw her real appearance was when he'd appropriated her webcam and got a good view of a small and apparently undernourished girl wearing camo pants, a white tank top, and a mop of dirty blonde hair sticking up at crazy angles around her head. With a single glance into her dark brown eyes, he was in love.

An involuntary sob broke from his throat.

Embarrassed, he quickly looked up to check no one had heard. Apart from a large family on the far side of the room, the diner was empty. The two youngest kids ran around the tables, hitting each other with their spoons, while the older three were stuck to their phones. Mum and Dad stared out of opposite windows in silence, watching angry flies buzzing against the panes.

Another sob. Billy couldn't help it. He didn't want to kill her; he loved her.

The tears rolled down his cheeks, and he rubbed at them roughly with his palms, then leaned his forehead on his hands, elbows resting on the table.

"Refill, darling?"

A sixty-plus woman in full fifties waitress outfit, complete with a tiny ruffled apron, a paper hat that seemed to hold no particular purpose, and smelling strongly of hair lacquer stood in front of him. She proffered the glass coffeepot she was holding. Her nameplate declared "Julie."

Without waiting for an invitation, she winked broadly as his mouth fell open, put the coffee pot down, and slid onto the bench opposite him.

He looked at the family. The kids had halted mid-run, the one behind about to apply his foot to his brother's backside, and the one in front caught hitting himself on the head with a spoon. Mum, Dad, and the older kids looked the same. The room was in stasis, though Johnny Cash still sang on.

"How're you liking LA, baby?"

"I'm bloody well not."

"Oh, come on, Billy. That attitude won't help nothin'." She sighed, but her pursed lips made it sound like a throaty growl.

"I don't know what to do."

"Yes, you really do." She nodded energetically.

"Don't make me kill her."

"I'm not going to make you do anything, honey. You have to do what's right."

"Murder an innocent girl?"

"You know, Billy, there's so much wrong with that sentence, I don't know where to start." Julie sighed. "Yeah, I do. She's not innocent. And she's *not* a girl!"

The words hit hard. "She's half a girl." He pursed his own lips and frowned, still sulky.

"And half a demon,' she added, leaning in as if sharing a juicy piece of gossip. "The literal spawn of... well, you know who. Not exactly our team mascot, is he?"

She sat back at the same time he did, their movements in perfect unison. Silence hung in the air again, apart from Johnny, while he fiddled with the coffee.

She took the cup from his hand and refilled it. He sipped and winced; the pain of the burn broke through his thoughts. "If I don't kill her, she'll destroy the world. She won't mean to. She probably won't even realize at first. But she will, won't she?"

Julie nodded. "It's one possible outcome."

He looked up sharply. "One possible outcome? There are others where she won't destroy the world even if she lives?"

"There are always options, Billy."

He sucked in a breath and lifted his head back to stare at the ceiling. Each of the little popcorn plaster bubbles sprang into focus. It was incredible how precise his vision had become; he hadn't put his glasses on for days. "That doesn't help," he said.

"I know. But you see, I can't say more because I don't know. We'd prepared plans for an outcome if Tazia looked like she would obey Jegudiel. That plan was you—*is* you. What you decide to do, well, that's up to you."

Billy rubbed his hand over his face. It stank of spilled coffee and the sanitizer he'd used on the plane after the water in the washroom sink had failed to flow. "I don't want to kill her. I love her. But at the moment, she'll say yes to the Advocate before I can fully control my power. If I go up against Jegudiel now, not only will she laugh in my face, she'll pull me limb from limb and take Taz, anyway. I have no choice." The last words came out softly.

"Okay then, baby. Looks like the decision is made. Oh, and by the way, they're not in LA—they're in Vegas." She winked again.

There was a scream as the kid's foot collided with his sibling's butt. Julie was standing beside the next booth along, tending a newly arrived customer. "Would you like fries with that, honey?"

14

TWITCHING REMAINS

THE JEEP WRANGLER was an older model. Battlefield green, it had two doors, a soft top, and a manual transmission, which Billy was cranking for all it was worth. He loved it!

As he drove, the loose canvas top flapped noisily. The wind whistled in and swiped him across the face, cooling him down. The heat in LA had nothing to do with rising demons and everything to do with the Californian midday sunshine.

Thanks to Julie, he now knew which city to focus on. He got organized, shopping for the equipment he'd need to pinpoint Tazia: two powerful laptops, a supplementary router, two additional hard drives, battery packs, and a variety of cabling. He needed some serious firepower.

He also needed Joshua.

Billy was still smarting that the necromancer had abandoned him. He didn't really expect much loyalty; after all, he'd kept him a prisoner in his computer for over a year, but total betrayal? *Not cool, bruv.*

It hadn't occurred to Billy that Joshua helped the others because he believed the plan to kill Tazia was wrong. (Well, it had, but it was easier to ignore that pang of doubt.) He preferred to believe it was because Joshua liked Tazia. *Really* like Tazia. She'd captivated him straight away: "Dude, she rocks!" He once said she reminded him of someone he used to know, but refused to give more information.

Shaking off his doubts, Billy took his purchases and drove to the coast on a whim, hoping that the sea air would reinvigorate him. He parked between the ocean and Starbucks, for when he needed a sugar laden pick-me-up.

For a while, he got lost in the world of wires and hard drives. He connected the hardware together and then hacked into a satellite orbiting the Earth, mostly through technomancy. His spell was charged to find any digital trace of either Tazia or Hux. It would search every electronic connection in the Vegas area: security systems for images, cell phones for calls or texts, point of sale and booking systems for credit card transactions. It would pick up physical energy, too. The sound of a voice hanging in the air, the touch of a hand on a countertop, or an image imprinted on the ether.

He also wanted to try out the one new angelic trick he'd gained since turning—boosting the spell with his own energy. Would it work? Would it hurt like hell again?

He'd discovered the ability by chance on the night flight from London. After the electric light stabbed under his long dark lashes for more than an hour, he'd lost patience and angrily wished he could switch it off. To his surprise, the lights went out. Delighted, he played ping-pong with the stewardess for an hour. She turned it on, he off, over and over.

Billy's inane grin and audible chortles finally attracted her attention, and he'd stopped wishing for darkness. Instantly, a quiet buzz had filled the air, and a shimmering ball of yellow translucent light had manifested in front of him. When it hovered level with his eye line, the light pulsed, lowered, and whammed back into his chest with an impact that forced him back in his seat. The pain sliced through his chest and left him gasping.

In the rented Jeep, looking out over the ocean, Billy hoped he could create that same energy again. This time, to boost the location spell.

Focused, and still fuelled by heaps of caffeine, he started to form a vision of his magickal intention: Tazia. They sat opposite each other on his bed back in his flat in London. In between them was a game board. Her eyes were round as she rolled the dice and then turned a card.

In his vision, her eyes narrowed as she figured out her strategy. "Suck it, arsehole!" she said, her usual insult before making a move. He heard her voice as clear as a bell in his mind. She waited for his response with a hopeful smile.

He imagined that, as always, he'd just made some minor move to set up his own failure and give her the win. It was worth it. He felt her kiss on his lips and heard her impromptu rendition of "Walking on Sunshine"—

The sound of a passing rollerblader shouting at his companion brought Billy up short, and the vision crashed from his mind. Nothing had happened. He was still sitting in the Jeep with his energy intact and a stupid grin on his face. *Bugger!*

———

Two hours later, the sun was going down. Apart from peeing twice and slurping back another Venti Macchiato with caramel syrup and whipped cream, Billy had achieved nothing.

He blew out a long breath trying to calm the racing in his chest, unsure whether it was caused by caffeine and sugar, or the pulse-racing fear that he would fail and all of humanity would be destroyed in a despair-laden spiral of demonic doom.

Another out breath, this time puckering his lips

dramatically like he did when he fantasized about kissing his latest celebrity crushes.

Thoughts of Tazia drifted through his mind again. Where was she? Was she eating properly? Did Hux remember to take her medications with them in case she had a panic attack? He shook his head. *Not helping.*

Instead, he thought about the flight when he'd messed with the light switch. How had he felt? Manifesting the energy had been unconscious, spontaneous.

He retrieved his coffee, got out of the car, and walked around to the bonnet. He leaned back on it, lighting a cigarette and watching the sun dip behind the horizon; a beautiful pink and orange blaze spilled onto the ocean.

Off to his right, a young man loitered by the rubbish bin. Actually, more like fourteen or fifteen, he sorted through the bin, and found some sort of Asian concoction in a takeout box. He peered at it cautiously, as though expecting something to jump out at him. *Sensible thinking, bruv.*

Billy had already clocked a rather large cockroach, or possibly a small evil-looking turtle, sitting in the gutter hissing indiscriminately rather than running for cover when cars got too close.

The boy dumped the carton back before reaching down further, up to his armpit in newspapers, food wrappers, and condoms (*most likely*). This time, he seemed to come up trumps. He grinned and pulled out—a rat. A full grown brown rat, which was very much alive and wiggling, dangled by his tail from the tips of the boy's fingers.

Even from his safe distance, Billy lurched backwards. He didn't have any particular phobias, but rodents generally were a sticking point, and rats especially.

He continued to watch in fascination.

The boy held the rat above his head and looked deep into its eyes. The animal twisted away, bucking its body almost perpendicular to the fingers that held it tight, a position it could not maintain for long before gravity pulled it down.

As the rat fell, the boy opened his mouth and bit its head right off.

Billy's mouth also dropped open.

He stared in horror as the boy threw the still twitching remains into the garbage bin before picking the severed head out of his mouth. He examined it closely, stuck in a dirty finger to gouge out what remained of the neck, and sucked enthusiastically through the hole he had made.

Even at a distance, it sounded like chunky soup being sucked through a wide straw, stuck pieces suddenly releasing with a satisfying slurp.

"Bloody hell!" Billy couldn't help himself.

The boy looked up at him and shrugged. He added the remains of the rat's head, now just empty bone in a furry brown skin bag, to the body in the garbage and shuffled over.

Billy instinctively moved back around to the driver's door, not wanting to get too close to this rat-eating teen.

"Whatchadoin?" the boy asked.

"Erm, nothing much." Self-preservation made Billy feel he should be noncommittal, but he couldn't stop himself adding, "Nice supper?"

"Nah! I like them younger. Not so tough." He was still chewing.

Okay then!

"You gonna finish that coffee?" the boy asked.

"Probably not now, no." Billy was feeling decidedly queasy and held it out. "Do you want it?"

"Yeah. Thanks." He took the remains of the coffee, smelled it, and sipped at it cautiously, as though it might be quite distasteful.

Oh, the irony.

It met with his approval, and he nodded. "Later." He

briefly flashed deep red eyes in Billy's direction, then turned and wandered back down onto the beach, kicking sand and picking at his teeth with his black-filled fingernails.

"Bye."

Billy climbed back into the driver's seat of the Jeep and reflected on his experience.

He wasn't fully demon; Billy was sure of that. A half-breed, maybe? Or just some poor possessed kid. Another family out there right now, pinning up "Missing" posters for a boy already lost.

Demons were on the rise here. He'd spotted them in the streets and sensed them in back alleys. The guy working in the computer store mentioned a club to avoid if he was new in town. He'd assumed drugs. The sales assistant had laughed and said that was the last thing to be worried about. Now Billy understood. This… rat boy was just a symptom of the bigger problem taking hold.

His anger grew warm. Stomach and chest grew tight.

The abuse of human souls was disgusting. They'd committed no crime. It was too cruel for demons to take them for their own.

The soul's development was a beautifully slow process. It didn't take one lifetime to perfect; it took hundreds. It required mistakes and misdeeds as well as experiencing true happiness. Then it would finally emerge, pure, strong. *Infallible, for chrissakes!*

Billy loved the human soul. Guarding its existence was the reason he had been created. It was his responsibility, and he believed in it. It was his Faith.

Heat rose up through his stomach. Teeth ground together.

How dare they! It had to stop.

This abuse of beauty. To see them rip out those hard-won souls and discard the remains. Throwing it in the garbage, like the possessed teen had disposed of the rat.

There was just one thing that stood between those same demons achieving their victory over the human miracle—Tazia's death.

At last, Billy knew he could do it. Fury surged through him. He *could* sacrifice his friend in order to save the millions of souls that had been so meticulously crafted and—

"*Arrgh!*" Pain ripped through his chest like his heart had been clawed from him. Energy flowed from the spot. It collected as a golden ball of light ten inches in front of his eyes.

Holding his chest with one hand, he reached for the closest laptop with the other, and pushed RUN. He groaned and pulled back his hand to clutch at his chest with that one, too.

The golden light hovered for a moment before funnelling into the laptop. Both computers instantly lit up, and the hard drives he'd networked together whirred into life. The complex code-string coursed over the screen at speed, operating algorithms and churning out calculations so fast he couldn't recognize them even though they were of his own creation. The magickal elements of the code manifested as an intricate location spell.

A stream of luminous gold shot out of the laptop and leapt to the streetlight he'd parked under. The bulb flickered brightly as it received the surge of energy, then it whizzed down the cable to the next, where it lit that one up, too.

The spell progressed along the line of light posts to his right, hitting each one in turn with a mass of sparks. It jumped into the junction box that stood on the sidewalk before disappearing underground.

It was done.

With his chest still burning and his anger spent, Billy fixed the canvas roof of the Jeep in place, and climbed wearily into the back seat. He curled up on the blanket he'd placed there earlier and started to cry for his friend.

15

____

PREPARATIONS

BILLY WOKE at the sound of his own snoring. It vibrated loudly in his head, deep low notes through the layers of dried snot and tears. He was slumped sideways onto the seat, arms thrown over his face to protect himself from the giant rodent in his nightmare, its claws digging into his skull—

He shot upright. Climbed into the front seat, yanked open the driver's door, and tumbled head first onto the pavement. *Bloody hell!*

Fresh morning air cooled his lungs, allowing a breath, but he couldn't resist a quick glance back into the depths of the vehicle to double-check. Rat?

Sweat-sodden t-shirt now in hand, he looked around.

It was early, about six thirty. Serious runners and the more leisurely joggers bounded past him either singly or in groups of two or three, each of them attached to earphones or checking the pace monitors on their arms or watches. They ignored him as he stretched out cramps, half-naked, by the car.

Billy remembered the rat boy from the night before and shuddered, the nightmare suddenly making sense. Then the rest came flooding back—the location spell!

He jumped back in the vehicle to check the laptops on the passenger seat. With the help of the battery backups, they were still whirring away. He already knew his energy hadn't returned. The hole ripped in his chest by the golden ball of light from the night before still pulsed, like it was emitting a constant S.O.S.

Would he find Tazia that day? Or would he have to spend another night camped by the open sea and sky, linked to the only working satellite he could find?

No, he would not think of Tazia.

If the mission—*Christ, I sound like Hux*—was going to be successful, he needed to get a handle on his emotions. He was teetering on the edge already.

With a Starbucks breakfast on order, Billy popped into their bathroom for a clean-up. In the washbasin mirror, a very different reflection gazed back at him. His light brown skin had peeled in patches, revealing new blotches of subtle colour, pinkish in some places, bleached creamy in others, and yet deeper tones of brown. What the hell? Was he becoming some sort of abstract representation of the whole human race? Or a tortoiseshell cat!

His hair upset him the most. It stood up alarmingly in different directions, making him look like an electrocution victim. And were there strands of grey? Of red! *No bloody way!*

He dunked the top of his head in a basin full of water, squeezed the extra out, and shook his head like a dog before layering in a fresh amount of wax and gel. The odd-coloured hairs continued to stick out like beacons in the night. Would he grow three in each place if he pulled them out? He'd read that somewhere. *Fuck!*

Doing his best to stop staring in the mirror, he cleaned his teeth and headed back to the counter to pick up his order before returning to the car.

For the next two hours, Billy sat in the Jeep running the

engine to recharge the laptops and, at the same time, had his cell phone plugged into a USB port, getting a full charge while he could. The heat from the engine, the laptops, and the sun made it sweltering inside despite the open top. He felt like a puppy locked in a car by a bastard owner, and had instant sympathy for those sad stories he'd read online.

He didn't even like puppies.

Billy's cell phone bleeped: a text message.

DUDE?

Briefly, his heart leaped. *Josh!*

Loneliness had lain heavily on him since leaving England. He was used to having Tazia and Joshua as allies, even Hux. Cut off and alone like this sucked. But, then again, Joshua was no longer his ally.

He picked up the phone. Should he? But there wasn't any point in not responding. After all, Joshua could find him just by following the cell phone signal. You can't hide from a roving ball of energy. So, he decided to reply: WHAT?

YOU OK?

I'M NOT DEAD. And after a thought, Billy added: WHERE R U?

BRO, COME ON!

He knew Joshua wouldn't fall for that easily, but he'd had to try: R U IN VEGAS WITH HER?

For a minute, there was no reply. Billy knew Joshua was digesting the fact he'd known Tazia's location.

Joshua's energy had a distinct signal, which Billy had programmed a thousand times into the codes that held him in the computer back home. He knew it by heart and added it into the working he'd sent out yesterday. If the spell found him, it would reveal his whereabouts to Billy. If he was with Hux and Tazia, they'd be vulnerable.

The phone beeped.

NO, BRO. NOT STUPID!

Billy immediately typed and sent before he could stop himself. SHE OK?

Fuck! Not thinking of Tazia!

DUDE! BEST FRIEND WANTS HER DEAD!!! :(

Joshua added another little sad-faced emoji, then the phone beeped again: SHE'S DEVASTATED!!!

Billy sucked in a breath: DON'T WANT TO. NO OPTION. JULIE AGREES!

YOU'VE SEEN YOUR ANGEL FRIEND?

Joshua's coding couldn't express misgiving, but the speed in which the text appeared sent a strong message to Billy that he thought this was a bad thing: YEAH.

SHE HELPING YOU NOW?

Billy paused. What was he doing answering all these questions? If he really was on a mission, he needed to keep his plans secret. He could almost hear Hux groaning at his unprofessionalism.

Talking of him... IS HUX WITH HER?

YEAH. YOU DIDN'T ANSWER.

IT'S JUST ME

Fuck, this is so hard. I want my friends back.

HOW YOU GONNA DO IT?

Billy read the text and felt the blood drain from his face. The one question he didn't want to think about. Of course, it would be a two thousand-year-old necromancer asking. Joshua had killed a lot of people. It was part and parcel of maintaining his soul at the expense of others. It made sense the question would come from him.

Before he could text a reply, Joshua had sent another: VAMPIRE INNIT.

Billy was still stuck in panic, staring at the phone and unable to make his fingers type.

Joshua continued: SHOOT BETWEEN THE EYES. CUT OFF HEAD. REMOVE HEART. FIRE. He even helpfully added a little flame emoji to illustrate the last option.

Billy finally replied. I KNOW WHAT UR DOIN.

WHAT?

UR TRYING TO STOP ME.

Now, Joshua was quiet.

HAVE TO DO THIS—NOT EASY—LUV HER. The three texts tumbled from Billy's fingers before he could stop them.

WE'LL STOP YOU DUDE!

U'LL TRY. Billy turned off his phone.

He sat for a moment, listening to the ocean flowing in and out. The waves sounded like his laboured breathing, the in-breath loud and forced, the out-breath quiet and weak. His face itched; more tiny pieces of paper-like skin fell. In the distance, a mass of seagulls called.

While other wildlife had retreated away from the areas where demons were increasing, birds had been drawn to them: seagulls, pigeons, magpies. They were everywhere. They brought down planes, stripped trees, collapsed roofs under the sheer weight of numbers. No one yet seemed to understand why. *Perhaps Julie knows?*

Billy's thoughts were a deliberate distraction. While he was thinking about birds, he could forget about killing Tazia. At least for a moment.

The streetlights to his right started to hum. They were off in the daylight, but electricity still flowed, passing from one to another. It sounded like someone was playing a vintage Stylophone one note at a time, getting increasingly higher as it got closer.

As the sound pierced Billy's thoughts, a flash, like a ball of lightning, hit the front of the Jeep. It flowed into the vehicle as a long golden stream.

The light stretched and wove its way around the inside of

the car, pausing in front of Billy before finding the laptops and pouring into them. Immediately the processors went crazy, whirring and flashing.

Billy grabbed the one closest, the one he'd set up to control the program, and wrote code in a haze of speedy fingers. Magick took control as he typed faster and faster, his mind empty. The spell had brought back data which had to be decoded.

Eventually, he stopped typing, and the golden ball of energy emerged from the laptop and reformed in front of him. He went stiff. This would be bad.

It blasted him full on the chest. With no flex in the back of the seat, he had nowhere to go and took the full force. It struck him like a hammer blow. His solar plexus contracted, and his breath was knocked from him. He screamed for air as the angelic essence reformed and twisted within his flesh, scorching a path to his centre like the blade of a scalding dagger.

Blackness.

Unconsciousness lasted just a moment before Billy opened his eyes and sucked in air. Big, ragged breaths grated against his throat and burned his lungs. He gripped the sides of the laptop so tight, the bones in his knuckles strained against tightly stretched skin.

As the pain subsided, five words appeared on the screen of the laptop: Laser Ridge Motel, Las Vegas.

16

SHAMPOO AND SWITCHBLADES

BACK AT THE MOTEL, Soren was deciding if it was time to move on. Staying in one place for too long was risky. He'd asked Joshua to check up on Billy, find out where he was, whether he was on their tail.

While he was waiting to hear back, Anastasia finally hit the bathroom for her first shower since their arrival in America.

Her refusal to wash had become a battle of wills. His hints had been met with shrugs, forcing him to a blunt. "You stink!" That earned him only a stubborn silence. His patience—never a strength—stretched taut.

A look at her hair hanging in greasy rat-tails, her waxy skin, and the clothes that hung loosely off her shoulders, meant only one thing: she'd given up on herself. The lack of hygiene was part of it.

He needed the demon back. He needed her strength. There was a battle coming. Now was not the time for hugs and sympathy. When he was forced to sit next to the open window, just to escape her body odour, he snapped: "Shower. Or I'll scrub you down myself."

She'd complied, barely even raising her eyes to his as she

trudged past and into the bathroom. As soon as the shower was running, the motel phone rang. Soren snatched it up to hear Joshua's message rendered in a flat, digital voice.

After listening to it twice, he sat for a moment, processing. Billy was coming. Alone. But another angel was helping him. His angel *mojo*—whatever the hell that was—wasn't fully charged, but Joshua was sure he'd be at full power soon. And the kicker? Billy still wanted Tazia dead.

Decision made. They would fight. He had to prepare her for a war. Cruel to be kind, and all that.

"Anastasia, are you done?" he called through the door of the bathroom. The water still flowed. No reply. After calling again and getting no reply, he pushed the door open and went inside.

She sat in the small shower stall, naked and hunched in the corner, hugging her knees up in front of her. She looked up but didn't move or speak. The hot water was all gone and now ran slightly tepid. She shook a little, and her skin had risen in goosebumps.

Soren took one look and switched to autopilot. He turned off the water, grabbed the bath towel, and pulled her to him. As he leaned closer to wrap it around her shoulders, he could hear her teeth chattering. She still didn't move.

He took his switchblade from his pocket and placed it on the floor in front of her. Then he retrieved a plastic tooth mug from the cabinet above the sink and, after pulling off its cellophane wrapping, also put it in the shower stall.

Settling on the battered pink bath mat, he took up the knife and made a deep cut with the tip into his left forearm, just above the wrist. He made no sound, not a gasp nor even a slight intake of breath. He didn't feel the cut at all.

As the blood started to flow, he left the tip of the knife in place and angled it over the cup. He kept watch on the cup as the blood trickled in a narrow stream so that it didn't overflow, his eyes also flicking frequently to her. Why had he left it this long? Another failure.

Likewise, she watched him, and when their eyes met for a moment, he noticed her dark brown irises flashed with a few orange sparks—the most life he'd seen in her since they'd left London.

When the cup was full, he removed the knife, and the cut in his skin instantly healed, the action of the wards flowing over his skin.

He held out the cup. The deep red blood sparkled in the overhead light of the bathroom. Life giving. "Drink it." It wasn't an order, not this time. He was trying for kindness, nerves light in his stomach. *Please.*

It was just food, needed to restore her strength and health, but it felt like more to him. If she accepted, it could be the start of the reconciliation he needed. No, he couldn't wish for that. *Just food then.*

But she didn't move.

"Anastasia—Tazia—listen to me. Billy. Is. Coming." He emphasized each word carefully, but kept his voice level. "I want to keep you safe, but right now, you're the best weapon we have. You need to get strong. Drink it. Please."

The smell of the blood seemed to animate her. Even he could discern a metallic tinge in the air. For her, it would be stirring up something primal. Billy had told him she'd not had one drop of blood since Detroit, surviving instead on human food, but human food couldn't sustain her long-term.

As her eyes flecked bronze, her pupils widened and her mouth opened a little, the tip of her tongue moistening her lips. She took the cup, hand shaking so much that he couldn't let go, but instead leaned forward with her, guiding it to her lips. There she stopped and stared at him a moment longer.

He nodded, encouraging her. "Drink."

She sipped at the warm blood. Then, as her eyes became

fully bronzed, she gulped it down in long pulls, which he watched pass from her mouth to her throat and even into her stomach as her abdominal muscles tensed and relaxed. It was as though she was sucking the blood inside her flesh to be instantly assimilated into her physical form.

She lowered the cup and let him take it back. "More!"

Soren nodded and repeated the process as before. This time, as soon as he'd finished, she seized the cup from him and downed the contents in one long gulp. The cup wasn't big, and he filled it twice more before he had to cut her off. Too much in one go would make him weak. He promised more later— also a fresh burger and fries. To that, she gave him a little half smile.

"Did you wash your hair?" he asked. She shook her head, so he stood her up, hung the towel back on the shower rail, took off his own clothes, and stepped into the shower stall with her.

The water had heated again, but not to the usual scalding temperature he preferred. He worked quickly, using the free motel shampoo to lather her hair, then move her head under the trickle of water to rinse. Twisting her around, he changed places so that he was now under the faucet and did the same thing to his own.

Soren killed the spray, then reached for the towels. He secured her wet one around his own waist before taking the second dry one and gently squeezing the water from her hair. Once done, he wrapped it snugly around her body, tucking the end to hold it in place.

They walked back into the bedroom, tracking wet footprints onto the carpet, and sat on the bed. Using his comb, he gently worked the knots out of her hair. It was a big job, and he tugged her head down more than once while he battled with the tangles. She didn't protest.

The touch of her hair thrilled him. A smile perked his lips. *Focus.*

Mouth set, he turned back to the coming battle. "The only way to get through this, Anastasia, is to treat it like a mission. First, we plan, then we prepare. Then we fight if need be. We've done this a hundred times. Nothing new."

She was silent for a moment before stating bluntly, "Apart from the fact we have to fight someone I love."

"I didn't say it would be easy." Soren paused the comb. "I need to know something first, though."

"What?"

"Has Jegudiel been here since we arrived?"

"No." She didn't hesitate.

"Is that the truth?"

She turned and looked at him straight in the eyes. "Yes!"

"Okay. Keep your head straight."

She turned back. "So what's the plan, lover?"

The smile sparked again. It was nice to hear a little spirit back in her voice. "We don't run. We wait for him."

She spun back around. "You want to fight an angel? Don't we already know that won't work?"

"He's still weak, Joshua said, still acclimatizing. I don't think he'd actually be able to do anything yet apart from trying to shoot you, burn the place down, or come at you with a knife. All those things we can be ready for. We've fought worse."

There was another pause, longer this time. Then she said without attitude, "When did you know you'd have to kill Cuinn?"

Soren stilled, comb held mid-way to her hair, and breathed deeply. "I knew it may have to happen in Detroit. That's why I tried to get you away from him there. Why I hurt you." He resumed combing.

He saw her flex her right hand a little. The bones he'd crushed outside Cuinn's bar had healed a little crooked. She had two pronounced swellings just below her knuckles. He'd avoided looking at them, but now, he put the comb down, took her hand and kissed it.

He'd said sorry to her so many times. The beating he'd given her was nothing she couldn't physically handle a thousand times over; she'd had worse injuries. But it stung them both.

At the same time, he remembered the moment he'd woken up under the rubble in the cave in Turin, nursing his own wounds, and facing the realization that she'd led him there to die. Did one cruel deed excuse another? He'd pondered that one over. So far, he'd only found excuses, not justification. Over the years, they'd both played games that ended in hurt.

"And when you did it?" she asked.

"What?"

"How did it feel to kill him?"

"I thought I was saving you…"

"I know that. But how did it feel?"

He had to give her a better answer. "Like I was killing my brother." His fingers wobbled.

For a while, only the smooth raking of the comb through her hair could be heard, all knots now gone.

"So, when Billy gets here?" Anastasia wriggled under his hands.

"We subdue him—somehow. Together. You'll be stronger by then. We'll try to talk him out of his plan."

"And if not?" She chewed her nails.

"Well, we might not be able to kill him, but we can disable him for a while." He pulled her around by the shoulders to face him. "Then, we get the hell out of here. Your hair's finished."

"Do I smell better?" She gave him a small smile.

"Much. Can you do it, Anastasia? Help me fight him if need be?" Her answer was pivotal.

"I'll try."

Despite the weakness of the words, it was the most focused he'd heard her. The blood circulating in her body was starting to have an effect. Vampires may be the leeches of the demon world, but they were survivors. Given the choice between life and death, they'd always choose life. They'd fought far too hard to let it slip away easily.

So, for once, he didn't chastise her for being non-committal. "Good. I'll get you those fries."

17

HOW TO KILL A VAMPIRE

THE YOUNG MAN who jumped in front of Billy's Jeep was covered in blood and wearing a ripped, low v-neck tee. Billy noticed his smooth chest and the brand of the shirt a split second before the blood.

No one had stopped to help him. This was Los Angeles. Usually, guys flagging you down at the side of the road were trying to shoot you, steal your car, or jump your bones, and since the demons arrived, there was always the chance they were trying to eat you, too.

Like everyone else, Billy tried to drive on past, but there was something about him, and he instinctively slowed down. The man took advantage and leaped out, terror plastered on his face.

It was evening, and Billy was finally out of the traffic that clogged up the suburbs. The interstate stretched in front of him. He should get to Vegas before midnight. He was pretty certain that Tazia and Hux would have moved on, but was determined to try. Now that his spell-work had found them once, it would track them again more easily. Anyway, there was only so far they could go in five hours, four if he put his foot down. He didn't need a delay.

The man banged on the hood of the Jeep. "Help me! Please!"

Billy considered the situation. It was clear that this guy was in trouble. He was already bleeding. If he drove off, he could be leaving him to his death. He was pretty sure no one else would stop for him. Silently grumbling, he pulled over so that the cars behind him could at least enjoy the free road. He heard "sucker!" as they drove on by.

He cranked the passenger window down slightly. "What do you need?"

"Need-to-get-out-of-here-man." Terrified, he couldn't get the words out fast enough.

"What happened?"

"Fucking-guy-came-at-me-slashed-me-for-no-reason." He was yanking at the handle of the car door and looking over his shoulder at the same time as though he was about to be jumped. "Please-man-please!" Cheeks shiny with tears, he seemed frantic not to let Billy drive off.

"Get in." Billy reached for the door lock, threw his stuff from the front passenger seat into the back, and let him into the car.

"Oh-God-thank-you-man-thank-you!"

As Billy merged the Jeep back into the traffic and continued onward to Vegas, he asked, "Where do you want me to take you?"

The young man didn't answer. He'd hit the lock the moment he got into the vehicle, and craned his neck to see out the window. Though it made Billy apprehensive, he was pretty sure he wasn't being set up. The guy was just too on edge. He was younger than he first appeared—eighteen or so—just a kid, really.

"Hey, mate, I can see you've been through something, but you need to tell me where you want to go."

The kid still didn't reply. He peered into the darkness, twisting his body round to check back the way they'd come.

"Ok, I just saw a sign to the hospital, I'll drop you there."

"No!" The kid made a grab at the steering wheel just as Billy put on his blinker to turn off the highway.

Alarmed, Billy wrestled to get back control of the wheel. The guy hung on with all his strength. There was a surprising amount of it! Although quite small and young, he had a big set of arm muscles. Cars swerved around them, honking horns at the idiot who was all over the road.

"Let go!" Billy ordered.

"Sorry, I just don't want to go to the hospital. *He'll* be there." *This is getting bloody complicated.*

"Ok, I won't go to the hospital. Let go and we'll just drive and you can tell me what happened, all right, bruv?"

The young man let go of the wheel and sat back in the seat. He was crying again. Not big sobs, just a continuous weak flow of tears that dripped down his face.

It was an attractive face. Though he had smooth brown skin very similar to Billy's own, his face was entirely different, with larger eyes, a broad brow, and high cheekbones. His hair was short everywhere except on the top, where it stuck up proudly. Billy was impressed. "What's your name?"

"It's… Ricky."

What's with the hesitation? Couldn't he remember?

"Hey Ricky, I'm Billy." He flashed a smile to break the ice. "What were you doing out here? There were no houses around where I picked you up."

"I jumped… from the car. He just went for me, man. Cut me. *Crazy!*"

"You said he was a doctor?"

"Yeah, he had one of those ID badges on the dash."

"So, you didn't know him?"

The young man turned and gave Billy a hard look. "No."

Billy caught the undercurrent and took another look at Ricky.

As well as the good looks and great hair, he'd been right about the t-shirt—a good brand. His jeans too were designer and stuck to him in all the right places. He also had boots, great boots! They looked new, shiny, black, and expensive. Not what the Average Joe would wear.

Billy turned back to the road. "He was a client?"

"Yeah. Picked me up downtown. Said it was just a short drive to an apartment. We didn't get there, though. He pulled up, said he changed his mind. Wanted to get started right away, so I did. And when I got my head in his lap, he stabbed me." His voice broke, tears flowing again.

The poor kid would be feeling vulnerable. Billy wanted to make him feel more comfortable. "Hey, mate, s'all right. If we were in London, I'd probably be your best customer."

He was half joking, but Ricky took him very seriously. "I thought so. Moment I saw you."

Pretending shock, Billy said, wide-eyed, "Really? Is it the hair?" He glanced back at him and grinned, hoping to put the young man at ease.

Ricky caught the grin and returned it with a little smile of his own.

"You said you'd been cut. Are you still bleeding?" With one eye on the road, Billy quickly looked him over. There was a smear of congealed blood on the side of his head, and more pooled on his neck and chest. It looked dry.

Ricky raised his hand and touched his neck and upper arm. "I don't think so." He looked confused. "I don't know why I'm not dead. He stabbed me. First my arm and then my neck. Just crazy!"

"Looks like he just side-swiped you. A lot of blood, but just a scratch. You were lucky."

"But it only just happened. He *just* did it. There should be more blood." Ricky put his hand up again and checked it. No fresh blood, just dried stuff scuffing off onto his fingers.

"Perhaps the jump knocked you out for a bit, bruv? You woke up and thought it had just happened?"

The kid put his head in his hands for a moment. "I... don't... know. Can't... remember."

"What day is it?" Billy wasn't sure why he was asking. They always held three fingers up when they suspected a concussion on the medical shows, but it was tricky in the dark. If he had a concussion, he'd need the hospital.

"Umm... Monday." Ricky thought about it. "Yep, Monday. I had to work the counter at my day job. Only do that on Mondays."

Billy looked at him again. "It's Tuesday. I think you've been out of it for some time."

"Really? Explains why I'm so fucking hungry."

They continued in silence. A sign to another medical facility came into view, a smaller clinic by the look of it. Billy turned off the highway and followed the signposts. He was right; the building was just a single story, long, low, and boxlike, but there was an emergency room to the left.

Halting the car in a spot on the far side of the parking lot, he said, "We should get you checked out, anyway."

Ricky didn't move. It was so dark inside the car that Billy could only just see his silhouette by a flickering streetlight.

"Ricky?"

"You got money?" the young man asked him.

Billy's heart beat a little faster. *Seriously, bruv?* "No."

Ricky turned and looked at him. In the shuddering light, his expression flashed as skepticism and then darkened to a frown. "That's a nice jacket you've got there, Billy. Cost you a bit. I'm not stupid. You got cash," he said.

"So, what? You gonna take it? After I've helped you out like this?" *The nads on this guy!*

"I'll work for it." He put his hand on Billy's leg and looked him straight in the eye, his chin raised.

Billy recognized the look: the pride, the determined tone of voice. He'd been there himself in the past.

He considered the offer. It had been days since he had last felt the naked skin of someone else. He missed it. It wasn't so much the end result he was looking for; it was the intimacy. But it wouldn't be right, not with this kid. "Mate, I can't. You're all banged up. I'll give you the money." He dug around in his back pocket for his wallet, pulled out a hundred bucks, and gave it to Ricky, who nodded his thanks, but still didn't get out of the car.

Billy waited.

"Can I at least kiss you?" It was an odd request, delivered in a small voice. He sounded shy for someone who'd been working the streets for a while, but maybe that was part of the act.

"Why?" Billy asked.

"Dunno. You've been good to me, man. Wanna say thanks."

What could it hurt? *I'm an angel—not a bloody monk.*

"Okay."

Ricky reached a hand behind Billy's head and pulled it toward him. He seemed gentle, sweet—until their lips met. Then, the urgency took Billy by surprise. The kiss was rough; violent even. He could feel Ricky's teeth pushing against his lips in passionate, almost desperate, need.

It was the sort of connection that was usually accompanied by soft sheets and candles, not in a hospital parking lot against the scents of dried blood, left over latte stewing at the bottom of a cup, and Billy's not-so-fresh body odour from sweating it out in a car for two days straight.

The smell saved him.

Unable to relax knowing he wasn't exactly giving off the Axe effect, Billy tried to pull away. Ricky held the back of his head tight, and wouldn't let him go. With the other hand, Billy heard him drag something against the plastic dashboard of the car. It hit the metal gearshift and clinked, metal on metal.

Oh, crap!

Without thinking, Billy moved with lightning-fast reflexes he didn't recognize as his, and grabbed at the object with his left hand. He didn't make contact. Instead, he found Ricky's wrist and gripped it fast.

At the same time, he shoved his right hand in between them and pushed hard against Ricky's chest. He couldn't budge him! Billy grunted with frustration; his angelic transformation seemed to be giving him speed rather than strength.

The tussle that followed was a desperate one, each man pushing back and forth, each trying to get their weight against the other; the centre console stopping both of them from getting any real purchase.

"Hungry!" Ricky's voice sounded more animal than human. He'd jammed his head against Billy's shoulder and now used it to push forward and gain some momentum.

"Give. It. Up!" Billy slammed Ricky's wrist off the dashboard with each word. The metal object fell into the footwell: a knife. The serrated sort used to cut up a juicy steak.

Fucksakes!

"Hungry!" This time, Ricky pulled his head away from Billy's shoulder as he shouted. His breath came in heavy pants, saliva misting over Billy's face with each exhale. His tongue was red and swollen. The boy blinked, and his eyes shone amber in the darkness.

A fucking vampire? Seriously?

With a surge of strength and desperation, Billy rammed his left foot against the accelerator and levered his whole body up and over to the passenger side. In neutral, the engine howled, almost drowning out another desperate shout for food from Ricky, before Billy threw his weight onto him.

With his hand over Ricky's chest, Billy leaned down, trapping him. The boy snapped his jaws, biting at the air a fraction away from Billy's face, and struggled to get up. Equally determined to keep him there, Billy pressed down harder.

At first, he didn't notice the heat accumulating in his hand. But then the burn strengthened, and a dull blue glow spread under his palm. Billy wriggled his fingers, trying to escape the heat and unstick them from Ricky's chest. He couldn't! The light intensified. It seeped between his spread fingers, brighter and brighter, until an electric-blue light burst from his hand and bleached out his sight. For a moment, Billy thought he'd gone blind, and manically blinked over and over.

As the light intensified, Ricky's screams got louder and more desperate. He kicked at Billy's shins in a last-ditch effort to get away, jerking his body this way and that to release himself. But Billy couldn't let go.

He couldn't even stop when he heard Ricky's flesh sizzle under his palm, or when the stink of burned flesh engulfed the vehicle, and grey smoke choked him. He still couldn't free his hand when heated blood bubbled under his palm, hot splashes coming up through his fingers and spitting onto his face.

After one last convulsion, Ricky fell back, silent, and still.

The light faded, and finally his hand was free. Under it lay the charred remains of the boy's blackened heart.

Shrivelled to the size of a peach pit, it sat in a handprint sized hole in the boy's chest. The edges of the surrounding flesh were shrunken. The ribs and lungs burned through, and the blood had dried to dust. Billy exhaled. His breath reached the heart, and it crumbled to hard black granules.

Expecting burns, Billy turned his hand over. There was nothing there but greasy black stains on his palm and fingers. The stink of warm, burned fat wafted up to him.

Trembling, he forced his eyes up to the boy's face. Ricky's expression was caught *in extremis*, eyes wide, the whites washed in red, and his mouth twisted in agony. The soft young lips Billy had just been kissing were now puckered, rolled back, and dusted with ash.

He gagged.

Without taking his eyes from the boy, he backed away, fumbling behind him for the lock on the driver's door. When he finally got it, he pushed the door open and backed out. His legs gave way. On his knees, he puked in violent waves, his body shaking and saturated with sweat. The broken street light strobing over the vomit on the ground.

Shivering despite the warm night, Billy took a deep breath, wiped his mouth, and circled the car. Gingerly, he opened the passenger side door and pulled out Ricky's still smoking corpse.

Now, Billy knew how to kill a vampire, and his heart was as broken as the pile of black ash he left on the ground.

18

SHAKING THE SERPENT'S TAIL

TAZIA HACKED at her hair with Hux's knife. She'd persuaded him to leave it while he went out to track down some takeout food. It had been surprisingly easy. He seemed pleased with her desire to finish her clean-up, though he'd raised his eyebrows and suggested scissors might be a better option until her fingers stopped shaking quite so much.

Bending double in the bathroom of the motel room, she'd cut at least three inches from it all around. She figured she'd tackle the bangs afterward. It was her normal approach to styling. Hux would hate it, of course. His own hair always looked like he'd just stepped out of a salon.

Her stomach growled at the thought of freshly grilled meat and some authentic American French fries. The crispy sort with very little real potato inside but some sort of reconstituted pulp flavoured with God-knows-what to make them delectable.

She stood up straight. The hair fell around her head like a star, sticking out at all angles. She shook her head to exaggerate the spiky look and blew a kiss at her reflection.

It'd been so long since she'd felt this unencumbered. It wasn't just a lack of hair. For the first time since she'd regained full access to her soul, she felt in control. Confident. As though she could handle whatever life would throw at her next.

The blood had helped. The strength in each of those tiny red droplets surged through her body. She felt she would burst if she stayed still too long.

As she smoothed her hair down with her fingers, Tazia decided to keep the long bangs after all. They were almost at the length she'd be able to tuck them behind her ears. Billy would say, cute. She laughed at the absurdity of it.

Next, she got to work scrubbing her teeth to get rid of the last of the rank odour Hux had complained about earlier. The mint set her tongue and gums tingling and matched the singing in her flesh. She rinsed, spat, and grinned at the mirror to examine her handiwork.

The High Advocate looked back at her. "Beautiful, pet." She combed fingers through her own long red locks.

Tazia didn't even blink. "I wondered when you'd turn up."

"I was waiting for that blond, giant man-god to go out. He's not keen on me anymore, Anastasia." She looked wistfully into the distance. "He used to love me so."

"No, he didn't. He just liked that you made him stronger."

"Oh my, Anastasia, you sound full of gumption today? That's unlike you. What happened?"

"He fed me."

Jegudiel raised her eyebrows. "That was very… nice… of him." It seemed she chose her words carefully. "Why would he do such a thing? Is that something left over from back in the day?" Her eyes widened, and the little smile on her lips implied firsthand knowledge of such delights.

Tazia blurted out a laugh. "Never our thing. Besides, I didn't have any trouble finding my own food." She paused. "But I've not been myself recently. You made sure of that."

"I never told you to stop eating, pet. And I've always told

you your place is by my side. If you just do what you are told, Anastasia, you'll never be hungry."

"I've always done what I'm told." Tazia held her eyes steady.

"Yes, and I'm sure you will again." The angel matched the stare.

"We'll see." Tazia glanced away. "Billy's coming. You knew he was an angel, didn't you?"

"Of course."

"Will you let him kill me?"

"Why would he do that?" Jegudiel pursed her lips.

"To stop me doing what you say."

The mirror creaked, and the Advocate's expression froze. "He was always such a do-gooder!"

Tazia leaned forward onto the washbasin, her nose just an inch or so away from the mirror, her skin tingling from the angel's energy. "Can you stop him?"

"If you say 'yes' to me, Anastasia, I can take you to safety. We'll set you up to have the power you were born for. He won't get you there, pet." She was smiling again, a wide, encouraging smile.

"We?"

The Advocate winked at her.

"And if I say no?"

The smile dropped, and she shrugged. "He can kill you if he wants. He has the power."

Tazia's head dropped. "But he loves me."

Jegudiel laughed, the mirror vibrating audibly against the hinges of the medicine cabinet it was mounted on. "But he loves God more. He's an angel now, after all."

"If what you want me to do will save people, why is he against it? Why is God against it?"

"Because it is not part of their plan. I'm offering people the ability to fight. Billy and his friends want Fate to play out.

They're spineless, pet. They want to see Earth destroyed, then they can swoop in to pick up the pieces. That's what they do." She bent closer to her side of the mirror. "That's what they call 'free will,' my dear. Stack up the odds, then force people into one-sided decisions. Save the planet when it's all over. That's what the whole ark thing was about way back when. Make the people bad and then save the few."

"I just can't believe Billy would do that."

"He's not Billy anymore, Anastasia. He's an angel. There's no Billy left."

Despite the blood, Tazia's mind spun. She grabbed onto each thought to try to find the logic. Each time it ebbed away. She grasped onto Hux's argument from earlier. "Hux and me —we'll be ready for him."

Jegudiel glared. "I've been very patient, Anastasia, waiting for you to come around and make the right decision. I may not be amenable much longer."

"You'll force me to say yes?"

"I can't do that, dear. But I can separate you from your friends." She counted off on her fingers. "Conn O Cuinn is dead. Billy's gone already. Soren Huxford would be very easy for me to destroy—"

"No! You've done enough to him!"

"But he never learns, my dear, does he? And all for the love of you."

"Please. Don't." Her energy plummeted. Normally she'd bluff it out, never beg. But images circled: Hux's face, their jobs together, leaving him in the cave in Turin to die. Her cruelty. His smile…

The Advocate continued with her list of targets. "That new ally of yours, the Seer? He's already talking to those he shouldn't in Boston. I could end him—"

"Stop!"

"And that just leaves your little necromancer. He's never

loyal to one person for long. I've been aware of him for a very long—"

The front door closing sounded in the other room, then Hux called to Tazia to come eat while the food was fresh.

"Coming!"

"What do you say, Anastasia? Us or them? Survival with me, or death with them?" The angel sounded like an angry rattler, hissing and shaking her tail at the same time. "It's time to choose."

Tazia leaned in, so close her breath fogged the glass, hoping her rage would burn right through it. "Fucking promise you will leave them all alone."

Jegudiel's smile was serene. She gave a tiny nod of her head.

The single word she uttered felt to Tazia like she had swallowed glass. When she turned away from the mirror, the angel was already gone.

19

ROOM SIXTEEN

BILLY PULLED the Jeep into the parking lot of the Laser Ridge Motel just after one in the morning. Out on the Strip, Vegas was still in full swing: coloured lights blazed, music bleeding from every doorway, and half-drunk revellers lurching along the streets. He'd finally turned off the highway, the drive a blur of exhaustion and guilt-slicked images of Ricky's dead body.

The motel looked sketchy. The sign out front read Value For Money. Sure, if that meant bedbugs and sheets you wouldn't want to take a black light to. It looked like all the motels ever featured on American TV cop shows: rooms in a row, doors facing outward onto a walkway, and parking spaces for vehicles right outside. The green-tinged petri dish swimming pool had a large closed sign. *Thank God for that!* Adjoining the motel was a Claire's Burgers, where the aromas of bleach and rotten lettuce blended with the gasoline in the air from stop-start traffic.

He'd assumed they would be gone, but checked at the reception desk, anyway. The twenty-four-seven service sign was a lie. It took thirty minutes for someone to answer the doorbell.

From the moans travelling out of the back office, the clerk was ensconced in front of some sort of sexy movie. At least Billy hoped he was watching a movie. If not, he wondered how he could get an invitation.

When the attendant finally came to the door, he told him that a tall blond guy and a small stinky woman were shacked up on the ground floor. He gave Billy the room number.

A few doors down, Billy settled into his own room to think out his next move.

He perched on the end of the bed, head whirling, looking for some sort of slick, organized plan. He had nothing.

Frankly, he was sick of it. The high stakes, the cruelty, the loss. The next steps were inevitable. The survival of humankind had to come first. Now, he could see the long game, the top of the mountain view, the bigger picture. Whatever metaphor worked.

He paced, a last faint hope rolling around in his mind. Would Tazia being half-human save her? Perhaps if he could persuade her to accept her fate, he could negotiate for her soul. To go to Heaven, not Hell. To be reborn into another life. Julie would help, surely? The thought of killing her made his guts twist, but if he knew it was only temporary, and her soul would get another chance at goodness next time—

He stopped short and sank back onto the bed, wrapping his arms around himself, wishing they were her arms hugging him. She'd been all he had. In those moments when he'd woken up beside yet another warm body feeling cold and alone, he'd call her. They'd talk and joke, maybe plan a job or play *Call of Duty*, taking out that dude with the semi-automatic who was impossible to get in single-player mode, and he'd feel good about himself again.

This back and forth went on for an hour before Billy finally realized he'd never be able to kill Tazia without it killing him in return. He needed to get on with it.

He headed to room sixteen.

The door was ajar, so he gave it a little push. Inside, only darkness and silence. "Taz?" No reply. "Hux?" Still nothing.

He eased his way around the door, peering behind it to the place where the baddies lurked in TV shows. No one was there. The bathroom door was open, light spilling into the main room. "Come on, guys! I've got no weapons. Let's talk." Again, no response.

Billy went inside and up to the bathroom door. The light flickered as a few large flies buzzed around it. The room was empty.

He blew out a breath, his heartbeat slowing. He'd just been handed the Get Out of Jail Free card. Gone. They must have left while he was in his room, having far too many moments of existential angst.

As he turned to leave, he felt the cold nose of a gun push against his temple.

Hux's large form loomed over him, still mostly in the shadows of the darkened bedroom.

"You were outside?" Billy said.

"Yep."

"And followed me in?"

"Yep."

Billy laughed, acknowledging his own stupidity. Sweat broke on his brow. The loud thumping beats of his heart started again—half felt, half heard—blending with Hux's steady ones. *Christ, is this actually happening?*

"Turn around slowly and put your hands behind your back." Billy instinctively obeyed. He felt a zip tie tightly secure his wrists. Her heart added to the chorus. It pattered like rain while she positioned the restraints. "Taz?"

"Sit on the bed." Hux was still giving the orders, and Billy obeyed, backing up to the bed. The front door closed, locking with a loud click, and the lights came on.

Billy shut his eyes against the glare for a moment, then opened them cautiously. Tazia leaned against the front door, and Hux, shotgun still aimed his way, had taken a seat in an easy chair placed six feet away from the bed. But Billy only had eyes for Tazia.

"You cut your hair." He smiled at her. "And looks like you ate something. Good."

She dropped her gaze to the floor.

"Forget the small talk, Billy. Do you still want her dead?" Hux demanded.

"Straightforward as always, Hux. I don't *want* her dead, no. Of course I don't. I keep telling you that—and her, and Joshua, and anyone else who'll bloody listen. I love her."

"Then why?" Despite her defiant eyes, Tazia spoke in a low voice. He'd heard her scream, shout, curse at him before, but this… little voice? It cracked his heart open wider.

"Because it's not up to me, Taz. I swore I'd protect you from the Advocate. But that promise was part of something bigger. Bigger than you and me. It was part of a promise to save everyone from her plans, not just you." He let out a big breath. "I failed, love. I'm so sorry, but I failed. You said you'd do exactly what she wants you to. And I can't let you. Because if I do, everyone dies. I've seen it." His mind flashed back to the vision of the future Ezequiel had given him.

"She's not doing anything, man. She's here, with me. Not Jegudiel. She hasn't even seen her since we arrived."

Billy's heart broke for him too. "Of course she has, Hux. Do you think the Advocate would leave her alone to run away with you when all her plans are resting on Taz saying yes?" He looked at her. "Tell him, Taz. Be honest."

Hux looked at Tazia, frowning. "Tell me."

"She was just here—for the first time." She scanned the floor.

His chin dropped a fraction, then he shook his head slowly.

"It's no matter." His voice was a little too loud. "You're not going to kill her, Billy, and the Advocate isn't going to take her."

"Hux, just how strong do you think you are, bruv? You're one guy. One human man up against angels and demons. Do you really think you can stop this?" Billy couldn't suppress the incredulity in his voice, enough to make anyone doubt themselves.

"I could kill you now—" Hux raised the shotgun "—or cripple you. Your choice."

"Try it!" Billy couldn't believe his own confidence. Would a shot this close cause serious harm, or just bounce off his skin? He had no option but to call his bluff.

"No!" Tazia left her place by the door and pushed the barrel of the gun away. "You said we'd just subdue him. And he's right, Hux. A gun won't stop him. Even if it did, don't you think there'll be another angel to take his place?" She crossed to the bed and sat down next to Billy, immediately resting her head on his shoulder. "If you kill me, will it all stop? Will the Advocate give up?"

"She'll never give up. But her biggest weapon will be out of play," Billy said.

"For Godsakes, Anastasia, don't listen to this. There's always another way." Hux let the barrel of the gun fall further and leaned forward in the chair. "Billy, work with us, man! Together we can do this. Jacob's already onto something in Boston. Just stop."

"Hux, if she agrees to this now, there's a chance her soul will be saved. No Hell. Reincarnation down the line. This sacrifice may just cancel out everything else."

"That's stupid! She should allow you to murder her to maybe—possibly—save her soul long-term? What if we keep her alive? What if we find a way for her to cancel out the bad in *this* lifetime?" He pointed the gun at the floor and walked toward him. "Come on, man. You have to see it doesn't make sense?"

Billy's eyes flicked to Hux's. Blue, honest, and of all the things he didn't expect to see, trust. *Fucksakes.*

It had to be now.

Strength pulsed through his body, the raw angelic power he remembered from long ago. He pulled his arms apart behind his back, stretching the plastic tie until it snapped. Up and out of Tazia's reach in an instant, he snatched Hux's gun from him, and smashed the stock onto his jaw.

Blasted across the room, Hux hit the far wall, forehead first. The plaster shattered, and his head rested against a deep depression. He slumped to his knees and groaned. Teeth gritted, Billy brought the gun down on his head again, directly on his temple this time. *Sorry, bruv.* He didn't want to kill him, just disable him for a while.

For now, Hux was out cold.

Billy turned back to Tazia. She hadn't moved from the position by the bed. Her eyes flashed amber, but she looked relaxed, almost serene. Billy adopted the same authoritarian tone Hux had used. "Come here."

Without hesitation, she walked to him, eyes back to beautiful deep brown. But empty. No life. The fight in her already gone. Did she actually want this? He opened his arms wide, and she came to him. "You know I love you?" His eyes were dry, but it was taking all he had to control the shaking in his limbs. Power circled inside him, ready to spill.

She nodded.

Smiling, he wrapped his arms around her and put his right hand to her upper back, level with her heart. The blue light surged from his palm and burned ice-hot into her skin.

Smoke rose. She shuddered.

Then she screamed.

20

DARKNESS

BILLY DROPPED HIS HAND. *I can't!*

It wasn't just her physical pain. Her very soul screamed for him to stop. *This is not the way.* Something spoke through him.

The material of her top had burned away, flesh melting under his touch, and the smooth surface of her rib bones made contact with his hand. In the air, the acrid scent of smouldering cloth mixed with the stink of scorched flesh. The hot tang of her blood touched all his senses at once.

As he let her go, she swayed, then her legs buckled. He reached forward to catch her—

A surge of dazzling white light exploded in front of him. The force of it swept him up and hurled him across the room. He hit the wall where Hux still lay, and slid down to the ground, dazed. *What the hell?*

"YOU WILL NOT TOUCH HER, ANGEL!" Barely coherent, the words shook the motel room, and a crack snaked up the wall next to his head. A huge pitch-black shadow loomed over him, throwing him into darkness. He backed away from it, and snapped his head around to face its source: the solid form of Jegudiel, bending over him. Blotches of red and purple stained her white skin; her features pinched and sharp. She growled through gritted teeth, "She. Is. Mine."

She swiped at him again. He flew the other way, crashing into the bathroom, taking out the wooden door as he went. He ricocheted off the basin, breaking it in two, before landing with his head rammed into the toilet bowl. The scent of the green pine freshener, hanging under the rim in its little white plastic holder, revived him. *Get up, Billy!*

He scrambled to get one foot beneath him. Before he could rise, the angel dragged him by one leg back into the bedroom and threw him down beside Tazia, who'd crouched on the floor moaning and twisting to reach the deep burn on her back. On his stomach, Billy stretched out a hand to her, but before he could make contact, Jegudiel snatched her out of his reach.

She carried Tazia to the bathroom, all the time cooing baby talk, and propped her forward against the wall. Water fountained from the broken basin and showered onto her back. Tazia moaned louder. When the burn stopped smoking, her cries subsided.

To his horror, Billy saw a handprint visible on her flesh. The burn was deep enough in places to have etched black into the white flashes of her rib bones. The surrounding skin remained scarlet and cracked.

He dropped his head onto the revolting carpet. Waves of sadness and shame rolled through his heart. Then, like a switch flicked, anger. Pure rage surged and burst from his body. A pure white flash of energy that rivalled Jegudiel's own. It burned in him, around him, through him. Ice-fire sparked from his fingers and blistered through his bones.

The energy propelled him to his feet, and he stomped into the bathroom where the Advocate still leaned over Tazia. She turned her head just as he grabbed a handful of her long red hair and jerked her backward, dragging her from the bathroom as she had done to him only moments before.

Her shrieks shattered both the bathroom and bedroom mirrors, showering Tazia in a cascade of silver slivers.

With the Advocate's hair still wrapped around his hand, Billy forced her over onto her back. He sat astride her, looping the long hair around her neck, and pulled. Her cry abruptly silenced. She thrashed beneath him, eyes bulging under the pressure of the tightening hair.

Under duress, the hair started to snap, and he switched to his hands, squeezing her throat. The fingernails of his thumbs pierced deeply into the flesh until blood seeped from the wounds and he could feel the taut tendons under her chin.

He choked her with the frustrations of hundreds of years waiting as an unborn human soul to serve as Tazia's protector. He choked her with the frustration of his failure. He choked her with his own guilt at hurting his girl in such an abhorrent way.

And he prayed: *Help me, my brothers and sisters. I have her. Come to my aid!*

"You're solid, bitch. You think they won't all be here soon?" He spat the words at her.

Blood bubbled from the corner of her mouth, her eyes rolling back in her head, while a manic grin formed on her face.

The smile confused him. "What? Why?" He blurted at her, but he'd already felt it.

A chill metal blade slid beneath his shirt. Its tip pierced his flesh and sank slowly deeper until it hit resistance. Then it cut a line from his back to his left side, grating over each individual rib. Billy grunted his pain, feeling the heat of the wound.

He let go of her neck to twist away, to grab at her hand, anything—

Too slow.

Jegudiel's arm already stretched above her head, the dagger ready to drop. The blade caught the flickering light of the bathroom just in time to warn him, and he raised his left hand. The Advocate struck, and the knife pierced through the centre of his palm.

Billy's scream spiralled into the atmosphere. It blasted out the remaining window glass, sending fractured pieces flying into the air outside the motel. Reverberations set security systems and car alarms screeching.

The Advocate pulled out the dagger, leaving a jagged hole in Billy's palm an inch wide. Electric-blue light sprang directionless from the wound, illuminating the motel room in another blinding flash.

Holding his hand, Billy gasped and dragged himself away from her, his strength seeping from him with each movement. Breath gone, he sheltered on the floor at the foot of the bed and vomited yellow bile as the agony of the wound hit his empty stomach. When the blue light ebbed, the wound gushed blood into the pool already formed from his slashed back.

He had nothing left. He was just a boy again. Weak and thin, waiting for his mother to get home, scared and alone. As then, he wished with all his might someone would come and rescue him. Where were the angels? Where was Julie? Wasn't there anyone to help him?

Falling sideways to the ground, he clasped his injured hand, and looked desperately around. Hux was still out cold. Inside the bathroom, Tazia had collapsed to the ground. She appeared to be miles away from where he lay, his vision tunnelling in and out.

With a last-ditch effort, Billy tried to rise, but his legs would not hold his weight. He crashed down again.

A foot wearing a perfect three-inch-heeled purple ankle boot came into focus. Laces were secured around exquisite golden grommets, and the suede leather was smooth and even.

The boot was joined by another. Together they stamped close to his face before travelling into the bathroom.

The Advocate picked Tazia up and carried her back. This time, she paused by his face and leaned over him. "She said yes to me, Billy. Even as she was agreeing to your stupid plan to kill her, she already knew I was coming to save her. She wanted *me*, Billy. Not you. Or the boy. *Me*. She's mine now, pet. Free choice, remember! All done. Your Father's precious world is about to die."

She raised her boot, droplets of his own blood dripping from the sole.

He caught the movement as she dropped her foot, heard the crack of his skull.

Then, darkness.

21

———————

WITCHES

TRICKSTERS WERE EVERYWHERE IN BOSTON. More than even Cairo, and that city had been overrun. Jacob flattened himself behind the wall, his leather coat catching on the broken brick. He'd been forced to rely on his sight at every intersection, pushing energy ahead of his steps just to avoid blundering into the demons who darted and flowed as dark shadows. It was exhausting work, and he resented it: his gift should be used for strategy, not for keeping him from colliding with vermin.

It had taken him three full humiliating days to zig-zag through a city that should have taken hours. Three whole days!

By now he was almost used to the humid air. That, and the incessant caws of the crows that owned the sky. A grim comfort, at least. It meant the city wasn't truly lost yet. A mixture of salt and smoke coated his skin, his hair, his tongue. *Filth.* Cities should be neat and tidy.

The long route up to Charlestown from Logan airport had been at an impasse. Its narrow streets and dead ends now served as perfect nests for the city's new predators and, sadly, their victims. Streams of still-human refugees escaped the city, blocking bridges and tunnels in their hurry to get out. Alongside them, the demon-possessed dead blundered around each corner.

Jacob wanted to spit his disgust, but settled for wiping his hand over his lips; all he could manage if his presence was to remain unnoticed by the demons across the way.

Umbrae. Two of them, right beside the unlocked security gate to the Wormwood Street warehouse, his aptly named goal. They merged with the darkness, but if he stared hard, he would see an occasional shift, a movement of deeper ebony.

He knew of ones like these from his homeland. They travelled the wind currents, burned in fire grates, or spewed from water pipes; trading elemental energies for whatever they needed to survive. In his village, children were taught to ward such things before they could walk. Here, people left themselves wide open, embracing ignorance, even calling it a right. *Liberté* indeed.

A few words travelled to him over the wide expanse of road. He felt for their resonance. When a wave of static prickled over his body and images shifted into his mind, he had them locked in.

"The father?" The taller shadow was questioning his stockier companion.

Another demon joined them. This time, female. Jacob had tracked her energy creeping up the road a full minute before she appeared. Her presence rippled into the bubble the others occupied in his mind.

The conversation continued; snippets of words batted between them. "Hush! Witches inside… Tell me what—"

"The blood was—"

"Lost? No!"

"Six burned! They—"

"Stupid vampires!"

Jacob probed deeper trying to fill in the details. Sight gave him fragments, never the whole, and he hated how quickly his assumptions rushed to fill the gaps. But he could feel their emotions alongside the words. He should lean into that for interpretation. Glee that the plan had been scuppered by the loss of the victim's blood. Now, retribution was coming, and a new plan had been triggered. To that they seemed nonchalant, as though this plan had nothing to do with them. Just a vampire plot, perhaps?

They continued speaking, and this time, he turned his head toward them directly, listening intently, eyes shut tight, visualizing them standing before him. It was a risk to press so close against the bubble; he might be seen, but he *needed* the clarity.

A sudden spike: "The angel doesn't know?" Shaking heads, the energy of the agitation and… fear? Yes, fear. Could they be speaking of Jegudiel? Or Billy? Did they know yet of Billy? Surely too soon.

They crept further down the street. Their forms slid over the walls of the warehouse, slithered across the road, and blended into the shadows of the building opposite. Their conversation echoed on, but now turned to mundane matters and TV soap operas.

He let them go, wincing. A sharp pain struck behind his eyes. So much effort for just snippets and guesswork. He did spit now. A nasty taste they had left behind.

Jacob waited for thirty more seconds, then crossed to the open entrance gate. A faint light glowed from the lower windows of the warehouse, the shiny new apartments above silent and empty. The ground floor door was jammed open. Good. Aideen's coven met in the bowels of the building. Usually solo, her last email had conceded power (and survival) now lay in numbers.

He smoothed his linen jacket, then his hair, dislodging a fine layer of ash. At the thought of her, knots shifted in his stomach where there used to be only butterflies. Six years since she'd left, just as the Rising took hold in Detroit. He sighed. The past didn't matter now. Finding allies did. Those like him who would stand against the monster *he* called *L'ange Noire.* Here, they called her the Advocate. Her end was coming; he already felt it. Soon he would see how.

He pushed open the door and stepped inside.

———

The energy in the basement gathered with the subtlety of a summer storm. Reckless and raw. It was nothing like the circles of his youth. The calm, measured rituals with his father and the elders. That was water over smooth stone. This? This was not patient; it was violent. What sort of entity would respond to such a crude invitation?

He glanced at Aideen. Still beautiful. Still fire. From her red hair to the spark in her voice. He'd reached out when the city's boundaries looked threatened, his professionalism masking the regret he'd never stopped feeling. They were on the same side again, but her magick, a gentle and earthbound rhythm more like his own, had never felt like this raw summoning. The stiff hug they'd shared confirmed it. It wasn't just her discomfort at seeing him again; it was this place, with these people. This alliance was a compromise, born of necessity.

He'd offered the circle (nine women, two men) the formal request to join, and to his surprise, no one had demurred. Aideen had clearly prepared them. A few had offered wide smiles and hugs, as if he were a long-lost relative. Jacob accepted their welcome but kept his distance. He was here to assess, not to belong.

The circle was formed for their working to begin.

He recognized the first stage of the ritual. A woman

stepped forward. She paid respect to, and asked the assistance of nature's entities, naming each them. The Elementals, he knew. The others made him pause and wonder. All demons? She took a seat in the centre of the circle.

Instantly, the air thickened. Like her positioning was part of it, as much as the words had been. Pressure built, first thickening then solid. It pushed against him from the centre, forcing him to take a step back before he shifted to stand forward to meet it. He would never cede ground.

The witch began to tremble.

He reached for his sight. Was this the entity he'd heard they consulted? He stretched his mind forward, but a curtain had been drawn. She glanced at him and smiled. He wrestled against it, looking for an opening, a way to clear the view. His failure left him gasping.

While Jacob struggled, her tremors increased in their intensity and propelled her from her chair onto the floor, jerking uncontrollably. The other participants chanted softly, ignoring her sufferings. Their voices rose as they swayed back and forth, jerky, discordant, as though they were all dancing to different music. Aideen's voice remained strong, sweet. It brought images of the earth opening. Smells of leaf-mould and pine needles. It tethered him.

The energy intensified. Not demon. Not Elemental. He did not know the signature. His sight remained screened, but he tracked it, circling the woman on the floor, pressure building as it moved faster. It tested the limits of her flesh and bone, not with curiosity or even animal instinct, but with the crude force of a hammer. Flipping her from front to back, dangling her by a single leg. Forever faster.

The witches' chanting got louder, their voices matching the intensity of violence the woman was enduring.

But over the chanting, another sound: high-pitched, grating. The drawn out screech of an owl in the night, but almost mechanical. Like microphone feedback or the highest pitch of an old-fashioned modem.

As the sound continued, Jacob's chest tightened. The entity whipped around the members of the circle, their clothes and hair flying in the breeze it made. That was it! The screech. The noise it made as it circled, ripping into this plane from another. His sight dropped; he could not track it anymore. Could not concentrate. His stomach locked. What was this thing?

The scream got louder. The doors and windows rattled, and each member battled to stay upright. The woman in the centre now hung prone in midair, spinning in time with each rush of pressure.

Jacob slapped his hands over his ears just as both sound and movement reached their crescendo, then—

The lit candles extinguished. Dark. Silence.

A thump vibrated up through his feet. The pressure released.

The candles relit all at once in a single wave of magick.

He glanced uneasily around. The light had brought with it a very different presence. Calm emanated from the centre of the circle. The woman sitting in her chair again looked serene.

Aideen smiled a greeting, her eyes locked with the witch. She looked from her to him, and nodded. It was more than confirmation, she granted him access, and his mind momentarily swarmed with images of green fields and mountains.

Jacob's senses recognized an entity sitting in the place of the woman. Despite the beauty of the images, to his tongue, ash; to his nostrils, freshly turned grave dirt. This was not a spirit of the land or air; nothing rooted in the earth's cycle could feel so black, surely. It must be demon, but he also sensed… friendship! He was at a loss, and the ignorance stung.

Jacob focused on the witch. Reaching to get past her flesh and see into the entity beneath.

It turned its eyes toward him.

Jacob held his breath, instincts screaming that he should not allow himself to be seen by this being. But at the same time knowing that only his submission would be acceptable to it. He dropped his gaze. Ashamed.

The entity settled, eyes forward, and Jacob let out his breath.

The witch standing to the left of Aideen spoke. The language was ancient, one he didn't recognize. The possessed woman appeared to listen, her head slightly bent on one side. She replied in the same language.

He'd expected deep, guttural, terrifying. But it spoke with a lyrical cadence. Light and comforting. Helpful, he guessed.

The questions and answers continued back and forth for some time.

Then the witch asked a final question. For a reply, the entity looked directly at Jacob, raising a poker-straight arm at him, its finger pinpointing the middle of his stomach. It spoke again, more of the soft lyrical tones it had used before. Yet, he felt the content of its words was anything but delicate.

Several of the others in the circle turned and looked at him, too. With their eyes, a wall of solid energy hurtled forward. He felt the impact. His sight flared scarlet. Unbalanced, he stumbled back, confused. Should he run? His instinct said so. He could not back down again in the face of this-this thing, and the people who'd invited it.

Before he could act, they all looked away and the wall collapsed.

Quiet chanting lifted the air. The woman on the chair slumped over, and the candles went out, this time for good.

22
____

BOLLOCKS

BILLY WOKE up in an ambulance charging through the streets of Vegas, sirens wailing. He was strapped to a gurney, hooked up by the arm to a bag of blood and another of saline, with an oxygen mask clinging to his face. For a moment, his vision lurched between blinding white and a deep scarlet. He closed his eyes and turned his head and the colours transformed to jagged, gut-wrenching waves of pain. For a moment, he believed Jegudiel's fashionable heel was still firmly wedged in his skull.

Gagging, he waited for the throbbing to subside enough to risk opening his eyes again.

Hux lay on the other side of the vehicle. Also on oxygen, he still appeared to be out cold. His eyes were sealed shut, with one hand hanging limply off the side of his trolley.

As long as Billy remained still, the pain in his head settled to background noise. Through it, he heard the conversation of the two medical staff who travelled with them. They were discussing an earthquake.

"Only downtown, apparently." The taller of the two men had heard blasts of information from his radio.

"Where we picked up these two?" While he was talking, the older, broader man adjusted Billy's saline bag.

"Yeah. Weird, though. Only one room, sixteen. Just flying glass everywhere else—and cracks in the walls."

"Did you hear about the noise?" Billy's guy paused and glanced at his companion. "The howling? Fucking creepy, man. Never heard that in a quake before."

Billy groaned. Those howls had been his.

When the EMT closest to Billy saw he was awake, he started reeling off questions: "What's your name, buddy? Do you know where you are? Where's the pain?" Receiving no reply, he started over.

Can't speak, dickhead. This bloody thing's on my face!

As if to save him, Hux started to thrash around. Eyes wide open, he fought against the straps, kicking and punching, his arms and legs jerking beneath the blanket.

The EMT, who had been questioning Billy, launched at Hux, trying to hold his massive shoulders down. One of Hux's straps burst open and released an arm. He punched, swiping at the man who dodged and crashed against Billy's gurney. The other was filling a syringe from a small dark bottle. Thankfully, the straps around his thighs and ankles held.

Hux sat up, pulled his oxygen mask off and looked around with glazed eyes. He spotted Billy, and his eyes narrowed.

He snarled.

Bollocks.

Both EMTs dived on him in unison, but were not quick enough to prevent him from reaching across the narrow space and grasping Billy's neck with one hand. "Where is she?"

Billy struggled against both the oxygen mask and Hux's steel-like grip, grunting urgently. At the same time, he jerked to back away from the angry man. Pain cut through his whole body, making him cry out.

The muffled scream seemed to break through Hux's anger.

He relaxed enough that the two EMTs were able to wrestle him back down, but not quite before he'd managed to pull Billy's mask and dislodge it. "Where is she?" he repeated.

"Alive! She's alive." Billy wanted him to calm down, mostly for self-preservation, but also because a further head injury might kill him. Hux sighed and went limp in the arms of the medical staff. The older guy pulled out the syringe.

He didn't fall back to sleep, though. He lay on his side and stared at Billy before whispering, "Has she got her?"

Billy nodded.

They rode out the rest of the journey in silence.

———

Glass jars stood on shelves cut out of the cavern wall and shone brightly with coloured lights. When Tazia tapped on the sides, the contents made high-pitched hums. She turned one over slowly, like it was a large hourglass, and the sound intensified. What was that noise? Was it pleasure or pain?

She was feeling better. The pain from the burn on her back had subsided, thank God. Her flesh had regenerated with the help of Jegudiel's magick and her own demon healing. She'd examined the wound in the reflecting pool outside of the cave. The scar was hand-shaped. When she saw it, she gulped back the cry.

And all this time, you thought he loved you, pet. The Advocate's voice was a continuous, silken whisper in her mind, even when the angel wasn't present. *You're special, Anastasia. One of a kind.*

As the days passed, she'd put Tazia straight on a lot of things. *Unique is not something allowed to exist in that world of yours. If you'd said no to my proposal, he would have killed you, anyway.*

For the first time, Tazia felt she fully understood the role to which Billy had been assigned all those years ago. She tried not to blame him for what he'd done. She tried to hold on to the numbness she'd been cultivating since the events in room sixteen. But tears continued to fall, regardless of her efforts to stop them.

Hush, pet, it'll be over soon and you'll be whole again. Let your soul guide you to the right path.

The right path? What the fuck was that? She'd not known the right path since she'd been left at the hospital in London. Longer. When Cuinn died. No! Even further back. From the moment Hux had shot her father and she'd briefly felt freedom. "What is the right path?"

The one where you become a shining light for all those lost people to follow. Let them see your example, Anastasia.

"Shining like the lights in the jars?"

A million little stars, my dear.

"How will I recognize my soul?"

It will sing to you, pet.

"And when I hear it sing?"

You'll be ready!

"For what?"

To meet your people and show them how to live their lives free of the demon scourge. Now, sleep and heal, my dear.

But Tazia didn't sleep; too many thoughts buzzing, twisting.

She lay on her bed, watching the lights flicker on the walls and the sun and moon set and rise.

How long had she been there? A day? A week? A year? It seemed like forever.

She tried not to think of the friend who had betrayed her or the man who thought he was protecting her. She just focused on her soul, waiting to hear it sing.

Then she heard the noise. A faint high-pitched hum came from the beautiful jars on the wall, with their shining moving lights.

Tazia picked another one off the shelves. It glowed so

brightly when she went near it, like it was calling to her. She shook it a little. The humming got more urgent.

"It's singing to me!"

Tazia darted along the shelves, shaking the jars violently so that her soul could use all the lights to sing to her. The sound rose loud around her, reverberating off the crystal walls of the cave.

She ran outside to find the angel, to tell her that she was ready, that her soul had started singing.

23

A REMARKABLE RECOVERY

AFTER SEVENTY-TWO HOURS in Nevada Central, Billy was ready for the showdown.

Across the sticky canteen table, Soren Huxford, professional killer, met his gaze over a tiny straw. His jaw worked grimly, sucking up the weak orange-flavoured water from the juice box. Billy matched him, suck for suck, until both their boxes collapsed with simultaneous, pathetic wheezes.

In front of them, lay the other spoils of their epic hunt for spare change; empty Twinkie wrappers and a half-eaten bag of Cheetos. *Bloody pathetic. And he still owes me for the Cheetos.*

On the first day of their recovery from the events at the Laser Ridge Motel, they'd been confined to side-by-side beds in the emergency ward, separated only by a cheerily floral-patterned curtain of blue irises and yellow daisies. After an hour of staring at it, Billy had sworn the blue and yellow shapes merged into greenish dragons flying across a landscape of giant white snowballs. It was one of the better trips he'd had. The heavy dose of pain medication still dripped into his arm, though the blood bag was finally gone.

Dr. Taylor, a young (and hot) intern with sparkling teeth, had moved them to a side ward after twenty-four hours. "Amazing recoveries," he'd said, winking at Billy. But insisted they stay for another day for observation. Convinced he would get a phone number, Billy grinned back, until Taylor bent over the bed to adjust the sheets and asked if Hux was single. *Perfect. Kick a man when he's down, Doc.*

Soon though, the doctor's smile faded. The silent death-stares Hux was trading with Billy were enough to unnerve him and post an armed security guard on the ward. A bloke whose weapon was practically the third person in the room.

Initially, Billy had done his best to avoid Hux's thunderous expression. It aimed right for the soft spots still raw with memories of Tazia. But after a few hours of painkillers, he no longer gave a toss and matched him glare for glare.

At the end of the third day, they were both discharged. Hux's concussion wasn't worsening, and Billy's injuries seemed to be healing at enormous speed, proving to him angelic healing abilities were every bit as effective as Hux's more magickal charms. They still hadn't said a word to each other.

Wading through the endless bloody discharge paperwork, Billy finally cracked. He suggested the hospital canteen to hash things out. Hux just grunted, the frown lines on his face looking like dark crevasses.

Hux erupted as soon as Billy sat down. "So, Jegudiel beat the living shite out of you?"

"That's a great opener, Hux. Well done."

"True?"

Reluctantly, Billy was forced to agree. "Yes."

"And you let her take Anastasia?" Hands curled into fists, the hairs on Hux's knuckles stood up as though an electric shock had passed through him.

Wary of the body language, Billy countered, "I didn't *let* her take Taz. I fought like hell!"

"Did you, Billy? Or did you think it would be easier if she wasn't around to confuse the issue anymore?"

"What?"

"I know you didn't want to kill her. So, with Jegudiel taking her you were off the hook, right?"

"No!" Billy stopped. He tried to get the events clear in his own head. He pulled the straw from the final juice box and bent and twisted it round and round until Hux grabbed it from him and threw it on the floor.

"What then?" he hissed.

"There's stuff you don't know. You were out cold. You didn't see… or hear!"

"What?"

"I nearly killed her… Tazia. She wanted it. She agreed. Said it was the only way. She came to me, Hux. Voluntarily. I put my arms around her and started to burn into her heart. But… I… couldn't." His voice broke as he remembered that moment and how he couldn't finish the job. He'd left her in agony.

"You burned into her heart? Like with fire? You set fire to her?" Hux jumped up—

"No! There's this thing I can do, now. Angel fire, I guess. It's blue. Comes from my hands. Anyway, doesn't matter. I didn't do it!"

Hux looked like fire was about to blast from his own eyes.

"Sit down, Hux. Let me finish. Please." Billy held his head in his hands. "I just need to get this out!"

Hux sat. Mouth clamped shut, breath coming in and out fast through his nose.

Billy rubbed his eyes roughly. "Next thing, Jegudiel was there. She dragged me away—and yes, she beat the shit out of me! I couldn't stop her taking Taz. I couldn't even get up once she'd finished. But the worst thing wasn't what she did, but what she said to me."

"What?"

Billy met his gaze, not knowing the best way to say it.

"Billy. What?"

"She said that Taz had already chosen her. Already agreed. Already… called to her for help. She did it before I even got there."

Hux peered at him, his voice hollow. "She… chose her?"

"Yes."

"But I was protecting her." Hux continued to stare, his face a mask of disbelief.

Billy held his breath. Would he accept it?

"She was lying, man, surely? That's what Jegudiel does!"

"No, Hux. Taz didn't fight her. She didn't fight me. I thought it was because she'd accepted the truth, but it wasn't. She didn't fight me cos she knew the Advocate was coming. She knew she'd live. She'd already said yes, bruv."

Hux was silent for a few seconds more, but Billy sensed the next thunderclap was coming. *One elephant, two elephants…*

Still seated, Hux swiped his arm across the table and knocked the juice boxes and food wrappers to the ground. It looked incidental, like an accident. Blink and you'd miss it. But he sensed it was just the warm up.

Billy moved back, scraping his chair away from the table.

The big man stood, picked up the round table in both hands, and hurled it away from them. It coasted just above the floor in silence like some huge Frisbee and passed through the windowpane as though tearing rice paper. The glass shattered with a crash and sent broken glass out onto the pavement in great jagged sheets. The table hit the ground outside and careened over the pavement, straight into one of the vehicles parked in the lot, setting its alarm screeching.

Hux's expression didn't change. His eyes were dead.

Screaming people charged for the exit while Billy stood up and retreated to a safer distance to watch. There'd be no point trying to intervene. The meltdown was already in progress. Frankly, Billy preferred that it happen now, in a public place, a hospital no less, where he could be tended to if Hux decided Billy would be next through the window.

But Hux had other ideas. His hands spanned one side of the vending machine and pulled it forward, the weight carrying it to the floor. It crashed onto its front. The hard-wired electricity cord ripped from the plaster wall, and released from the back of the machine as it fell, sending a shower of sparks into the air.

As it hit the ground, Billy felt the floor jolt under him.

A second machine followed suit. This one fell onto its side, slid, and twisted forty-five degrees before coming to rest. The glass front smashed, and boxes of juice cascaded out, spilling in a neon orange and yellow stream. Quarters flowed too as the cash collector broke apart. They clattered onto the floor, skidding away in multiple directions.

The first orderlies on the scene seemed unsure whether to grab their hypodermics or call for Security. One look at Hux and they did both. They circled him warily, staying well back, while their radios chattered back-and-forth, the pounding footfalls of the guards getting closer.

Billy took a few steps closer. "Hux, we've got to get out of here, bruv."

Hux had stood stock-still after the second machine hit the floor, his arms now hanging loosely at his sides. At the sound of Billy's voice, he looked up, eyes wide. "What happened?"

"Bruv! We've got to go!" Billy gestured as two security guards, edged around the door, weapons drawn.

Hux nodded at him and then looked toward the broken window.

Finally on the same wavelength, they bolted across the room and jumped the low windowsill crunching on broken glass. They zipped into the hospital car park with Billy putting on a surge of speed to avoid getting sideswiped by an arriving ambulance.

He spotted an open gate to the side which led to the park next door. Trees—hundreds of them. "This way!" He sped off with Hux pounding behind him.

24

LUCKY COW

THE DEEP RUMBLE of Hux's snores echoing inside the Jeep had driven Billy from the vehicle. Long drags followed by a series of stuttering snorts. Each sound grated in Billy's chest.

He stood in the deserted campground, kicking sand and small stones up and down the path that led from their parking spot. His arms were crossed, and he kept his eyes down as he walked.

After the hospital, they'd driven northeast out of Vegas and into the deserts of Nevada's national parks. He thought it beautiful, the red rocks, the canyons, and dried river beds, and insisted to the surly Swede that it was the place they should stop to plan their next move.

The energy of the ancient glacier-carved land hung in the air, moving subtly on the tiny breezes that sprang up in the night's chill. Everything cascading in whorls of light blue and pale purple. It encouraged him to breathe and relax. These colours always triggered memories. His mother had adopted the use of English Lavender soap when she'd arrived from her homeland. She'd wanted to fit in. *Not that it had ever done her any bloody good, mind you.* He'd grown up with the smell, but she was in the colour, not the scent.

Billy circled his neck warily, hearing clicks for two complete rotations before they subsided, then gazed at the sky, his arms hanging loose. The atmosphere washed over him again. Cleansing him.

The bright moon cast alien shapes on the ground. Its light stretched reddish shadows from the huge rock formations, even at midnight. Was this how Mars looked? Had he been there? It was part of God's creation, after all. Perhaps angels didn't need space helmets.

The snoring stopped abruptly.

Billy jerked his head toward the Jeep again, waiting. It bounced slightly under Hux's weight as the big man readjusted his position inside. This happened regularly throughout each night.

Tension rose in his chest as the calming energy he'd been absorbing shot back out of his body and returned to the rocks. Like a stutter, the rumble started again, then back to the long-drawn-out growls that reverberated in Billy's head.

For fucksakes!

It wasn't his fault. Hux was slouched across the back seat, shoulders and head jammed vertically against the window on one side, his feet hanging out of the one opposite.

This latter arrangement was at Billy's insistence. He'd objected to the stink of the man's unwashed feet, made worse as each day's sweat got soaked up by his thick army socks. Once his boots were off, the putrid stench had made Billy gag. The first time he'd objected, Hux had begun a long discourse about him "toughening up" if they were going to "win this fight." The last time, that very evening, he'd just snarled, "Grow a pair."

Despite the bluster, Hux had shoved his feet out into the open air every night since the first complaint, and Billy had seen him rinsing his socks at the water pipe earlier in the day and drying them on the car's bonnet.

The days were long and hot. The nights cooler, but equally drawn out. Nine of them spent waiting for inspiration to strike. For a plan to become obvious.

For a bloody sign! Do ya hear me, God?

Billy kicked some more stones, this time with gusto. He narrowly missed a scorpion that had scuttled up to his boot while he'd been reflecting. He didn't much mind them. They made him laugh. He loved how they zigzagged in the sand, pincers up, always spoiling for a fight. They were tough little buggers. Scorpions and Hux had a lot in common.

Foot stink aside, life with the ex-soldier hadn't been a bed of roses. He'd been grouchy and distant. Apparently, undecided about whether he could trust Billy.

They'd discussed what the High Advocate said about Tazia choosing her until Billy wanted to throw up. The conversations always ended with the acrid smell of her burning flesh in his nose while Hux made him go over every single detail again and again.

Gradually, though, he'd stopped asking. Then he went quiet altogether, preferring misery over action. His nightmares had started then, too. In the short periods of peace between snores, Hux would wake up shouting or lashing out at an enemy who'd infiltrated his dreams. Billy asked him gently if he wanted to talk about it, his sympathy mixed with curiosity. The "No!" was unequivocal.

He'd also tried to engage Hux in conversation to figure out a plan. But after being told to: "Shut the hell up," one too many times, Billy had zipped it. Both of them remained walled in their own silent pain.

After ten days they still had no idea what to do next.

Billy crouched and peered at the track, hoping to find one of the little quartz crystals that were littered about. At night, he could spot them more easily, shining in the beams of moonlight. If he was lucky, he may even find a small pebble of turquoise. That would be a treat.

As he picked up a rock with a greenish tinge to examine it more closely, he heard footsteps approaching and looked up. It was a young woman. They hadn't seen any other campers since they'd arrived, and there were no other vehicles. Where had she come from?

About the same age as Tazia, her black hair was pulled back behind her head, but the front sections had escaped and hung down, obscuring her right eye. Dressed in an ensemble of combat trousers and a black tee, he couldn't tell if she was army or police.

She smiled as she walked, talking quietly to herself. Her feet were bare, and she dragged them slowly over the sandy gravel, kicking the dust as she went, leaving a trail of bright specks in her wake.

If she'd been holding her arms out in front of her, he would have sworn she was in a zombie trance. *Lucky cow, she's stoned!*

"Hey!" he said softly, not wanting to alarm her. He approached druggies as he did strange animals—cautiously.

She stopped, looked around for the source of the voice and spotted him. She attempted to straighten up. "Sir. Yes, Sir." *Army then!*

He laughed. "Having a good night?"

"Yes, Sir. I'm spreading the word, Sir. Singing her name." The girl raised her arms to the sky and grinned. "Do you hear the singing?"

"Erm, no. Can't say that I do." *Wow, that's some trip!*

"I hear her voice, Sir. And the angels that sing with her." Her arms flopped back down. She caught his eye and frowned. "Do I tell you my orders, Sir?"

"Yes, tell me your orders, Private." What could it hurt?

"I'm to spread word of the Saviour, Sir."

Billy blanched. "Saviour?"

She nodded and smiled again. Her eyes widened and seemed to light up like the little quartz crystals he'd been searching for. For a moment, she forgot herself and spoke dreamily, "It's a wonderful story."

Billy stepped toward her and forced a smile. "Tell it. Please. I'm Billy, by the way. What's your name?"

She was having trouble standing without falling and put a hand out to him for support. She wasn't stoned; she was exhausted.

He took her hand in his. "At ease, soldier."

She relaxed, and he pulled her down so that they were sitting cross-legged and knee to knee on the pathway. A small cloud appeared to drift across the moon, and moving shapes patterned the surrounding ground. Billy shivered at the tiny drop in temperature.

"Private Miller, Sir."

"First name?"

"Kristina, Sir."

"Good. Kristina, you can relax. Tell me about the Saviour."

She shuffled a little, getting comfortable, and released a long breath through her nose. Her eyelids were heavy, but as she started speaking, they widened again. Energy bubbled around them. Billy felt it pleasantly fizz and pop.

"I met her in Sedona, Sir, the Saviour. She was there to speak to those who'd listen. There were hundreds. Some said thousands! All gathered on the rocks and down in the river valley. We saw her arrive, guarded by her soldiers—demons, of course—but now devoted to just her. Serving her! It was amazing, Sir!"

She leaned forward and gave what seemed like a drug-infused grin. Billy peered into her eyes carefully. He could see the scene she was describing reflected in their surfaces. He could even see Tazia there. Was the memory carved into her eyes? This woman wasn't afflicted by drugs; this was magick. This was how Jegudiel was spreading the word.

"She walked up the river, picking through the rocks and wading through the water. We could hear her boots clicking on the stones, getting closer and closer! She smiled and waved at us all. Such love, Sir! She was so beautiful! She sat on a big rock in the centre of the river, and told her story."

Billy peered closer. He looked directly into the eyes of his best friend. She gazed back at him; Tazia, speaking from her very soul, believing every word of her sermon.

Private Miller shook her head, and her eyes dropped.

Billy lost his view of Tazia and panicked. "Look at me again, Private!"

She did, her grin now gone. "The poor girl, Sir. Treated so badly by her father. Abused by his hand and others. Her poor soul, twisted for evil. The lives she took, Sir. The murders. The pain she gave! It left her used and broken." A tear formed in her right eye and trickled down her cheek. "But then the angel saved her. She showed her—"

Billy's eyes hardened. He didn't want to see; didn't want to find Jegudiel in Kristina's eyes. But there she was, red mane flying behind her as she appeared beside Tazia on the rock.

"—how to embrace her humanity. The Saviour revealed her secret to us, Sir. She's really a demon. Yes! A demon with a human soul. Isn't that amazing? Isn't that beautiful?" She smiled widely again. Another victim of the Advocate's deceit.

Taking a breath, Billy felt his energy build. He set his teeth in an effort to control himself; the ground below him quivered.

Kristina didn't notice; she was too caught up in her euphoria. "The angel had shown the Saviour her purpose."

"Which is?" He bit his lip to silence himself.

"To save us all!" She looked again at the sky, dropped

Billy's hands, and raised her own. Her voice rose as the shadow, larger and darker this time, flowed across the moon.

"If she can beat her demon to become a being of pure, God-given light, how can we fail, Sir? How? She'll stand beside us and show us how to fight. We can beat the demons! We can beat them!"

There was a noise to his left. Billy turned to see Hux standing in the moonlight, his tall form clothed just in his combats and socks, t-shirt in one hand hanging to his side, plastic bottle of water in the other.

He pushed his hand through his hair. "I heard voices."

Kristina didn't notice his presence. She was still joyfully staring at the sky, a moment of pure transcendence alight on her face.

Billy held a palm up to Hux. "Do you know how she will lead you, Kristina? How she'll defeat the demons?"

The soldier reluctantly gave her attention back to him. She shook her head, but gripped his hands tight, urgency in her tone. "We have to trust, Sir. Follow orders. Wait and watch. The birds will guide us to where we're supposed to go and the music will tell us what to do."

"The birds?"

"Yes. We must follow them, go to the places they gather. Follow them when they take flight. Then she will come and she will show us how to fight."

"She? The Saviour? The half-demon girl?"

"Yes. *Our* Saviour, Sir. Yours and mine." Private Miller stood and pulled him up to stand in front of her. "Will you come with me?"

"Where?"

Kristina pointed, and both Billy and Hux followed the direction of her finger.

In the air above them, the darkness Billy had seen earlier and taken to be a cloud was now visible as a huge flock. The birds circled high and moved in one mass. Looking closer, Billy could make out each one swooping and weaving. Blue jays, crows, and magpies, and the music Kristina could hear was the sound of the birds' cries as they flew.

To her ears, it was a beautiful symphony, music sent by her Saviour. To them, a cacophony of squawks and screams.

He looked back at her. "I can't follow, love. Not yet. Things to do. But soon, okay?" He kissed her cheek. Her skin smelled of soap; her hair was soft against his face. That was beauty. True beauty. He tensed. This was what the Advocate was out to destroy.

Kristina made a huge effort to stand up straight and then saluted him. She ambled on down the path, back in her zombie state. With shock, Billy realized the shining drops that reflected behind her as she walked were not newly turned shards of quartz, but drops of her blood catching in the moonlight. The soles of her bare feet were covered in deep drills and cuts. She must have been following the birds for miles, making ribbons of her feet.

Hux breathed hard, gripping his t-shirt tightly in his fist. As Kristina walked past him, he shoved the nearly full bottle of water in her hand. She barely noticed, too busy gazing at the sky and singing softly to herself.

Billy met his eyes and nodded. It was time to act.

25

THE SAVIOUR TRIP

TAZIA SAT on a bench picking mud out of the sole of her boot with a sharp stick. She pushed the tip around each tread in turn, fascinated by the hexagonal pattern. The boots weren't her usual Dr. Martens. These had most likely been made by some kid in a sweatshop in China.

She pushed against the mud again, forcing more to fall onto the ground in front of her. There was quite a mound.

The Advocate had told her to stay put, so when not picking at her boots, she sat at the end of a causeway marked by a fancy gazebo staring across Boston harbour. A few feet away stood two Soldier demons. With broad builds and army cut hair, they reminded her far too much of Conn O'Cuinn to get comfortable.

She'd asked the Advocate if they were guarding her against danger or to ensure she didn't get away. Jegudiel had just laughed and said she could leave any time she liked.

She hadn't considered it.

Since leaving the cave the Advocate had taken her to almost six weeks ago, she'd felt less confused. Another dimension? Heaven? *Whatever!* That place, in all its shiny happy glory, had done a real number on her: made her fucking soul sing to her. But now she was clear; she was the people's Saviour. It felt good. Useful. Like she had a purpose. That was new. She didn't count being her father's muscle as purpose.

Shivering slightly, Tazia walked a few paces to the end of the jetty. It poked out a hundred feet or so into the murky ocean, waves lapping lazily at the concrete piles.

Only a few months ago, there would have been yachts lined up here, the big expensive kind with shiny chrome railings and curved wooden decks. Now, though, there were very few boats. Despite her best efforts to persuade them to stay and fight, many Boston residents had hitched a lift on the first sea-worthy vessel they could find.

Some had stayed, though.

Yesterday, she'd met with a big group in an old meeting hall north of here. They'd listened to her words, the ones that Jegudiel told her to use, about how her soul had survived. How, despite the atrocities that her demon self had forced on her, she'd fought the battle and won. How her own redemption was coming and that of all humankind, as long as they fought like she had. Sure, hadn't God even sent her one of his angels to guide her?

This was always the point when the Advocate made a grand entrance. In a flash of light, she'd smile benignly at Tazia, red hair flowing like she stood in a perpetual breeze. Sometimes, she swore she heard fucking harp music playing.

Despite her initial skepticism, she'd started to feel she was making a difference. Fighting the Risings was the only way to save the world. The people couldn't give up.

She surveyed the stunning expanse of water spread out in front of her. Islands dotted her view, but beyond that was the Atlantic Ocean. She imagined it beautiful, blue, calming. There was too much to fight for to give up.

So what if Jegudiel had to add a few special effects to get

their attention. If she could save a few more souls from the oncoming tide of demon-kind, it was worth a little magickal trickery. Right?

The crowds had grown daily. About a month ago, they'd started to beg her to touch them and would hold out their hands for her to save them first. She'd resisted such craziness. But the Advocate pointed out that if it gave them comfort, she should do it. For the people. For *her* people. For her *children.*

So, she *had* touched them and promised healing along with salvation. Anything that would give them the strength to save themselves. What harm could it do?

The sun dipped below the horizon, and just as she did every night, she heard Jegudiel's voice. She held the mirrored pendant, which she now wore at all times, up to her eyes.

"You did well today, pet." Jegudiel stretched in the mirror, uncurling each luminous limb. Shimmering gold with flashes of long, red hair as her form morphed from her true self to the body she preferred to wear. "Do you think it went well?"

"Yes, I think we saved a few!" Tazia smiled, her taut cheeks filling out to offer a couple of dimples. She returned the admiring glances from the two guards with a quick wink.

"Good! We can't save them all, but we can try." Jegudiel's enthusiasm was tempered by a loud yawn.

Not for the first time, Tazia felt the Advocate was acting more and more like a showbiz mother. Pushing her daughter into the limelight. Basking in the reflected rays of her youth and beauty. Or in this case, the whole Saviour trip.

"It's time we took this show on the road again, Anastasia. Arizona was great, but Boston has been especially good to us. We have ten meeting places filled to the brim with yummy humans ready to turn on their demon oppressors as soon as you say the word. We'll deal with these and then move on." She rolled very human eyes before they changed back to dark almond-shaped depths.

"Do we just leave them?" Tazia had never been too sure of this part of the plan. People had gone where she'd told them to, gathering in specific places, getting ready for some thing or some sign she wasn't clear on. Or else, they followed the birds that drew them to the demon-stuffed cities, though why, she didn't know. When she tried to logic it out, her mind seemed to get woolly with the effort.

"Do we start the fight now?"

Jegudiel smiled. "Sort of. You lead the fight, my dear."

"Against the demons?"

The Advocate sucked on her teeth, and fluffed her hair, but said nothing.

A red aura sparked from the pendant. Tazia dropped it. *What the hell?*

From behind, the two guards grabbed her arms, pinning them behind her back. She struggled. "What the fuck?"

With a quiet ripple in the air, Jegudiel slipped into the space beside her, solid. Recently, she'd taken to appearing this way. Tazia preferred it when there was a loud fanfare or flash of light. She got a heads up.

"Don't fight, pet. There's no point. There's a piece of the plan I needed to keep from you. Just a bit of magick. A little switch to flick, if you like. Something I placed in your soul a long time ago. That's why it was so important you had it back."

Like Billy before her, she put her hand on Tazia's back and light flowed from her hand. But unlike Billy's magick, this light was deep red and seemed to hug her warmly.

There was no pain. No burning or cutting. Not even a drop of blood. She relaxed into it.

As the red light flowed into her, she felt she was fading, losing herself. Nothing recognizable as her own anymore. Her senses too became indistinct. Happiness, sadness, joy, pain, all merged into a nondescript sense of calm. And what's more, she didn't care. Was she floating? Did it matter?

It was over in seconds. She stood perfectly still, grinning at the angel, lids half shut until her smile and shoulders drooped.

The subtle cloak of red energy clouding her changed. It thickened and swirled. Became brighter, more intense. It seemed to move in time with her steady heartbeat. In… and… out. In… and… out. Until it quickened, and her heartbeat followed suit. In. Out. In. Out. In. Out. In. Out. Scarlet now, the aura spun around her. Shrieking, whirling. She could no longer register where it ended, and she began. No sound. No vision. No Tazia. Only red.

It surged, forcing its way into her body from all directions, targeting her heart. Raw energy vibrating, digging, eating her alive!

She didn't feel it end. She *was* simply new. Light was brighter, sounds louder, clearer. She felt each particle of air float over her skin. Each drop of water in those particles dampen her hair. She could feel her hair! It seemed to breathe with her, to dance around her head and yet it still hung as straight as before.

Tazia shook off the Soldiers' hands and took a step closer to the water, testing her newfound senses. The waves still lapped against the jetty, but now their inner form, their true strength, was visible to her. They surged and crashed and roared. A fine spray sizzled on her skin.

But the change was more than physical.

Now, every hidden desire she'd ever had was clear: unboxed, extreme, and exposed. Every thought or need she'd ever squashed down in order to be reasonable or controlled ran amok in her mind unchallenged. Morals, modesty, decency, humanity, all gone.

She didn't want to feel love; she wanted obsession. She didn't want respect; she wanted total devotion. She wanted to control the lives and actions of her followers. She wanted death, disease, and destruction just because she knew it would be created in her name.

Tazia wanted power. Raw, unharnessed power.

The Advocate watched her carefully. "Feels good doesn't it, pet? Are you ready to work?"

"When do we start?"

26

FIFTY-FIVE DAYS LATER

THE VAMPIRE SOUNDED like the bit of an electric screwdriver skating in a stripped screw—dog-whistle thin one moment, then stuttering into choked, ratchety grunts. Billy had no place to hide from the sound. He'd tried. Up to the attic and down to the disgusting basement. Both infested with vermin: bats upstairs and God knows what form of rodent down. He'd valiantly eyed the latter for all of two minutes before going back to face the noisy demon again.

From the kitchen doorway he glared at the captive secured to his seat with thick wire they'd found in the garage. Hux stood in the corner, leaning against the back-door frame. He calmly wiped the barrel of some sort of automatic weapon that Billy didn't recognize. He wasn't good with guns.

The demon looked at him with wide yellow eyes and recommended begging. "Help me, please!"

The hole from the bullet wound in his shoulder was two inches round and expanding. Along with the blood, clear liquid trickled from it and ran down his naked chest and stomach where his shirt had been ripped open. From there it diverted into his trousers, running along the edge of a heavy leather belt, which Hux had helpfully undone, as well as the zipper.

Wherever the liquid flowed, a blaze of red was visible on his skin. Little blisters formed and popped, leaving the holes to fill with the acid-like holy water and drill further into his skin.

The vampire's chance of recovery was high, but his opportunity to ever bump uglies again was looking remote if he didn't start talking, and quickly.

Hux stopped polishing his weapon and dripped a little more water into the wound. The vampire screamed.

"For fucksakes, Hux, can't you shut him up?"

He looked up. "This was your idea, Billy. If you can't stand the heat..." He nodded at their surroundings and smiled slightly at his own joke.

"Very bloody funny!"

The vampire had said nothing useful in the four hours he'd been their guest, and Billy was beginning to worry that the idea to detain and question him was a bust. His companion had already been dispatched.

The two demons had jumped them as they settled into the abandoned house they'd found on the east side of the Vegas Strip. They'd headed back into civilization after their sojourn in the desert ended, to wait for the latest intel from Jacob.

The African helped them get their heads back in the game, pointing out (using a lot of metaphors) that their personal falling out would not aid Tazia or the fate of the world. It pissed Billy off that Hux took notice of this man, but rejected his attempts at reconciliation.

Jacob called frequently, giving updates from Boston. Since his first meeting with the witches, he'd passed on helpful information from the coven's communications with an unidentified entity. At least, that was what it was supposed to be. Jacob shared that he felt the dark energy was asking more questions than it was answering. "The coven's source was...

illuminating this time, William," he'd said. "It asked us, if we knew how to kill an angel."

Thanks to Joshua's research from way back at the beginning of this nightmare, they already had the answer: only an angel could kill another angel. "And you told them we have one of those?" Billy asked.

"I did. But it… laughed."

"Rude!"

"Indeed. It told us it is not enough to be an angel. The blow must be struck with a weapon forged in Heaven."

"An angelic weapon?" The words felt heavy, but familiar. *He knew this!* "And did your entity know where the bloody hell we're supposed to find one of those?"

"A question I am currently pursuing," Jacob had replied. "But be aware. This means you are vulnerable. But it also means *L'ange Noire* is not invincible."

It also meant that despite the agony of it, the Advocate's attack on him in the motel could only have failed. If that knife had been angelic, she would have killed him. Did she know? Sure as shit she did. So why hadn't she used one? Was she deliberately saving the kill for another time? The knowledge left Billy feeling terrifyingly vulnerable.

Jacob had also passed on accounts regarding activities in the Boston area. The reports were disconcerting, mainly about a young woman accompanied by an angel. They both preached salvation to the humans who would listen. It was ominous news and backed up what they'd learned from Private Miller in the desert.

It was Tazia, Billy was sure (he'd seen her in Kristina's eyes), but until they knew how to defeat Jegudiel, Jacob suggested they stayed put. No point in Billy coming to demon central with a target on his back until there was no choice.

To his surprise, Hux had agreed. It was always the same with him. The longer he was away from her, the further he ran.

If only his angelic senses allowed him to see into the man's heart.

He spent the days researching angelic weaponry and fantasized about the feel of Jegudiel's neck between his hands. When he thought about it, they glowed blue and fired little sparks.

Now, they waited in this skeevy part of town pretending they were still in the game. Torturing the odd demon for information wasn't part of the plan, but this one had jumped them. *So, fair play, right?*

Avoiding the pool of water and blood on the floor, Billy headed over to the paper calendar hanging on the wall of the kitchen. It featured crappy pictures of Vegas tourist attractions, one for each month. Currently, it was turned to a blurry picture of a Tudor revival-style mansion house and declared: Visit The Ghost Museum For A Halloween Seance With Charlie The Cursed Doll!

Billy drew a thick black line through the twenty-first with a marker, his evening habit. It had been fifty-five days since Tazia had been under the direct control of Jegudiel. Far too long. This watch-and-wait policy was pissing him off.

"Do you think he'll talk?" His gaze moved back to the demon in the middle of the room.

Hux shrugged. "Sometimes they die before they say anything of use."

The demon tried to shift slightly in his seat. He eyed the trickle of holy water that was about to descend below his zipper.

"Come on, mate. You want to keep your tackle intact, right?" Billy said.

"Man, please! I don't know nothin'!" He was an older white guy, fiftyish, flabby, receding hairline. Billy wondered why the vampire sire had chosen this man to gift with further existence. He hoped he'd led a good life and his soul at least had found a way to Heaven.

As the thin river of holy water finally found its target, he started to moan again. A stain of light red leeched through the top of his grey underwear.

"Please, please! It hurts so bad!" The vampire squirmed and started to sob.

Hux walked over to him, towel in hand, and dangled it just above the offending stain. "Who are you working for?"

The vampire shuffled in the seat, trying to stop the flow. "Okay! I'll tell you—*aargh!*" The final words were distorted by a scream as the water found a particular tender spot and a new bloom of deeper red stain appeared.

"Who?" Hux lowered the towel.

"It was the angel. Please!"

A stink of rising sweat and warm piss, the latter now soaking through his jeans, rose up.

Gagging, Billy stepped back. Hux didn't blink and threw the towel down onto the vampire's lap where it formed a barrier to the holy water and also sucked up the bloody urine. Billy had a distinct impression that Hux had seen this a hundred times before.

"Which angel?" they said in unison.

"Red-haired bitch!" The vampire was still peering between his legs warily.

"What exactly were her orders?" Hux asked.

"Just to distract you, man. We were supposed to just distract you!" He shifted again, double-checking the towel was still doing its job. Suddenly cocky, he glared at Hux. "She said she had special plans. Needed you out of it!"

"Special plans? Like?" Hux picked up the towel again and threatened more water.

"I dunno. Something about a girl and… a switch." He tried to shuffle back.

"Switch?" Billy exchanged a look with Hux. Jacob had reported overhearing a conversation between demons talking about losing someone's blood. Julie had told him, they programmed him to wake him up. Could all these things be connected? "What about a switch?"

"I dunno anything else. Just that…"

"Yeah?" Again, in unison.

"She said you were a couple of assholes!"

"Did you get that, Billy? We're arseholes!" Hux pulled a revolver from his holster, lowered it to the vampire's forehead, and shot him cleanly between the eyes. No time to whimper, he was dead instantly.

"Good." Billy blinked at his own cruelty. The idea that he could now get the revolting mess out of the kitchen overcame his usual sensitivity. "Do we have disinfectant?"

"You sure you're not a girl?"

"That's sexist, Hux. But why am I not surprised? You could use some, too. Maybe, dip your feet in it."

"My feet do not—"

The satellite phone rang.

They both reached for it, but Hux snatched it up. He paced back and forth through the pool of blood and pee as he listened, spreading wet boot prints across the floor. Billy shuddered.

"Are you on your own? … Where are they? … Fucking witches!"

Billy didn't flinch at the vitriol. It was a sentiment he'd heard a thousand times, and one he couldn't entirely disagree with now he knew the history. When it came down to it, witches only ever looked out for themselves. They'd proven that often enough.

"Ok, man, we'll get there as soon as we can." Hux put the phone down. "Boston has completely fallen. The coven has gone. Just Aideen left, Jacob's friend. The female demon at the focal point has been confirmed. It's her, Billy…" His face hardened.

Can't you even say her name, now? "Is Taz inciting it or trying to stop it?"

"She and her guards rounded up a hundred or so people last night, under the pretence of helping them. She led them to a warehouse where they got jumped. There are now a hundred more demons walking around Boston." He held Billy's look for a second more while the news sunk in. "You ready to go?"

Billy nodded. His stomach lurched at the thought of what was coming. If Tazia was all in, it must mean she was completely under the Advocate's control. Was this the switch? Could he get her back?

As he closed the door on the sticky, stinking mess in the kitchen, he felt a pang of relief that at least he wouldn't need to face the clean-up.

27

HORROR STORY

THE KNIFE TAZIA used to slice deep across the boy's throat was an ordinary yellow-handled construction knife, the kind seen on any building site. From his hiding place, Billy wondered what had happened to the hunting blade she'd preferred before her father's death.

She'd loved her Bowie knife. She would clean, sharpen, and shine it for hours, lovingly polishing every groove and serration. This one she just left hanging in the boy's open throat and let the body drop to the ground. Then she pulled a replacement knife from her back pocket. The same yellow plastic.

Christ, what's happened to you, love?

Just a few moments earlier, he'd seen the blade reflecting in the few streetlights left unbroken. It shone between her fingers, handle pointed down, looking as though she was about to launch it like a carnival knife thrower. But her target wasn't a spinning disk. It had been a young kid, trapped and frantically scanning his surroundings for a way to run or someone to help him.

As she'd walked toward him, she flipped the knife from handle to blade and back, all the time staring him down with a slight smile.

Billy and Hux were in an industrial dockland area of Boston, holed up between massive double-decker metal containers that looked like they'd been dumped by a nearby crane in a vague U-shape, like a huge cattle pen. Inside, a small crowd of people—a mixture of men, women, and several young children—were trapped by twenty or more demons, mostly vampires.

Following the sounds of screaming, they had slipped down between two container walls and watched.

The human renegades had a choice: they could allow themselves to be captured, fed from, even possessed by the demons, or fight and most probably die. The hope of their faces when they recognized Tazia as the Saviour faded as she flashed the knife. Confusion replaced it. Then fear.

The boy was the bravest. Just in his teens, he'd shown amazing courage pelting the demons with broken brick, before running at Tazia, arm raised. Maybe he thought she was the weakest link?

He was wrong.

Billy was transfixed by her. She was expressionless; skin dull and smooth, mouth set. A perfect puppet.

Hux couldn't take his eyes from her, either. It was almost too painful for Billy to see his suffering. His eyes were round and lips pinched together, he shrank back into the shadows. Disbelief? Shock?

In that moment, a horror story was made real, and it stood not twenty feet in front of them.

Billy risked another glance at Hux. He'd cemented his ice-cool stare back in place. He mouthed, "Stay down!" and, "She stays alive!" This final message was accompanied by a look that said: *Don't even think about it!*

Unnecessary. He'd agreed that this time, Tazia lived. He'd nodded his reply. This way had to work. The alternative was no longer possible for him to contemplate.

Now that the boy was dead, Tazia turned her attention to the other humans who cowered at the far side of the pen, all hope fading from their faces. The men and women formed a barricade in front of the children, but it was futile.

Billy was close enough to Tazia to hear her sigh before signalling with her hand, a tiny gesture. With it, she released a handful of the demons. They overcame them easily enough and systematically broke the necks of the remaining adults in the group. The dead bodies were dragged away while the children were left alive, picked up, and carried off. Would they feed on them? Occupy them?

There was no screaming.

Tazia stayed where she was. Moonlight lit her pale face, and the weak glow from a streetlight behind her created a halo-like effect around her upper body.

Her hair was different, the bangs completely grown out, and she'd cut the back to the same length to meet them. She'd lost weight, her cheekbones standing proud, and her flesh strong and rippled with muscle. Blood powered her now.

It was her eyes, though, that caught Billy. There was no trace of dark brown left, just constant pure amber. He'd never seen that before.

Standing beside her were two guards who ghosted her every move.

She took a step forward, peering into the darkness where both he and Hux were hidden, her head tipped to one side. Did she smell them? See them? He didn't want the confrontation yet. He wasn't ready. Besides, with Jacob scouting elsewhere, they would have even less of a chance against the Soldiers.

Tazia took a step back and issued a quiet order to the men. All three set off at a jog.

Billy and Hux exhaled at the same moment.

28

FACING OFF

HOLED up in the basement of an abandoned house in Boston, Billy listened as Hux and Jacob animatedly discussed the next stage of the plan. They had yet to meet Aideen who had apparently been called back to the coven, outside the city. The argument was one Billy was trying hard to avoid.

For him, it was simple. They would find Tazia, take out her guards, and bring her in. When he'd voiced this opinion, both the former soldiers in the group frowned at him and continued their debate. They seemed obsessed with "reconnaissance" which they spoke of with reverence, appropriating several big guns, and maybe even a… flame-thrower. *What the fuck?*

"You do know vampires are flammable, right?"

"It's not to use on her, Billy. It's for her guards." Hux paused before asking with exasperation, "Have you ever been up against a Soldier demon?"

He was trying his best to be patient, Billy could tell, and had asked several times for him to leave the planning to them. But with every passing tick of the clock, and more tellingly every cut of her knife, Tazia's soul was closer to eternal damnation.

Billy wandered up into the kitchen, the only modernized space of the detached historical home. He absently tested a kitchen drawer—soft close. *Nice.*

Still hearing loud voices coming from the basement, he headed for the door. Maybe fresh air would settle him.

The house was set back in a private subdivision (aka urban village) which, up to a few weeks ago, had a working security system that said, *have a nice day* in the morning and *welcome home* in the afternoon. With the power out, the white box on the wall was silent.

Outside, the air was warm for autumn. Not a flake of snow had fallen yet this year; with so many demons at large, it would only get hotter.

Regretful that the leaves from the ornamental trees were unlikely to unfurl again, Billy ran his hands over the brittle branches. Powdered bark collected in his palm. It already smelled of death.

In the moonlight, he couldn't make out any animal life, but he knew it would be there. Demon cities attracted rodents, snakes, lizards, and birds of course. Mostly magpies at this stage, spying from the bare trees, rooftops, and dead telephone wires. He could feel their eyes on him even in the dark. Occasionally they made a quiet squawk or whistle as he passed by, whispering his presence to whoever was listening. *Little fuckers! Better than GPS.*

He left the yard and walked slowly down the main street into the village. A solid decorative metal gate marked its entrance. Each half had been pulled off its hinges and abandoned, one half in a flower bed and the other leaning against the quintessential white picket fence of the first house on the block. It looked as though it had been rammed by a ten-ton truck, the thick vertical bars bent in a wide slew across the middle.

Next to the remains of the gates, a sign declared ANGEL'S

LANDING. It also lay on its side. He'd burst out laughing when he saw it the night before, and spent a few precious minutes of satellite-hacking time to Google it.

The village was named after a local hilltop not far away, where an angel had once appeared to accompany the souls of twenty settlers to Heaven. They'd apparently suffered a hideous death at the hands of a local native raiding party. *Revisionist bollocks!* Besides, he knew better now, there was no chance any angel would drag themselves away from whatever crucial "watching" they were doing to intervene.

It was creepy on the abandoned street with no cars in the driveways, no people shouting "hello" or popping out to their mailboxes. Despite the warm evening, Billy shivered and pulled the hood from the sweatshirt he wore over his head. It was a garish orange he wouldn't usually be seen dead in, left in the clothes dryer by whoever owned the house.

A faint rustle sounded in the bushes to his right. "Who's there?" Billy squashed the anxiety and stood his ground. He heard a giggle and recognized it instantly. "Taz?"

"Hey, Billy." She stepped out from behind the bush. Her grin plastered like it had been painted except for the shine on her teeth. Her eyes caught a little of the moonlight. The rest of her skin was dull, yellowish, like she was wearing a rubber mask. It gave her a surreal look.

For a moment, he doubted whether it was really her or someone dressed up in her clothes. Then, a slight breeze blew, and he caught her scent. A musky sweet Moroccan oil she used on her hair and skin to protect against sun damage.

She was alone, with no demon guards. "Are you okay?"

His concern threw her off a beat, and for a moment she frowned. "Of course." The smile snapped back. "I saw you yesterday. You and Hux. Watching me at the docks."

"Yes." There was no reason to deny it. "You killed that boy, Taz."

"Yep."

"Why?"

"He was resisting me."

The excuse came automatically, and he could tell it sounded perfectly logical in her head. "Is that what you have to do if someone fights back? Kill them?"

"Subdue or kill." Again, automatic.

This was a Tazia Billy didn't know. Even in the worst of her gun-toting, demon-killing days, when she worked contracts or under her father's orders, she never did so without thought. Back then, she didn't have access to her soul, but often it was hard to tell it was missing. She seemed to have a conscience. *That* girl would call an ambulance to save a man she'd fed from so he'd live. This one was different. Like she'd been… recoded.

He settled on the low wall that separated the median from the rest of the road. She wasn't here to kill him. So what was the point of the visit?

"Are you following orders, babe? From the Advocate?"

She didn't answer, just bounced up and down on the balls of her feet.

Both hands had been behind her back from the moment she'd arrived, but now she pulled them forward. There was a large dagger in her right one. It shone brightly in the moonlight, casting a glow that seemed to emanate from the blade where shiny studs were embedded in the dark grey metal. In contrast, the handle was wood, carved with symbols, and polished to a high sheen.

It was an angelic weapon, and he could feel it hum.

"You want to kill me?"

"I can't kill you, Billy. You know that. Not me. I'm no angel!" She laughed, almost identical to Jegudiel's evil titter.

He cringed. "So, what's the plan, Taz? You stab me, leave me for dead, then your boss comes and finishes me off? Or is this supposed to just be a warning for me to withdraw?"

She hesitated. *She's still in there. I know she is.*

"Taz? Love, you gonna let her kill me?"

"You were going to kill me, Billy."

He couldn't deny it. "But I didn't, did I? I couldn't do it. I love you too much."

She flipped the knife from blade to handle just as he'd seen her do before she'd killed the boy. It was something she'd not done before. "What is that?"

"What?"

"The knife-play?"

She hesitated. "I… don't… know."

"Do you feel anxious, Taz? I can hold you, like I used to, if you like?" He smiled at her.

"No! Last time you held me, you hurt me!" She flipped the knife even faster.

"I'm sorry for doing that, love. Really. I was wrong." He got up from the wall and walked toward her as naturally as possible. He didn't look at the knife. "She confuses you, Taz. She's made you think you're all-powerful. That what you're doing is for the good of… well… what exactly? Not the people anymore."

"Time for demons to take control."

"Under your instruction?"

"No!"

"Under hers?"

Tazia had no answer. She was becoming more agitated, the interminable knife flipping now accompanied by back and forth pacing. Tick tock. On and on.

"Under hers?" he repeated. There was something here, knowledge she had that Billy needed.

"Stop it!"

"Taz, I'm not trying to upset you. Let me hold you. We can figure this out, babe, it's not too late." He took another step toward her.

"Don't come any further, Billy. Seriously, I will hurt you." The mask was slipping, and her voice broke a little.

"Did she tell you to hurt me?"

"She gave me the dagger."

"But it's your decision to use it, love…"

"I…"

"Let me hold you." He took another step forward.

"Stop! I'll do it! Then…" For the first time, Tazia's eyes widened.

"Then, what, love?" Another step.

"Then she'll kill you." She moved back, banging against a garbage can left out God knows when. The lid loosened a fraction, and the flies buzzing inside escaped between the gap. She flailed at them.

Billy took the last step, holding out his arms. "I just want to hold you. Make it better."

With a sob, she grabbed at him. The hug lasted just seconds, beautiful. Then she stiffened, stepped back, her eyes wide, and her teeth clenched. Her arm swept forward.

The dagger struck his right side at an upward angle. She pushed the tip up toward his heart, reaching under his ribs and through his lung. The pain didn't hit immediately. She held it there.

Billy wobbled. *She did it.* He smiled. "It's… okay, love. I… understand." His breath already shortening.

Momentarily, her mouth turned upward in a toothy grin. Then that look faded. Doubt flickered in her eyes. She blinked. For a moment, he stared into those dark brown eyes he loved so much.

She brought her mouth up close to his ear, and whispered, "It's a demon running the show, not the Advocate. I don't know who." She yanked the knife from him and slipped back into the darkness.

Billy wavered again, trying to maintain his balance. A

sudden cough caught in his throat, a wet splutter, and he tasted metal. Shock hit just as blood dribbled from his mouth and he fell to the ground, his right arm crunching under him. Lying on his side, he stared at the ANGEL'S LANDING subdivision sign. His sight shrank to nothing.

29

STICKY MESS

THE MOON HUNG RIGHT OVERHEAD when Billy regained consciousness. The sticky mess of blood that poured from his wound and saturated his top had stopped flowing. The stain was almost invisible against the hue of the material, but he could feel the liquid wet and heavy when he shifted slightly. He wasn't too sure how much blood he had left, but the ice in his extremities wasn't normal on this warm night.

From his angle on the pavement, he could see the occasional rodent emerge from hiding places among the rocks and cracks in the road. The blood scent had made them brave. One came close and lapped at the puddle that trickled from him to the gutter. *Fucking rats.* Billy couldn't get away from them. Even here, thousands of miles from home.

He'd always spot them between the Tube tracks, or scampering down alleyways when out for an evening run. When he was tiny, and just arrived in London from Pakistan, they'd play on the floor of his bedroom. He would huddle under the covers, knees up, too scared to lie down, praying they wouldn't climb under the sheets when he fell asleep.

On the road, all he could do was hope they wouldn't nip at his flesh. Only the blink reflex of his eyelids worked fully. His limbs had frozen, resisting the waves of pain shuddering up into his head and down into his toes.

His breath had stalled too, dragging on his left side, absent from his right.

The human body was meant to give him human perspective, a tactical advantage. Some advantage! A ripped up meat suit and a front-row seat to his own fuck-up.

At that moment, with every shallow gasp for air, Billy knew only one thing: he had to save his girl from the bitch who had turned her into a monster.

Get back to the bloody house, Billy! He could picture Hux and Jacob still arguing about The Plan. Was nursing a sick angel back to health part of that? Could he even make it that far?

Sucking in what breath he could, he forced himself to movement. He rolled onto his left side, and reached out with his arm. Then he bent his leg to gain traction with the pavement. With the remaining strength he had, he pushed himself forward.

He screamed. The magpies shot up from the trees, awake and disoriented, their screeching joining his cry.

Pain flashed over him, wave upon wave of agony rushing over his body. He could no longer feel where his limbs were. One mass of purple gut-twisting pain.

"Poor Billy!" The Advocate stood beside him. Had the scream summoned her, or had she been there the whole time, just watching?

"Fuck... you... bi..." He tried, but was out of breath before the final word.

"You shouldn't be so nasty, pet. I could kill you here and now." He caught a flash of the dagger and, even within the shroud of pain, felt her trace the curves of his stretched-out arm, which now lay uselessly at a right angle.

He tried and failed to draw it back, tears of pain and frustration coursing from his eyes. "Do… it." He knew she could. An angel wielding an angelic weapon. In a second, he'd just be a flash of light whizzing back to his birthplace billions of miles away orbiting Earth. A speck of stardust. The image was so romantic it made him want to laugh. The sound gurgled in his throat.

"Ahh, why would I kill you, pet? You've proved yourself useless over and over again. You see, I was wrong, Billy. I thought you were a threat to me. But nothing—nothing—you've done has made me worry even slightly."

Then she said it. The words he'd been dreading.

"You drove her right to me!" Her high-pitched laughter echoed around the empty street, bouncing off each structure.

"I… failed." His shame found the little blood remaining and blazed in his cheeks.

"Yes, pet. You failed. Just like Soren Huxford did before." She tutted and drew her hands down the front of that bloody purple dress he hated so much, distracted by creases he knew she didn't care about. "Honestly, you men! All for the love of a woman. So predictable!"

The laughter stopped abruptly. "But I'm bored now, Billy." She got down on her knees in the pool of blood still leaching from him, and turned her face level to his so that even her hair sopped it up. Her face ebbed out of focus. "I'm bored with the games. The pathetic attempts to save her. She is mine." She spat each word at him. "So, give it up already!"

The sound of a door opening echoed down the road, and she glanced up. Her tone changed again. She playfully tapped him on the nose with the tip of the dagger, toying with him. "Time for me to go, pet. Your friends are looking for you. And I'm sure a few angelic Brady Bunch are on their way, too. Take care. Hope you feel better soon." The last was delivered in a sing-song voice.

The last thing Billy heard was Hux's heavy footsteps approaching at a run, and his cries for Jacob's assistance.

30

LIMBO

BILLY HADN'T MOVED for three days. Days spent just existing. His limbs pinned to his side as though they would break if he dared flex even a muscle. An oxygen mask cemented to his face, and his eyes open, but unfocused.

He'd seen nothing of the bustling nurses or the constant back and forth of visitors to the patients in the beds next to him, nothing but the look on Tazia's face as she'd driven that knife into his side.

She killed me.

She knew it wouldn't be death. Not by her hand. But the intent to leave him for the Advocate to finish off was clear.

She hadn't hesitated. Teeth gritted, excitement in her eyes. Flashes of red buried deep within the amber. She'd wanted the kill.

My best friend killed me.

He could still feel the strike of the blade. Strong. Decisive. Not a moment's hesitation.

God, she'd wanted it.

She'd wanted to take him out of the game. He could feel it

in the brutal finality of the act. His death would have been her release.

He'd spent three days telling himself she must have been compelled, that it wasn't her. A pointless argument. It didn't matter anymore. She'd believed he was truly the bad guy.

She actually wanted me dead…

He could see it on her face. The triumph.

There his memories ended, with pain. With that look.

When the shoe was on the other foot, he couldn't do it. In the end, no bullshit argument about the greater good was worth his best friend's life.

But you didn't fail, did you, love?

He wasn't technically dead, but Tazia had killed a part of him all the same. Now, he had no bloody idea what to do next.

LET'S PLAY PICTIONARY FOR IT

BILLY'S long dark lashes afforded him the opportunity to spy on the comings and goings of the ward without drawing attention to himself. If he didn't move or speak, he could remain locked up tight in a cell of his own making.

He couldn't check his injuries. Not even bend his head to look. When he tried, shuddering pangs of white-hot pain shot from his chest to every limb, forcing him to grab the oxygen mask and suck in shallow gasps until the agony dispersed. The injury was not healing at the speed he'd hoped; the drugs just tempered the torture.

Her knife had really done a number on him.

The shock was the worst. If he dwelled on Tazia's actions, he found himself caught between mutely staring straight in front of him or weeping with huge sobs that caught in his throat. There was no middle ground.

In his better moments, he would consider his own actions when he'd first found out he was an angel. How he'd convinced himself that Tazia had to die, that her life was inconsequential when measured against the survival of humankind. He'd valued Earth's unknown occupants more highly than his love for her, his best friend. Now, that logic shamed him.

It didn't matter how hard that decision was and how the implications had plagued him. He understood the betrayal she'd felt because her treachery had sucked him dry. He was left as nothing: a dusty husk. A body attached to an oxygen mask at one end and a pee bag at the other.

"Time for supper, Mr. Nadig." The voice sang its way into his consciousness; the tinkling tone sounded familiar.

He peered through his lashes at its owner—an orderly who usually brought him his meals. She was the Amazonian type: tall, well-built, and blonde. She could have been Hux's sister.

She busied herself pulling over the little rolling table that usually spooned the bed. As she picked up his supper from the bottom of the food warmer trolley, her scrubs snuggly grabbing at the curves of her bottom, he saw the unmistakable outline of thong underwear.

When she turned around with the plastic covered plate, bending unnecessarily low to place it on the table, her rather substantial cleavage was put on display, too, and Billy's interest went from mild appreciation to outright enjoyment. *Nope, I'm still not dead!*

She winked at him. "Thought you could do with a treat, Billy." She removed the lid from the plate with a gesture that declared, "*Ta-da!*" so that he was not sure whether she was referring to the food or her appearance. The food won. It was Shepherd's Pie, his favourite. English food in a Boston hospital? Hang on—

"Julie?"

She nodded, smiled, and settled on the edge of the bed, crossing her legs, the material of her trousers pulling taut over her thigh.

"Full… marks… for the… body… girl." He said the words, gasping for air in between, and immediately started coughing.

His hand jumped to his chest as pain darted from his midsection and travelled to his feet. He replaced the oxygen mask, but did not try to reach for the food.

"Do you need some help?"

"I can't… get up. I'm… pathetic."

Julie snorted slightly at the word choice and pulled him to a seated position. His face got swiped by her chest in the process, and for a moment he was lost in the sensation of smooth, soft, warm flesh against his cheek.

This time, his pulse genuinely gained a bit more momentum regardless of the pain shooting up his side and around his back. "You're… the medicine… I was—" Another round of coughing cut him off, and his pulse abruptly returned to normal, whatever "normal" was for a man who'd had a dagger stuck in his lung not four days ago.

"Just don't forget I'm your superior, Billy." She tried to look at him sternly, but whoever she was wearing ruined the effect by giggling.

The scent of the food was working. For the first time in several days, he was actually hungry. He reached for the fork and moved the pie around his plate, taking in the savoury aroma of potato, meat, and gravy. Eating took mixing-cement-like-effort, though. After a few mouthfuls, he put the fork back down.

"Got news of Tazia?" He avoided more coughing by taking a breath first to propel the words at speed.

"Same. She's rounding up the people she and the Advocate tricked into following her. Killing some, leaving others for demons to transform."

"Where?"

"Still Boston—north of here—I guess they're being thorough." Heavy irony coloured the last phrase.

They sat in silence for a little while, Billy making another attempt at his supper and Julie tapping her fingers on the side of his bed. "So, what's the plan, sweetie?"

He suddenly got busy shovelling food into his mouth and chewed rapidly, ignoring the pain the movement generated.

"Billy?"

He shrugged slightly and grabbed another mouthful.

"I can wait." She sat back, crossed her arms, and smiled.

He attempted an answer and sprayed the air in front of him liberally with pie mush. "Don't... know... innit." The flippancy was deliberate. The pain cutting into his heart had nothing to do with the injury.

While she mock-wiped her face from the offending food spray, he stopped eating and put down his fork. "I don't know what to do, Ju."

They'd been here before: him with no idea about his next move, and her refusing to lay it out. Her presence meant there was something he should be doing. But what?

Gasping a big breath, he spat the words out fast. "She knew she couldn't kill me, but she stabbed me anyway. Why?" No oxygen left, another big gulp of air grated in his throat. He grasped his chest again.

Julie raised her eyebrows. "Maybe she was doing it to prove something?"

"To who?"

"Whom."

"What?"

"To whom. Just a grammar point."

Who the fuck does this body belong to? Poet-bloody-Laureate.

Billy decided he preferred the wistful Julie. "Who... was she proving... something... to?" He re-jigged the sentence.

"Herself maybe. You. Or Jegudiel? I don't know, Billy. But just seems to me that either she was doing it cos she wanted you dead, and knew Jegudiel would finish you off, or else she was proving a point. Maybe she was pissed at you. Just teaching you a lesson."

"No way." In the years they'd known each other, he'd never seen Tazia hang onto a grudge. She lived in the present. If she couldn't deal with something immediately, she either lost interest and let it go, or even blamed herself. She wasn't Hux. That guy was like a dog with a bone.

"Well then, maybe they were just trying to get you out of the picture for a while. Distract you—" her eyes ate into him "—after all, it worked!"

The tone was critical, and he deserved it. He'd been lying around the hospital for four days, doing nothing but mooning about how his girl had hurt him. He had to shake this off and forced himself upright a little. "Ok. So, let's… say she was… going through… the motions… just for Jegudiel. What then? How… does that help us?"

Julie shrugged, still revealing nothing.

Billy shoved away the table and lay back on the bed too hard. The pain leaped in his back and chest as his breath left. He still managed a choice "c" word as he grabbed for the oxygen mask.

The outgoing expletive ended up muffled, but Julie got the point. "No need to curse at me, sweetie. You need to figure this stuff out. Your job—not mine."

"I… know." He didn't want to go there again, but forced himself to review what had happened in the street. What Tazia had said. Done. She was different. Fully vamp. Amber eyes— no trace of brown. Well, until the end—

Fuck! That's it!

Billy struggled to release his mask, but it had become wrapped around his ears. As he wrestled with it, it kept slapping him in the face, until Julie came to his aid.

As soon as he was free, he said, "She-told-me-there-was-a-demon-Ju!" The words came out in a loud rush, and he grabbed her arm at the same time. He gasped and pulled her to him, speaking a little more quietly this time. "A demon is in charge—not Jegudiel!"

He remembered Tazia's face. She'd looked at him, so focused for a second. It was not with triumph as he'd first thought; it was a look of determination, so he would understand. Her eyes had been brown again—no amber or red flecks. He'd watched her lips as she'd spoken. They were beautiful. "'It's a… demon running… the show. Not the Advocate… I don't know who.' That's… what… she said!"

Julie sat back and seemed to run his comment through her mind. Her blank face told him nothing. Did she already know?

"The fact she told you, Billy. That's key."

"Must mean… she's not… as under the bitch's control… as we thought."

"Yes, exactly, but there's more too."

Julie was back to giving him just hints again. It infuriated him. "What?"

"Jegudiel has two clear weaknesses. You can use them both." She was urging him on just like she'd done that very first time in the doctor's waiting room when she'd encouraged him to recognize his angelic self.

"Well, she's… not the boss. That's… clear." Too much oxygen addled his mind. Clarity had devolved into slightly blurry insight.

"Yes. That's key. But could be good or bad, sweetie…"

He had nothing. Her face dropped. It made him sorry he wasn't better at the "guess what Julie knows" game. Flippantly, he asked: "Can we… play *Pictionary*… for it?"

To his surprise, she smiled. "Why not!"

Julie got up, smoothed down her top, and collected his half-eaten food. She put the plastic plate cover, drinking cup, and cutlery on the food trolley then paused over the rest of the pie.

Picking up the fork, she carefully gathered it into the centre of the plate to create a little mountain.

"*Close Encounters!*" Billy blurted out, feeling a brief rush of genuine excitement. "Jegudiel is... an alien!"

Julie paused with the fork. "What? Don't be dumb." She squashed the potato into a long, thin shape.

Billy watched with interest until she stood back and admired her handy-work. "That... looks like... a penis, Ju."

"For fu—" Julie cut herself off and glared. She took the fork to the pile of mash again, this time ensuring the bottom end of the thin, soggy mixture was very pointed.

"The... dagger?"

She nodded briefly. Mushed all the food back up and started rearranging it into a round shape with what looked like a jagged crown around it. She gouged out two holes (maybe eyes?) and a wide smiley mouth.

Billy had an immense desire to smirk. This could be anyone. "A... queen?"

"For fucksakes!" With a final flourish, Julie added two upside down triangles dangling from the lips, then spun around the plate so it was facing him. "Tazia! It's Tazia! See?" She followed this up with another hearty curse word, but had the good grace to go slightly red.

"You... go... girl!" Billy was proud of her.

Julie patted his hand and mouthed "good luck" at him before picking up the plate and piling it on top of the trolley. As she walked away, the world surged into motion.

32

____

ON THE SEVENTH DAY

SOREN CAME to the hospital each day to sit by Billy's side.

When he'd found him on the street, slumped in the road, a river of blood still flowing from him, he thought he was dead. If he hadn't known he was an angel, he would have given him up as a corpse.

Instead, he and Jacob had raced him to an emergency department south of Boston, the only hospital still functioning in the area. In the Jeep Billy had briefly stirred, and said one word, "Taz." Nothing since. Just sleeping or staring with blank eyes.

Frustratingly, the doctor told him that yesterday he'd been awake, hungry, animated. Now he was out cold again.

Soren tried a whole slew of techniques to snap him out of it. Glaring into Billy's glassy eyes and pinching his arm so hard one of his wounds started bleeding again. When that failed, he whispered threats into his ear, and even, in desperation, crooned a few erotic promises. But nothing had forced Billy to talk.

He concluded he was either faking well or really was in some sort of sporadic catatonic state.

Today, he sat in the chair, resigned. Chin resting in his palm, he stared out the window, watching all the birds flying north toward Boston in the warm still air outside. Vast flocks darkened the skies.

Every now and again, he'd sneak a look at his... friend. The angelic transformation had pared him down to thin, sinewy muscle. Small in the bed, his stick-thin limbs poked out of the wide square armholes of his hospital gown. He looked weak. The fight all gone. Where was this angelic warrior they needed?

As he sat, Soren semi-rhythmically pushed a foot against the bedside table. The action shifted a glass of water resting against a metal jug and clinked in stuttered time as he flexed.

"For fucksakes... Hux stop... kicking... the bloody... cupboard!" Billy had finally come to himself. The effort of forcing the words out in-between shallow breaths left him flailing to change his position and find some air.

Soren jumped up to help and pulled him up to sitting. The coughing continued, and after fitting him with the oxygen mask, he stood patting Billy's back. After a few moments, the fit subsided, and Billy managed a few big breaths.

He removed the mask. "Just been... waiting to get... your hands on me."

"Arsehole." Soren sat back down.

"Did it get... that far? Were... you safe?" Billy questioned, eyebrows rising to accompany the smirk. He replaced the mask.

Soren gave him a pointed stare before a brief smile. If Billy was joking again, he must be okay.

The younger man rubbed his chest. The doctor seemed impressed with the healing speed. Soren knew better. He'd expected angelic-level recovery based on former injuries. Something was holding the process back. "How are you feeling?"

"Like… I've been… stabbed and… left for dead." His eyebrows jerked up.

Soren nodded. It had been a stupid question. "I have questions. More intelligent ones. Are you ready?" He forced a level of sympathy into his voice. It had been days since they'd last had news of the Advocate or Anastasia. This mission was slipping away from him.

"Sure." Billy spoke in-between taking breaths with the mask on.

"Who stabbed you?" He hoped for a different name this time.

"Taz." Billy looked at him calmly.

Soren shook his head. "Wasn't Anastasia, Billy. Was the robot that bitch has turned her into."

Billy broke eye contact.

"You know that, right?"

He gave him a one-shouldered shrug and winced.

Soren struggled with what to say next. Billy needed to heal. If lack of hope was holding him back, then he'd need to help him find some. Cuinn had been good at pep talks, maybe…

He'd have to dig deep.

They'd had their moments of reconciliation over the last few months since Turin, but there was still history they'd not discussed. Perhaps it was time?

He cleared his throat. "So."

"Yeah?"

"You used to be that techno-kid I hated. Anastasia ran to you for help. You were on the scene long before me." Was he listening? "Billy."

"Yeah. I heard… just confused—"

"This is hard, okay. I'm not good with… words."

Billy's eyes flicked back to him and, for once, he didn't crack a joke. He gave a nod—barely there—Soren took it as encouragement.

"She loved you. Clear. I was the dumb muscle. Convenient. A job." The tension in his body kept him stock still. He battled to control his neutral tone.

"Hux, she never—"

"Let me finish." Soren forced a slight smile. "I figured out in Detroit why it stung so much. She was a job to me, too. Supposed to be at least. But I fell for her. Just too stupid to realize. I was a fucking arsehole in Detroit. In more ways than you know."

He sighed, images of stalking her, cutting his own skin, crushing her hand. *Huxford, get to the point.* "But I did figure something out, right. She loves you and you love her. Maybe it's friendship, maybe more. I dunno. But it's real. Solid. And this bitch can mask it, but can't take it away. Unless you let her."

In his head, it was poetic. Billy's relationship with Anastasia was the most authentic of all of them. It didn't bite anymore. She had someone in her life besides him to take care of her. And that was a good thing. Beautiful.

Instead he said. "You can't lose her, man. You have to keep hoping. Keep fighting for her."

"I know… still hard." Billy replaced the oxygen mask.

"Okay. I get that. Next question. Why aren't you recovering quickly? Your angel mojo misfiring?"

"Nah. Angelic weapon." This time, he didn't even attempt to move the mask. The reply was muffled but still audible.

Soren nodded. "Okay. But Anastasia used it, not an angel, so—"

"She couldn't kill me… even with the weapon… but still more powerful—"

"So, it will take you longer to recover." Soren interrupted to save him from the explanation. *Shit.* He hadn't needed to reveal so much of his thoughts after all. The weapon was the delay, not the lack of hope. Not loss of love. He'd read it wrong.

"Yeah." Billy started coughing again, grating at the air with the in-breath and a chest that sounded like it didn't want to fill.

He grabbed Soren's arm and clung on while he struggled, his face turning red with the effort. It brought a little life back into his cheeks.

Soren put his hand on top of Billy's for encouragement and willed him to get control again, subconsciously breathing long slow breaths for him.

When the fit subsided, emotions boxed up again, Soren continued his questioning. They couldn't wait until Billy was well enough. "How do you know? About the weapon?"

"Julie."

"She was here?"

"Yesterday."

"She say anything else?"

Billy nodded, but struggled to catch his breath. Soren waited, tapping against the side of the table with his foot until he saw Billy's glare and stopped.

"She said not too late Taz not hers completely." He'd forced the words out in a rush, and now lay exhausted.

"Not the Advocate's?"

"Yeah." Billy held up a hand and took another big breath before continuing. "Something Taz said to me…" He pulled the mask away, and Soren got closer to him to listen. "There's a demon in… control. Not the Advocate. She said it just after… she stabbed me."

Soren sat back.

For the first time since he'd killed Conn O'Cuinn, he felt a change.

It crept up on him, rising from the bottom of his stomach. It was the feeling he got when he knew he'd almost completed a contract. All the cards were in his favour. The target didn't even know he was coming. "This changes things, Billy."

Billy's eyes held his.

He can feel it too. The shift.

"Hurry up and get well, man. We need you. Anastasia needs you." As an afterthought, he added, "Don't forget to hope."

———

On the seventh day, instead of resting, Billy left the hospital. He didn't feel much like God, anyway.

The death knell in his head had finally faded to a dull chime. That bloody pep talk Hux had given him—if he could call it that—actually helped. It was time to get to work. Christ, if the man-God could declare love would conquer all, who the hell was he to argue?

His angelic healing had kicked in since that chat, too. While pain still lingered, his chest felt clearer. He drew a breath, and it only hitched once. Sounding more like mild pneumonia than the sixty-a-day emphysema he'd been channelling.

The bench Billy sat on outside the hospital was the old-fashioned kind with curly metal legs and wooden planks. It reminded him of the one back home on his terrace.

The last time he'd sat on that one, he'd shared a cigarette with Tazia. She'd made the end wet because she held it in her mouth in between puffs and played with it with her tongue. *Yuck!*

They'd been engrossed in discussing her fears around Hux coming to hunt her down. He'd had such a hold on her. Billy hadn't understood it at the time and sided with her, of course. Was bloody outraged. But now, he understood. They'd loved each other, but completely oblivious, had betrayed each other just the same.

It was screwed up. If this was ever over, he'd get them in a room together to hash it out.

No, when this *is* over. Keep the hope, Hux had said. And he was right.

Billy's thoughts triggered more reflections. Humans were so flawed, and yet so perfect. Memories too, of the days before he was Billy. Visions of Earth from the sky. The soft wind on his skin as he'd shared space with the birds that skimmed past him. The awe of walking invisibly among humans and seeing their creation not just as flesh, but as intricate living architecture. He could sense bones, muscles, organs, blood, all moving together to create a simple motion. *A bloody symphony!*

He saw it now on the faces of the people passing through the hospital entrance: smiles and grimaces, anger, relief, fear. Each, a fleeting masterpiece. These were the survivors, fragile yet stubborn. If they could do it, how the hell could he give up.

Watching them, his focus tightened.

Julie had told him that Jegudiel had two weaknesses, weapons they could use against her. He understood the first: the angel dagger. He was sure they could come up with a plan to get that from her. Difficult but a clear mission objective. *Hey Hux, I'm a bloody soldier!*

The second thing, though, confused him: Tazia herself was Jegudiel's weakness. Another weapon, Ju has said. How?

Although Tazia had broken herself out of the Advocate's influence to whisper the words in his ear, the rest of the time, she was doing exactly what Jegudiel wanted her to do. That's not a weapon, it's an asset.

But a little voice nagged away at him. What if she didn't do what she was told? How would Jegudiel react? Was there even a way to turn Tazia back into herself, before the switch? Before she said yes to the beast.

The tightness in his stomach released into little butterflies.

Jegudiel wouldn't expect Tazia to turn against her. It was the very reason she'd fallen. Not passion for the Abbot, but pure, petulant outrage at being overruled by Ezequiel. At her judgement being questioned.

That's it! Her biggest weakness is arrogance—or pride if you want to get all Old Testament about it.

Tazia, like her father before, had triggered that weakness. When Billy was planning on killing her in the motel, Tazia had called on Jegudiel to help her. That cry for assistance had fed the angel's ego. That's what she had taunted him with at the motel, and again on the street. That's why she'd let him live; the Advocate wanted him to feel her superiority.

Well, he was on to her now.

If they could break her control over Tazia, they would break Jegudiel's spirit. It may just be enough to give him the chance he needed to kill her.

The Jeep pulled into the loading bay in front of him. Jacob got out of the front passenger seat while Hux peered at him from the driver's side and whistled to get his attention like he was a bloody dog.

The midday sun reflected on their faces, shining so bright on Jacob for a second that it bleached out his features as he walked forward. He emerged again, smiling widely, arms opened in greeting. His tall form moved so easily, so balanced. He was stunning.

Hux kept the engine ticking over and drummed his fingers on the outside of the door through the open window.

The sun shone on his hair, picking out the individual strands that had escaped capture from behind his ears. They were all different shades of blond. Even white in places after so much time in the demon sun. The escaped strands seemed to dance around his face as he looked at Billy, waiting expectantly.

Wow, they are both such beautiful human beings!

Hux interrupted his thoughts with a shout. "Billy! Get your arse over here!"

33

DOES SHE DO IT FOR YOU?

FROM THE OFFICE chair in the back of the Charlestown hardware store, long legs stretched before him and arms folded, Billy stared at the picture of the woman given centre stage on the wall. He'd been studying the nearly naked Miss September for several minutes, deliberately testing what remained of his human self under his angelic form.

The details—big eighties hair, slick fuchsia lips parted just so, and opaque white stockings—were the epitome of old-style soft porn. He was amazed someone had ever found it arousing. For him? Nothing. He might as well have been a dickless Ken-doll for all the excitement the image generated.

It unsettled him. Porn had never been his thing, but sex had always grounded him even in his darkest moments. He didn't want to lose that.

And then there was Thomas.

The man had been occupying his thoughts of late. Knowing they'd been at the beginning of something when everything blew up, frustrated him. If he ever got back to London, could it blossom? Grow into something. Would the guy even give him a chance, now, after so many rejections?

The room darkened as Hux entered. His large frame blocking the beams of sun cutting through the holes in the metal shutters, even into the back room. "Am I interrupting?" he asked and nodded at the picture.

"Nah." Billy looked from him to the picture. "Does she do it for you, Hux?"

Hux looked critically at Miss September for a moment. "Too much hair."

Billy nodded. "And the lips?"

"Sticky."

Another nod.

"Is he here?" Hux asked.

They were expecting Jacob any second, and he was bringing his friend with him, one of the witches.

Billy shook his head. "Can we trust this Aideen?" Having someone new in the fold worried him. It was hard enough coming up with a plan the three of them agreed on, let alone involving someone new.

"She's sound. Jacob trusts her. That's enough."

There was a quiet knock. They both followed the sound to the back door of the small store. Hux pulled out his pistol and looked through the security peephole. He kept the gun ready, but immediately opened the door. Both Jacob and Aideen entered, looking a little worse for wear. Blue demon blood spattered Jacob's t-shirt, and blood dripped down Aideen's face from a small head wound.

Billy forgot his concerns about Aideen's trustworthiness and led them both into the staff kitchen, where he wet a clean tea towel in the sink, and gave it to her.

"Thanks a million," she murmured, her Irish accent lilting gently. She pressed it to her head.

Billy passed another damp towel to Jacob. The blood was eating through the white top, creating little holes through which his skin shone, beginning to blister. It looked like a strange case of the measles.

"Trouble?" Hux asked as Jacob ripped off his tee.

"Thank you, Billy." Jacob took a moment to dab at the marks, then pulled on a replacement shirt Hux held out to him before answering. "Two lesser demons. Three blocks away. Filth from the gutters. An unfortunate encounter. Their approach was crude, but we were cornered. One got to Aideen before I could stop him and knocked her against the wall"—he smiled at her—"but she created her own opening. She is resourceful."

"He was a nasty piece of work," Aideen added. "But he learned his lesson. We made sure of it."

Jacob looked at her and smiled. "Yes. They are all dead now."

"Good." The drive from the hospital to here, a little strip mall in demon central, had been tough for Billy to see. The streets weren't empty, they were haunted with wandering soulless victims of the risen demons. Some naked, just skin and bone. All, broken. Vacant eyes seeing nothing but pain.

It made him want to take up a gun and shoot, just to end their suffering.

But they couldn't draw attention. They needed to be ready when Tazia showed up again. She'd last been spotted rounding up humans not five blocks away, and funnelling them towards the docks.

Jacob had kept a psychic watch for her since she'd attempted to kill Billy. She'd popped up close by, but the reports came from the demon conversations he'd intercepted rather than following the whiff of energy signatures. Just bloody dumb luck, really. He had to be in the right place at the right time to eavesdrop.

They *needed* Joshua. He'd be able to track Tazia just like that. Where the fuck was he?

At first, Billy thought the necromancer had just got bored, disappeared off to have fun elsewhere, and would eventually come back. Now he was worried. He'd used technomancy to look for him, and Jacob had tried his more esoteric methods. Nothing. Joshua had completely disappeared. Billy feared for his friend's safety.

Fresh coffee aroma dragged Billy away from his thoughts, and back to Aideen's report about the entity the coven had communicated with.

"It was hard at first, to know whether we could trust it. But then our own Guiding Spirit approved. It also became less cryptic and more helpful," she added.

"It told them *L'ange Noire* was not working alone, just before Tazia shared the information with you, Billy."

"You trust him, Jacob?" Hux asked.

"Reluctantly, I have got used to its bullish ways… and its smell."

"For goodness sake, Jacob. It is just a little rough around the edges." Aideen smiled at him, a teasing edge to her voice. He returned the smile and shrugged.

"And can the entity or the coven help us free Tazia?" Billy helped himself to coffee from the still brewing jug, while Hux did the rounds with the other. He always made two these days.

"The entity talks of Tazia with great gentleness, Billy. It's adamant we break the Advocate's hold on the poor wee girl." She paused and smiled. "We think we can permanently break this *switch*, Jacob overheard the demons talk about."

"We fight magick with magick." Billy had come to the same conclusion himself.

"Yes. But we don't override—we undo." Aideen put down the cloth she'd been holding to her head, sipped from the coffee cup Hux had given to her, and smiled into it like it was medicine. "Oh, this is good!"

She continued. "We think the angel tied a darker knot on her soul than the sigils the Abbot worked into her spine before. A contingency in the original magick when Tazia was born, God love her. A trigger. After the Advocate took her from you in the motel, she didn't cast a new spell, just pulled the root of the old one."

"So can we break *that* magick? That root, or knot, or the bloody switch?" Billy asked. This natural magick language was confusing.

"We can," Aideen confirmed. "The coven believes we can craft a spell to shatter that construct. It would break Jegudiel's direct control. It would give Tazia back to herself—the version after the tattoos were lifted, overwhelmed but at least free."

His mind worked. Would she be free? Only free enough to lead a half-human existence. She'd still carry a monster inside? It wasn't enough. "But could we do more?" His voice was barely a whisper. "Could we make her human?"

Billy pinned Aideen with his gaze, his eyes pleading for any hint of hope. Silence stretched on as they all waited. He was the first to crack. "Come on, love. We've all been thinking it, wanting it—can we actually make it happen?"

Aideen exhaled slowly. "We talked about it. Theoretically, we could, but it would be a fierce bit of work. The only reason her soul hasn't burned out the demon already is because the creation magick forces them into an unnatural truce—to exist in the same space." She seemed to pick her words carefully. "If we build on the first spell we may be able to do more than just break the switch. We could attack the bindings that make her a hybrid."

She looked from Billy to Hux. "Theoretically, with no magick holding them together, the soul will instinctively try to purge what's poisoning it. It would be a battle. Hard work, Billy. Exhausting for the witches. But if we could create a ritual to amplify that effort, to forcibly expel the demon half and let the soul win. It should leave her…" she sighed "…human."

"There is a but, isn't there?" She'd made it sound possible, but Billy didn't want to punch the air right yet.

Her eyes locked with his, again. "*But* there's a seal needed. A spell that powerful, that rewrites a person's very nature, it needs an anchor. It needs her permission. She has to *want* it. Voicing her agreement, choosing to be human, is the only thing that can complete the ritual."

"Her choice," Billy breathed. All at once, the pieces clicked into place. He jumped up, a hand to his chest as pain stabbed through him. "That's bloody it, Hux. That's her weakness!"

"Jegudiel's weakness? The one Julie talked about?"

"Yeah. If Tazia chooses to be human, it's the ultimate rejection of Jegudiel. The Advocate's precious Saviour turning her back on all that power. A soul she thought she owned, gone… The arrogance, the shock… it would be devastating. It could weaken her enough for me to strike." Billy tried to pace, but the nagging pain in his chest made him stagger, his mind already racing.

"If you can get hold of the angel dagger." Hux pushed the swaying Billy gently back down into a chair.

"I will!"

"You don't know that. What if it's not there when—"

"There are more holy weapons." Jacob interrupted. "They are in antiquities museums, held in a few private collections, or buried in graveyards all over the world. Just a few that we know about, of course, but they do exist. I've been listening," he said. "And demons like to talk." He grinned.

"Seriously?" Stunned, Billy shook his head. Why had Julie not told him this?

"You should be able to find them, Billy." Aideen smiled encouragingly at him. "You just need to learn how to listen for their call."

"Me?"

"Yes. They'll hold a magnetic attraction for you. The power is already in you."

"What do you mean?"

"I'll show you—I just need your blood…"

34

SWAGGER

THERE WERE two things Billy had wanted to avoid during his short human existence: getting caught with his pants down in a public place and having a face-off with an armed assailant.

He'd failed at the former five years ago when a guy he met in a club in Soho got a little rough down a dead-end alley. Truth be told, Billy was more than satisfied with the outcome, apart from when the police officer shone a flashlight in his eyes, looked at the trousers around his ankles, and shook his head in that "Jeez, not again" sort of way.

Billy was ridiculously embarrassed by the whole incident. It made him feel like an amateur when, really, he was a highly skilled Lothario. Clearly.

The second thing had yet to happen. Until now.

He didn't count the fight he'd had with the Advocate in the hotel room or Tazia almost stabbing him to death. Those incidents carried too much… baggage. This was altogether different. This was exactly the type of face-off he'd had bad dreams about.

His would-be assailant, a six-foot-five demon, appeared to be built from concrete blocks. He had the massive arms and shoulders of someone who dead-lifted a baby elephant daily, and solid pecs bulged under his tight t-shirt.

But unlike in his nightmares, the way he was presently bearing down on Billy in the hallway of the old Victorian library building was almost disrespectful. He walked with such a casual swagger that the angel was insulted. He even had a smirk on his face.

And his weapon of choice? A dagger. *Bloody perfect!*

Billy was starting to feel like a pincushion and couldn't stomach the idea of a blade slicing into his organs and scraping against his ribs, yet again. It would hurt. A lot. Again.

He called to the approaching demon, "What about a gun, bruv? Couldn't you use a bloody gun?" A bullet would hurt like hell, but a clean wound would take less time to heal.

The demon glanced from Billy to his knife, then back to Billy. He leered and waved the blade in front of him. "Sharp!"

"Fantastic." Billy shook his head and glanced to his left, noting Hux was having his own time of it. The difference was he looked in his element.

Hux lived with the perpetual expectation that he was about to be jumped. And, of course, if it happened, he was trained to deal with it. He was already crouched, ready for the attack from the demon thug circling him. The guy was stocky, looked like he ate a thrash metal diet and came complete with a shaved head, vicious tattoos scraping all visible skin, and sharp shiny horn-studs piercing through his lower lip.

The two of them circled using a side-step, moving their feet apart, then together in a vague approximation of a waltz. Hux never took his cool blue eyes from the demon's red circled ones. It wasn't a stalemate; it was foreplay, and Billy was waiting for one of them to get jiggy.

He dragged his attention back to his own suitor, who was still casually walking toward him. The dagger in his hand was long and thin, with multiple sharp teeth sticking up from the sides. Billy squirmed, thinking of flesh getting caught around the teeth, making pulp of the skin, blood, and organs inside him. "Look, mate. We don't want a fight. Just need to get to that room over there. We can make a deal, surely?"

The demon maintained the leer, never a good sign. "Sure, we can deal, pretty boy." He passed the dagger-skewer from one hand to the other and back again. "Deal is, I kill you."

Pretty boy? Billy's thoughts went back to the guy in the alleyway in Soho. He'd whispered the same words in his ear while holding him tight against the wall, squashing his face into the rough brick so hard that he had red dust-filled grazes for a week afterward.

He hadn't liked being called a pretty boy then, or now. He knew he was pretty; bloody gorgeous in fact. But there were implications when someone else said it. It was always delivered as an insult, like good-looking made you stupid. The words made him embarrassed and weak. All things he no longer considered himself.

"You need to work on your threats, mate!" The heat in Billy's palm started to build along with his anger.

The guy in the alleyway had legged it when he saw the copper heading toward them. A quick whispered, "Sorry, pretty boy" in Billy's ear, and he was gone. He'd been left trouser-less and abandoned. If he'd had his angel magick then, it would have ended very differently.

"I've changed my mind," Billy said. "Let's have at it, dickhead!" He gave a confident smile and a come-get-me gesture that wouldn't have looked out of place in *The Matrix*.

The demon hesitated as if trying to figure out what had changed. Then he charged, dagger raised. Face switching from confusion to determination.

Billy felt a surge of icy energy pass into him and build in his palms. He didn't look at the knife directly, even when the demon hacked at him. Instead, he grabbed his wrist, stopping the demon dead. He smiled into his shocked face, then rammed the flat of his right hand into the demon's chest, abruptly stopping his forward movement.

The blue light burned through Billy's hands into the demon's flesh: ice cold. He screamed, great high banshee howls that echoed around the large hallway and out into the night.

The dagger fell. In one hand, Billy clutched brittle bone and frozen blood. In the other, a blackened heart. The demon dropped to the ground. *Pretty boy, my arse.*

Taking advantage of the distraction of the howl, Hux had sprung forward and used his weight to push his opponent off balance and took the fight to the floor.

The demon's right arm flailed and hit the wall, knocking away his blade. Hux made no mistakes and struck him deeply in the stomach with his own. The first blow disabled him long enough for a second—a swipe across his jugular. Blue blood spurted wildly. It spattered Hux's face. Billy winced as he saw the acid raise red welts over Hux's cheek.

Already weak from blood loss, the demon punched, and although his fist found Hux's jaw, it was more a savage kiss than a strike, and did no more than cause the ex-soldier to wobble.

With his healing charms already taking effect on his skin, Hux slashed again. Probably unnecessary. The demon was already choking out a final gurgle before he slammed back to the ground. Dead.

Billy and Hux exchanged looks, then assessed each other's kills.

"That blue light thing. Effective." It was the first time Hux had seen Billy in fighting form.

"S'nuffin, bruv." Billy shrugged, but was ridiculously proud to receive Hux's admiration. He ran his hands through his already perfect hair to make sure the front quiff was still in place. "That double whammy you did with the knife," he said. "Very slick."

Hux nodded, seemingly appreciating the compliment, too. "Okay. Let's go."

Bonding finished, he was already walking toward the back of the hall to the room the demons had been guarding. They suspected the angel weapon was inside.

This part of the building was huge and confusing.

Half museum, half library, each exhibit was housed in central display cabinets within a huge double-height hall of books stretching down both sides. Old-fashioned desks split by Victorian and Art Deco lamps separated the central displays from the book covered walls, making navigation reliant on four long, narrow, parallel pathways running the length of the great hall. Once you picked a path, you were stuck until you made it out the top end.

The place had been wrecked. Obscene graffiti scrawled across the walls in black paint. Splatters had dripped down to the floor and mixed with the blood of the rotting corpses slouched beneath—some of the first kills from the Boston Rising. The rancid blood remained sticky in the heat and stuck dust even more securely to the soles of their boots. Billy's *ick* factor was high.

Marauding demons and half-turned humans had also left deposits of stinking excrement, attracting an army of rats and insects that crawled from every nook and cranny. Their squeaking and hissing made him jump and stamp his feet continuously to keep them away.

Before the demons stopped them, they'd been heading for a small Mayan exhibit housed in a room just off the hall. It was there they believed an angelic weapon was located.

Aideen had shown Billy how to use a drop of his blood smeared onto an ordinary kitchen knife to simulate the blade they were trying to trace, to create a focus. The rest had been surprisingly easy. She walked him through a brief ritual to guide his thoughts, and then he had seen a vision of the library building in his mind.

The two men crept down the hallway, keeping close to the wall of books on the right. Hux led the way, Billy following close behind. He was feeling the after effects of the fight and sucked in breaths in heavy pants, his head pounding.

When they reached the double doors to the Mayan room, Hux whispered to Billy to stay put. He then made some other military-style hand gestures, which Billy had no clue how to interpret.

"What the fuck does that mean?" His low voice travelled further than he expected when his words were caught in a sudden ragged breath.

Hux hissed. "Stay there until I signal."

"What's the signal?"

Hux's eyes threatened death. "Forget it. I'll come get you." As an afterthought, he adopted a brief motherly tone and said, "Keep an eye out for trouble, okay?"

Billy nodded, not really caring. He was glad for the support of the wall, but still found himself sliding down onto the hard cold floor. Five feet away was the rotting corpse of someone's pet golden retriever, and he watched numbly as a couple of rats chewed on a leg bone. The coolness of the ground felt too soothing for him to move regardless of his proximity to the ravenous rodents.

Dragging his eyes along the corridor to the left and right, he forced himself to pay attention. Both directions were empty.

Hux reappeared. "All clear."

He offered his hand and pulled Billy up from the ground. Not for the first time, Billy felt a pang of attraction for the older man. It wasn't his looks or his strength; it was his presence. He gave off an instant air of safety. Ironic, given that the very same attraction could easily end with a bullet.

The room they entered was a mess. Artifacts were everywhere, display cases had been smashed, and filing cabinets tipped over. The likelihood of finding the relatively small dagger in these shambles seemed low.

"If the demons were guarding the place, the knife is still here." Hux began to pick things up haphazardly. He examined each item and threw it to one side.

Billy, though, circled the room, trying to find some logic to the upturned cabinets and wall displays. Little old-fashioned typed labels were still stuck in some places, suggesting this area had been for eleventh century domestic pottery, while that cabinet had contained ceremonial clothing from a small tribe in Central America. "Stop, Hux!"

Hux scowled at him, but did as he was told.

"If it's here, bruv, it'll still be near its original display." Billy started to pick up the cabinets and shelving units, pushing them back into place, but the effort left him gasping. He stopped and bent over to pull in some breath.

"Okay, I get it." Hux picked up where Billy had left off. "Pretty boy's got brains." He smirked.

Billy jerked his head up, eyes blazing. "You fucker—"

"I heard him. Made you mad? Good. Use it."

"I did. Dead... demon, innit?" Billy struggled to right a cabinet. "Anyway, this... pretty boy has brains as well... as perfectly shaped biceps."

Hux raised his eyebrows and pointedly looked at Billy's arms.

Following his eyes, he said, "Just don't... say anything!"

In silence, Hux continued putting the furniture back so they had space to move around the room without stepping on things.

Billy scanned the items on the floor, but the knife wasn't among them. "If it's here, it's probably still in a drawer or cabinet somewhere. Look for a label that might help. Something like Ritual Items or Mayan Weaponry."

They both started beside each other on the same wall, and then slowly circled in different directions. After a few steps, Hux stopped and looked over at him. "I've underestimated you, Billy."

Expecting sarcasm, he nodded, but continued with his task. "Me too. You're not as much of a meathead as I thought you were."

"Billy!"

Billy looked up. *Christ, was this another pep talk?*

"I tried to say it the other day. But words are not my thing. So I'll keep it short. You were a pain in the arse. Just that magick kid Anastasia always ran to. You love her, though. I see that now. You were... good for her. Kept her human. While I... needed her demon." He stopped, looked back at the filing cabinet he was in front of, and read off a card stuck in the front of a drawer. "Ceremonial Equipment?"

"That could be it." Billy joined him, and they both studied the cabinet. The drawer with the label was locked shut.

Hux yanked on it, but the lock wouldn't budge. "Can you magick this open? Or do that blue light thing?"

Billy had recovered his breath. "The lock isn't electronic so, no, my tech won't work. Not strong enough for any more blue stuff. Can't you force it?"

"I'll need a lever, something thin and strong to slip into the top of the drawer."

They started looking around again.

"Why did you say that stuff about me and Taz?" Billy asked.

Hux shrugged. "Cos we have a fight coming up, and I don't know who'll survive it. If I don't... if it can't be me with her. Or if she chooses you—"

"You giving me permission to love her?" Billy stopped

sifting through the debris on the floor and stared at him. They stood just an arm's length apart.

"I don't have a right to do that. But if she makes the choice to become human, she'll need at least one of us."

"And if she doesn't choose it?"

"One of us needs to kill her." Hux maintained eye contact and spoke without hesitation.

"You telling me, now, that I may need to kill her? After all this. After chasing her across a continent, and getting my arse handed to me—twice! Now you're on board with the 'killing her' plan?"

Hux nodded. "We've got to be prepared." He spoke softly. "It's the kindest thing. If we fight her and she kills one of us, the other needs to be ready to act. She won't come back from it, Billy. All her humanity will be gone. She wouldn't want us to let her live. Don't get me wrong though, man. I'll fight like hell to keep her alive and you should too."

"And if we both live and she does, too?"

"If she chooses to be human?" Hux kicked a trashcan that was lying on its side. Balled-up paper and sweet wrappers spilled onto the floor beside it, but it revealed nothing helpful.

"Yeah."

"Then she decides. She may want one of us. Or maybe not. Up to her, man. But if it's you she chooses, you won't get a fight." He smiled at him. Not a broad smile, but one accompanied by a small sigh, his shoulders falling.

"There was a maintenance closet in the hallway. I'll go check it." Billy needed space.

For a guy who didn't like words, the conversation was intense. Hux was showing a side of himself that he'd only seen glimpses of before. He was making himself vulnerable, sharing thoughts about Tazia. Making plans. Billy had no doubt Hux was mentally preparing himself for the fight. Not only to die if he had to, but to make any sort of sacrifice that was demanded of him.

Could he do the same?

Being an angel had changed so much for him. Decisions used to be easy; the plastic paddle or the wooden one? The red shoes or the black? The Pilsner or the Stella-fucking-Artois?

Now? Would he give up his life to save the world or save Tazia? Or would he throw in the towel altogether, and go live in outer space? The stakes had been raised so bloody high. It was doing his head in.

The door to the maintenance closet was unlocked. Whoever had ransacked the building had ignored it. Nothing was taken. A toolbox sat off to one side on the floor. Billy searched through the contents and came up with a long-necked, thin-headed screwdriver and a hammer.

Returning to the room, he gave them to Hux, who used the combination to first weaken the lock on the drawer and then, when he felt it loosen a little, to pry it open from the top using the screwdriver as a lever. There was a brief groaning protest, and then the drawer popped open.

Both of them pushed forward, Hux's long blond locks brushing up against Billy's short, dark, gelled ones for a moment in their haste to see if the weapon was inside.

The drawer was divided into hanging files. Each one contained a bagged object with accompanying description. All the objects were thin and smallish, ranging from hair ornamentation to the remnants of a small woven blanket. Neat handwriting on the folder at the back announced, Ceremonial Dagger.

Hux pulled the entire file out and handed it to him. He looked expectant, as though he thought Billy could tell if this was the knife just by holding the file. Angel magick, maybe.

Inside the file was a black satin bag, and inside that, a beautiful piece of artwork. It was about twelve inches long and made of a solid piece of glistening black obsidian. A four inch handle shimmered with inset jade. It was in the shape of a single wing, carved to provide finger grooves for a right hand when gripped. The scalpel-sharp blade was thick, but the tip was long, thin, and curved slightly upward.

Running down each side of the blade were four small divots, eight in total. Nothing was mounted in any of them apart from the last hole in the far side of the blade, the one closest to the handle. It had a single sparkling black stone that resembled a cut diamond.

Billy remembered seeing similar stones in the blade Tazia had used on him. "This is it—it has to be." He turned the knife, feeling its weight, and it automatically fell into his right hand in a way that suggested the dagger should be used by striking out and up rather than at a downward angle. The upper part of the blade curved up so it could reach the heart even if the entry wound was at diaphragm level.

"Any way we'll know for sure?" Hux asked.

"I don't feel anything. Julie would know. But she never turns up on cue."

"Okay. We'll take the chance. Jacob is waiting for us." He turned to leave.

Billy replaced the knife in the bag and wrapped the extra material round and round the blade. He put it into the inside pocket of his jacket.

He pushed aside thoughts of what he'd do after the battle. With the blade secured, this one-sided fight was looking a little more hopeful.

35

BATTLE READY

TAZIA SAT on a bench looking out over Boston harbour, watching sheets of heavy fog undulate across her vision, mimicking the movement of the waves beneath.

In her mind, the other side of the fog bank was a distant world, the one she'd left behind months ago when she'd clutched Conn O'Cuinn's dying body to her. That moment was her measure. Before, he was alive and her hope intact. After, he was dead; her hope shattered into jagged pieces.

After her soul returned to her, it should have been the beginning of a new life, the freedom her father had promised. But it had never happened. She'd replaced one master with another, and here she was, months later, an ensouled human-demon hybrid with no freedom, no hope, and no control.

So, she thought of Cuinn. Tried to remember the stirrings of love forming in her heart. A long-lost kiss just on the other side of that curtain of fog. Even that little light was most often gone now. It blinked off when the Advocate took control.

Tazia released a long sigh, then gasped for breath. Drowning. As soon as she let go of the memory, she felt nothing. No loss. No resentment toward Hux. No anger against

Billy. Nothing. Not even a low burn of hatred toward Jegudiel. Numb to all of it except the fear her will commanded in others. All she had left was power.

It flamed in the base of her stomach and surged into her limbs when she wielded her knife or fed. When the bodies fell. What did death matter? She had been weak before. Now, it felt fucking good to be in control. The only thing that did.

In the last week, she'd hardly thought about Billy. She didn't know whether he'd lived or died by the Advocate's hand after she'd left him on the street. Jegudiel had returned a little while later, hair dripping with his blood and a serpent smile. She didn't reveal his fate, and Tazia didn't ask. Easier that way.

Jegudiel had told her that Billy's death would demonstrate Tazia's strength, gain her more respect from her followers. It had seemed to make sense before. Now, she didn't care.

That night, as she'd watched him collapse, the blood running from his wound and the air retching from his mouth, for one moment she'd wanted him to live. So, she'd told him the thing she thought he wouldn't know—that Jegudiel was a puppet, too. Just like him. Just like her.

Then the moment was gone. She'd felt the Advocate's arrival. Heard the praise in her mind, and suddenly she had a place in the world again.

The energy shifted next to her, like it had on that day. Purple washed over her skin. A splash of heat dislodged her hair. Fingertips tapped along her spine. Her body and mind shifted to silence. A single tear formed as she focused on the foggy ocean, forgetting her previous thoughts.

"You were thinking of your angel, pet. I could see it in the colours of your thoughts."

"Was I?"

"He did not die, Anastasia. I spared him." She clicked her boots together.

Tazia looked sideways at her.

"It's not over, though, pet. He'll be back soon. But this time, I will wield the knife. And he *will* die. And you will kill Soren Huxford. Are you ready, my dear? It will be fun." She giggled.

"Yes." Tazia looked back at the fog rolling toward her. "I'm ready."

The curtain had almost fallen.

———

"Why does it have to happen on the full moon? She isn't a werewolf!" Billy leaned against the door frame that led to the back room of the hardware store, arms crossed and his foot tapping dangerously. Natural magick frustrated him. Technomancy didn't rely on the moon phases or times of the year. If he needed to write a spell, he just got it done. The power was in the digits; not some naked old crone dancing under the moon.

He was grumpy and tired. His thoughts muddled, and his eyes stung. Every muscle protested when he moved. It had been a tough few days since he and Hux had recovered the angel weapon.

"We need to harness its power, Billy." The sigh Aideen mixed into her words said it all; they'd had this conversation ten times already that day.

"But if I enhance the spell, maybe we won't have to wait?" He was thinking in bits and bytes again. Logical intention focused into a nice digital package.

"That won't help. Returning someone to their human form is an act of *natural* magick." Despite trying to use a measured tone, her patience sounded worn thin.

Jacob shot her a quick smile. She returned the look before adding, "It's not a matter of moving an object or blowing a circuit. Your magick is perfect for that. But this is about manipulating DNA. Regenerating a soul. Not reconstructing computer architecture!" The last comment came out rather more snarky than she probably intended.

"Bitch." Despite the deadpan accusation, Billy smiled at her. "Sorry. I know I'm being frustrating, love. I just need to get this done."

"I know." Her voice softened. "Wait for the proper time. It'll work. I can feel it—"

"It *may* work."

Billy whirled around at the voice. A petite woman stared at him from the front of the store, a serious look on her face. He hadn't heard her come in.

Adorned in heavy black-rimmed geek glasses, and with a perfect dark bob hairstyle, she looked like she'd just stepped out of a preppy college movie from the fifties. A Letterman jacket with a large J, and a pleated skirt that stopped just above her knees. Shiny-black kitten-heeled shoes and high socks completed the ensemble. He liked the shoes.

"Or it may not work, Billy. You need to be prepared. Did you get the weapon?"

"Julie?"

"Who else?" This time she grimaced slightly, like it would disrupt her perfect hair if she actually smiled. "Did you?"

"Yes." As Billy walked over to his jacket hanging by the side of the door, and fished out the dagger, he glanced back at his companions in the back office. Aideen and Jacob sat together, coffees in front of them. Aideen, with her gentle smile and Jacob gazing back at her from across the table. For the first time, Billy noticed there was an energy frozen right along with them, soft pink ribbons travelling between them from heart to heart.

"They love each other." He spoke almost to himself.

"Of course." Julie grinned at him, a fully fledged smile this time. "It's beautiful, isn't it?"

"Yeah."

The two angels stood united, marvelling at human love freeze-framed in the scene before them.

On the couch, Hux was stretched out. He'd been napping when Julie arrived. His arms were crossed on his chest, defensive even in sleep, and his long legs rested on the arm of one end of the couch while his head rested awkwardly against the other.

A silver fan had been gently blowing his hair when Julie's stasis kicked in. Now it was caught perfectly still, the right side trapped in a billowing arch around his head like one half of a blond halo.

"Why does he look so tense, even in sleep? It's like he never rests." Billy felt a surge of protective instinct for him.

"He doesn't. Not fully." Julie pursed her lips.

"Why?"

"The past hasn't caught up with Soren Huxford yet, Billy. Until it does, and he finds peace with it, he'll be in this perpetual state of unrest." She turned her back on the sleeping man. "The weapon?"

Billy handed the knife to her. Its black blade and green handle glistened in the flickering overhead strip lighting that had escaped the stasis. Julie paced back and forth, matching the on and off motion of the light. She ran her hand over the empty divots.

"What's wrong?"

"There's only one stud left. One stud, Billy!"

"I don't know what that means. In my extensive experience, a stud is a good thing." He cocked his head slightly at her, knowing the time was wrong to crack an inappropriate joke, but did so anyway.

She ignored him. "To kill an angel you first must be an angel and wield an angelic weapon—"

"I know that. I'm an angel. This is the weapon." He took the dagger back from her and waved it around.

"—and then strike to the heart."

"The heart? Specifically?" Billy stopped. Another thing he hadn't known. *Bloody witches!*

"Okay. Well, there's her heart." He pointed roughly at Julie's chest. "And here's the knife. *Oomph!*" With a grin, he dramatically plunged the dagger toward Julie's body, stopping a good ten inches away from contacting her. "See? Dead angel."

She didn't move a muscle.

"This is the part when you clutch your chest and fall on the floor… *aargh!*"

Julie stared at his performance, saying nothing.

Billy's smile dropped. "Okay, what's wrong? I'm tired, and cracking jokes takes effort, especially when they're not appreciated."

"As I started to say, a stud from the blade needs to be transferred to the heart. It's the stud that kills the angel—not the actual blade."

"You mean those little black diamond things?"

"Yes. All blades have eight studs when they are first created. This one has already been used to kill seven angels. It gets harder to kill an angel the fewer studs there are—"

"Because the blade has to hit the heart exactly where the stud is so it can be transferred?"

"Exactly." Julie shook her head. "Basically, you've only got one shot. Miss and you're toast!"

"How many studs does her weapon have?" Billy was afraid to ask. He'd seen them glittering in the moonlight as Tazia used the knife, but hadn't known enough to count.

Julie wouldn't meet his eyes. The light in them softly reflected in her patent leather shoes.

"How many, Ju?"

She finally faced him. "All of them. She stole the knife from

Heaven when she left. It was brand new. And although she's killed many people and demons since she fell, she hasn't killed a single angel. It has all the studs."

Billy sank down on the chair behind the sales counter. The old-fashioned till was open in front of him. "I'd say that counts as a pretty major design flaw, Julie." He pulled out a handful of coins and started stacking them on the glass counter in front of him. The action was meant to soothe him.

All at once, he stopped stacking the coins and swiped them off the counter. They hit the floor with a crash, bounced, and skittered to a stop under the product display shelves to his right. *Every bloody time they got close!*

"Doesn't mean it's over, Billy." Julie crossed the floor and squeezed his shoulder.

"No, I understand. Just means I can't miss." He faced her, his arms collapsed by his sides. "Was I really the great warrior angel you told me I was? Cos I've not felt it. Not once. All this time since I've changed, I've had moments of strength, but they've always been followed up with just so much bloody pain."

"Billy, you've had twenty-seven years in this physical body, and a thousand before that locked away in a soul, waiting to be sent to Earth to fight this fight. Confusion, loss, fear, love. It's all part of being that soul. Part of being human. It's not all going to click into place in a couple of months."

"But I'm so weak, so tired. I need to fight tomorrow—it's the full moon!" Tomorrow he'd have to face Jegudiel, face the being that had taken away the love of his life, beaten him twice already, mocked him, and left him for dead. "I'm shit-scared, Ju!"

"I may be able to help." Julie left his side and walked to the plate glass door. She gazed through the metal shutters with her arms crossed, her lips moving, then tilted her head to one side like she was listening. She turned and walked back with a smile and a confident stride. "I can help. I *will* help."

With no further hesitation, she held his face tightly with both of her hands. "Are you ready?"

"Erm—"

Fierce heat surged through Billy's head, and his whole body convulsed from that point, like an electric current had him stuck tight. But almost straight away, his body released the stiffened posture, and his vision clouded with blue light.

Julie still faced him, but this wasn't a preppy girl with perfect hair and black-rimmed spectacles. This was a light blue shimmering form that danced all around him. She was flowing through him and yet also stood in his peripheral vision as a vaguely human shape. Two arms, two legs, and a head, slim and sinewy. Two stunning crystal indigo eyes gazed into his, and light trailed from her limbs as she moved.

He looked down at his hands. They were gone. Where flesh should have been, emerald green light sparked with silver. As he turned them, the movement left glistening sweeps of spring green and teal in the air.

Was that a flash of soft white wings? Could he hear them beating? Was he flying now, far above the pain of the Earth? Starlight was all around him. Calling. Welcoming. The scent of ozone filled his lungs. *I want to come home—*

The seat of the cash desk chair, solid under him. The moans of the half-humans stumbling along the street outside. Julie was gone.

But Billy was just fine.

Everything appeared sharp and vibrant. He could feel the hardness and softness of objects just by looking at them. He could hear the humming of the overhead light and discern the pulse of its flicker a fraction before it appeared to his eyes.

He wasn't looking at the world; he was feeling it for the first time.

He held his arms up in front of him: muscled, healthy arms, with perfect light brown skin. He flexed and felt his biceps pop. *Wow. I'm buff!* No aches, no pains. His breath smooth as silk.

"You all right, man?" Hux leaned over him, peering into his eyes.

"Yes. I'm fine." Billy spoke in a voice he didn't recognize. It was his; it was Billy's, but it was strong and true and determined. He felt alive. On fire.

He smiled broadly at Hux. "I'm more than fine. I'm fucking battle-ready, bruv!"

36

THE LAST STAND

BILLY ALREADY KNEW this battle scene would not look like a movie. There would be no big rolling camera shot swinging between the opposing forces: one army standing against a dramatic backdrop of a sunset or sunrise; the other—a smaller scrappy band—bravely standing ready for a death or glory finale. This battle scene would be altogether different.

But there *was* a hill, complete with a monument marking some famous last stand. Eighteenth century, apparently. The details were fuzzy. He'd had to Google it, then promptly forgotten. Other things on his mind.

Billy, Hux, and Jacob looked down from the roof of the blue clapboard house they'd occupied last night, along with Aideen. From where they stood, along the road to the hill, all they could see were the semi-lifeless bodies of leftover humans. Tortured people told to sacrifice themselves to save the world by Tazia and Jegudiel.

There were at least a thousand of them, swarming on the road in front of the house and over the hill. They weren't dangerous, but they could distract and disguise the movements of the demons that made up Tazia's true war party.

Billy's breath caught. He'd expected an army, not... this. Not a tide of broken people shielding the actual monsters. *For fucksakes, Taz.*

"We stick to the plan." Hux scanned the undulating movement of the crowd, trying to fix on a target—a Soldier, maybe, or a Leech. His face was neutral, showing neither fear nor consternation. This was Jegudiel's play, and he had accepted it. "We can't let ourselves be distracted."

"Sure, bruv. No distraction. At. All." Billy raised his eyebrows. He paced quick circuits of the rooftop, trying to get a feel for the extent of the chaos. He could see Tazia's bodyguards bossing the demons around. But where the bloody hell was she? He wasn't that surprised. Of course, Jegudiel would come up with a plan that didn't involve either herself or Tazia simply standing and fighting. The angel had spent two thousand years avoiding heavenly punishment. She hadn't done it by being predictable.

Hux didn't respond to Billy's sarcasm. Instead, he looked away and focused his attention on Jacob. "Witches ready? The moon rises in a few minutes."

The silence made Billy look back from the view. Jacob didn't seem himself. His eyebrows arched, eyes wide. This guy had seen many fallen cities. Was this so different? Was this too much?

"Jacob?" Hux asked again. Still calm.

Jacob dragged his eyes away from the scene long enough to say, "Yes, Hux. The coven is ready. I will stand guard as we agreed." He looked back again, eyes already scanning, steady but distant. Looking for the signs of success or failure, perhaps. Then he headed for the stairs.

As he left, Billy glanced down. He didn't need to ask if the working had started. The rooftop vibrated under his feet; energy building from the twelve witches in the basement. They'd arrived in ones and twos during the day, and now cooked up the bait for Hux's trap. A spell to turn a half-demon to human with magick loud enough to scream *'Here we are!'* across the whole bloody city.

The fight hinged on Tazia coming to them. To be too fucking curious—or insane—to resist. And then to seal the deal by choosing herself for once.

"Save yourself, girl," Billy whispered into the air, hoping the magick would fly directly to her heart—her soul. If she didn't say yes, and came spitting fire, those witches would be the first to die.

They all had roles to play. He would take the angel. The Mayan dagger was tucked in his belt. He could feel it now, singing to him. He had a weapon. Hux just had... history to fight Tazia with.

"So, Iceman, are we ready?" Billy looked at Hux.

Hux rolled his eyes, but nodded. "Ready, Techno-Git."

"Then let's get on with it." As Billy flew, he saw Hux's rifle flash under the light of the moon.

———

Tazia felt eyes on her. She knew which house they sheltered in, could feel the magick rising from it. That was new. It wasn't what Jegudiel had told her would happen. She'd said a straight one-on-one fight: herself with Hux and the Advocate with Billy. So what was the spell?

She'd watched Jegudiel become more agitated as the power of the magick started to rise and reach them in waves.

"They're goading us. Ignore it." Jegudiel spoke from the mirrored pendant Tazia always wore around her neck now. As soon as she became corporeal, Heaven would see her, and the race would be on. Billy needed to die before the other angels joined him and the fight. If Jegudiel failed, or they arrived too soon, she'd be dead regardless of whether he was the one to destroy her.

And where would that leave her? Dead at Hux's hands, most likely. Or he'd be dead, and she'd be, what… free? *Hah!* That was a hope she no longer carried. But this magick had her itchy; those old tattoos still seemed to grip her in its presence.

"What is it? What are they doing?" Despite her father's training, magick had never sat naturally within Tazia's skill set. Too much patience and control required. She could feel the power flowing over her from the boarding house. What did it mean? There were eyes on her. She could feel that at least. Was it one set? Or hundreds? She shuddered. "Let's start the fight!"

"No." Jegudiel's voice was shrill. "That's what they want, pet. They want you to go to them, where they have the advantage. By forcing them to come to us, they'll need to fight their way through the crowds and the Soldiers. Trust me, Anastasia."

"But what's the spell?" Tazia paced, dodging out from behind the memorial of some long-forgotten soldier she hid behind. Her guard crouched down, his gun ready, beside her.

He was a Soldier demon. Celtic, just like Conn O'Cuinn. He had the same freckled skin, crew cut, and stature of a well-muscled warrior. He had the same lilting accent, too. Sometimes Tazia would make him repeat his orders just so she could listen.

"It doesn't matter." Jegudiel hissed into Tazia's ear. "Remember, we have the depths of Hell on our side. No spell can stop us."

The angel's red hair flashed in the mirror as she turned her head to listen to something. "He'll be here soon, Anastasia. I can hear him stirring. Just stay focused. I'll go and see where he is." Her image disappeared from the pendant.

But it was too hard to stay still. Tazia needed it done.

She paced once again outside the boundaries of the base of the monument. One step, two. She heard the *whoosh* of the bullet a fraction too late. It slammed into her shoulder, passing straight through her flesh, and grazing the bone of her right clavicle.

She spun but stayed standing. Just an ordinary bullet? *Hux!* Not even holy water?

He was taunting her. He could have shot her straight between the eyes, but chose not to. Just proving his strength. *Arrogant arsehole.*

Images flashed. Turin airport where he'd promised to kill her. How he'd cornered her in the stairwell in Detroit and broken her hand. Slammed her head into the bar in front of Cuinn. *Alpha male bullshit.* Always taking the control he hadn't earned. For years now she'd walked on a fucking knife edge with him.

Enough!

Her rage became visceral, churning her insides. Her eyes flashed red. A long, low growl deep in her throat. This time, he wouldn't win.

Without a word to her guard, she broke cover and darted between the half-humans milling around, heading straight for the house. It was time for her to call the shots.

37

VENGEANCE

FROM HIS HIDING place in a discarded mirror, one of several lying on the ground, Billy could see the cave in front of him where Jegudiel hid. He'd heard her talking with Tazia as she projected her image to the harbour in Boston.

It was cramped in the mirror. He stretched an arm a little, and the glass creaked alarmingly. Jegudiel looked in his direction, so he froze again. If he cracked the mirror, he'd have to leave, and he wasn't quite sure yet how to jump out of it without her seeing. It was too soon. This battle would be on his terms.

Despite his concern, he couldn't quite keep the smile from his face.

Her super-secret hideout, a pleat she'd jimmied in the fabric of space, wasn't hidden well enough. Her energy had left a trail from the harbour a child could follow. With his newfound ability to whizz between planes, tracking her had been almost too easy. *Thanks, Julie.*

He could now fly through the universe unseen, tracking anyone just by thinking about them. He'd spent the last twenty-four hours doing just that with Tazia. His initial joy at the ease of it had curdled as he watched her, a mindless robot, issuing orders and feeding from the humans Jegudiel provided.

That sadness had hardened into cold, pure anger. Jegudiel had stolen the beautiful soul Tazia had mourned for so long.

When Billy got angry now, the sparking blue light no longer burst from him uncontrolled. He felt the intensity build, a storm contained within his chest, stomach, arms, ready to be unleashed. He was in control. Not the power.

Only one thing disappointed him: no physical wings. Just flashes of light as he translocated. Very dramatic, but not the same as feathers. He glanced at his arms and the mirror creaked alarmingly. He froze again. Jegudiel looked in his direction. She'd definitely heard him. *Crap! How do I get out of this bloody mirror?*

He wanted to maintain the element of surprise. Creep up and stab her, easy as. No heroics. Just "Surprise!" then *poof*, the end of the bad angel. That was the plan he and Hux had hashed out, anyway.

Now though, she looked suspicious. He'd heard her mention a "he" who was coming. Some demon ally? The guy running the show. He didn't care. That new fight could wait. This one was personal. And he would win. He was a warrior angel. He was in charge and powerful. He rocked!

So how the hell do I get out of this fucking mirror?

The mirror creaked, again. Jegudiel looked directly at it. He was losing the element of surprise by the second.

She walked slowly in his direction, even had her angel dagger in her hand. It caught the light of the full moon that glowed just as strongly in this universe, and glittered at him, boasting a full complement of diamond studs.

Billy barely breathed.

Jegudiel squinted, scanning the landscape in front of her. Another step forward.

It was now or never.

Before he could move, a tremor vibrated through him. The spell on Earth. Events were unfolding. Hux and Tazia. He focused, drawing on the rising energy. This was the optimum time. He flexed deliberately, the mirror cracked in one corner, and Billy grinned. *Come closer, bitch, I'm waiting for you!*

The Advocate pinpointed the noise, and walked abruptly toward him, glaring at the mirror. On guard, she gripped her knife with white-knuckles.

Billy clutched his own dagger.

Ready.

Jegudiel took one more step. The mirror was at her feet, but the light from the full moon shone right into it and blocked her view.

He lowered his chin and tensed. Ready to spring—

Now!

He flexed his body with such force the mirror exploded up into Jegudiel's face.

She put up a hand to protect herself a second too late, and a large piece of glass embedded itself in her right eye. Reddened fluid seeped over the lower lid and trickled down her cheek.

Billy crashed through the remains of the mirror and into her world.

Howling, she stepped back and raised her dagger.

He flashed behind her.

She spun around.

He shifted again to her blind-side. She slashed out with her knife just as he pushed forward with his. The weapons met, and the clash of the two angel blades echoed out. The sky exploded above them—a beacon lighting the heavens—a sign to all that the fight had started.

The two struggled, pushing the blades against each other until Billy used his higher position on the slope to force hers away.

She didn't drop it, but groaned as her wrist cracked and her arm twisted back against the shoulder socket at slightly the wrong angle. He heard bone scrape against bone as the muscles and tendons were pushed aside.

While she still moaned, Billy gripped her by the back of the neck and flung her back toward the cave. She hit the wall, just by the opening, and fell to the ground, taking white stone and dust with her. Cracks spiralled up the side of the rock face.

Before she could recover, he was beside her, his hand clamping onto her ankle, and dragged her along the ground behind him. The hard rock scraped against her white skin, leaving tiny crystalline pieces embedded deep in the flesh, and her blood smeared the ground in a long red ribbon.

As he dragged her, the humiliation of losing Tazia to her in Las Vegas and then again on the side of the road in Boston, came flooding back to him. He struggled against the memories, reminding himself he was a soldier, and just needed to follow orders—to get the job done. But he wasn't yet "soldier" Billy, not completely. Too many years as a human left him needing revenge.

He couldn't just kill her; he needed to make her suffer the same powerlessness he'd felt. That she'd made Tazia and Hux feel.

He lifted her by the ankle and threw her into the cave itself. She crashed into the shelves carved out of the rock, and a hundred jars stacked high tumbled down, smashing on the floor, the lights inside them scattering out into the air. Some zipped out of the cave and up into the sky. Others circled weakly or skirted the floor before floating away on updrafts.

Billy watched them rise around him like he was upside down in snow globe. What the hell?

Her leg cracked as it hit the wall, and her weapon spun out of her hand to land at his feet.

"*No!*" From her position on the floor, she grabbed at the

jars, desperate to save them. Only one jar remained untouched high on the top shelf, its light buzzing noisy and bright.

A shadow passed over her face. When she looked up at him again, her good eye was glassy and set. Without flinching, she pulled the glass fragment out of her other eye, trailing sticky threads behind it. She wiped away the blood with the palm of her hand and ground the mess into the hip of her purple dress.

The cave vibrated with her fury, and more cracks spider-webbed across the walls. Rock dust rained down from the ceiling. He felt a wave of raw power slam against him, but he kept his feet under him and stared her down.

Billy kicked her knife back toward her. He didn't want it to be over. No heroics, Soren had said, but this had been too easy. Not only did he want to beat her fairly, he needed to beat her spectacularly.

At that moment he wasn't only an angel seeking retribution on the enemy of his Lord, he was a man seeking vicious revenge for the pain and suffering of his friend. "Come get me, Jegudiel. Just you and me now."

A smile whipped across her face. She picked up the knife. Then, using her good leg, pushed herself off the cave wall, springing at him just as he made his own leap toward her. She reached him a fraction of a second earlier, and her momentum rolled them both over and out of the cave entrance, through the reflecting pool outside. Her access to the world below.

Reality screamed as they fell through it. The universe dissolving into blinding, celestial light.

In that final flash, one triumphant image burned into his mind: the cave entrance collapsing, sealed forever beneath tonnes of rock.

38

THE SAVIOUR

SOREN STARED AT ANASTASIA, waiting for her play. She stood before him on the pavement in front of the old clapboard house. After the rifle shot had hit her precisely as he'd intended, he'd raced down the stairs and watched her push her way through the crowd to get to him. He hadn't wanted to hurt her, just get her attention. To slow her down enough to give him the upper hand when the fight began.

Through the sights of the rifle, he'd watched her agitated pacing back and forth by the monument on the hill, and knew he'd soon have a chance. Her impatience had let her down as always. It was a difficult shot, uphill, through the branches of trees that lined the road up to the hilltop, in the dark. But he could do it.

As he watched, she'd held a pendant up to her face like a mirror, her lips moving. Billy had figured that one out. Jegudiel was talking through the pendant. That boost Julie had given Billy made him the angel he was meant to be: smart, strong, fast. Senses off the charts. It gave him hope he could take the Advocate down. But that was Billy's fight. His was here. And right now, Soren only had eyes for Anastasia.

He'd anticipated her reaction. He knew she wouldn't allow herself to be picked off from a distance, and certainly not by him. Not after everything he'd done to her. No, this time, she'd want to win.

She'd run through the half-dead people, shouting orders to her soldiers to stand down before she'd come to a stop in front of the house. She wanted him for herself. And here she was, knife in one hand, eyes determined, and a half-grin goading him on.

For a split second, he imagined her as she used to be in the days when they'd fought beside each other in Turin. Then she'd looked fit and healthy with glowing skin, rounded muscles, and full cheeks. She'd looked human. Now she was just a graphic novel version of herself: pinched and lean, with hard muscles on her arms, and prominent cheekbones.

Behind him, the members of the coven chanted louder and more intensely from the basement. They were doing their jobs. He had to do his.

"This it then, Anastasia? You and me?" He stepped forward out of the shelter of the front door, not six feet from her. He also had a knife: long, serrated. It wasn't his usual switchblade. He'd wanted something more menacing. Something she wouldn't be expecting.

"No less than you wanted, lover." The smirk left her face for a moment as she heard the chanting emanating from within. "Magick, Hux? Since when did you need magick?"

"Just to keep the angel out." He had a lie prepared. "I wanted a fair fight."

The full moon was high in the sky, and for a moment, it seemed to hover above the fog to shine down on her. It caught in her hair. Streaks of blood and mud painted her. So many lives she must have taken over the last few weeks since she'd chosen the life of the Saviour. So much pain she'd caused.

Were they right to save her, to make her human again? Would she survive it?

"I'll give you a fair chance. Look, I didn't even bring a gun." She indicated the empty chest holster that usually carried her firearm.

"That was stupid. I taught you better." He brought his hand to the back of his belt and grabbed at the gun he'd put there earlier, swung it around and fired.

She leapt forward just in time. His shot went wide and grazed her right thigh while she was still in flight. In the crowd, one of the soulless was put out of its misery.

Anastasia landed on Soren's chest, feet first, and forced him backward through the door of the house. He sprawled onto his back while she landed solidly on her feet and stomped forward to lean over his prone body.

Blood from her shoulder and thigh seeped through her clothes. Not heavy. Not critical. He felt a surge of relief. The chanting downstairs was louder. Soren scooted backward along the ground, putting space between them, then rose carefully, watching for her next move.

"*You* taught *me*? You always were so up yourself for a soldier who couldn't even keep a job! Always so angry, Hux. So out of control. Pathetic!"

His eyes hardened.

She waited for him to get up, her head tilted to one side. "So sorry, lover. Did I hurt your feelings?"

Knife at the ready, he circled her slowly. His eye on the open stairway that led to the waiting witches. He needed to distract her, edge her toward it. "We don't have to do this, Anastasia. I don't want to hurt you anymore."

"Hurt me? You haven't even begun to hurt me." She matched his posture and movements with her own, crouching and circling, never taking her eyes from his, half a smile on her lips.

He smirked back. "Remember last time we fought? Your hand does." Soren glanced at her right hand, the one he'd smashed against the door of Cuinn's Irish Club in Detroit. "Remember how I humiliated you in front of your lover? Left you for dead when he turned back to his Core? Sided with the angel against you?" He deliberately distorted the truth.

A snarl replaced her smile. "Liar." She didn't pause to question him; she lunged, her knife slicing through the air where his throat had been a half-second before. The tip just nicked his skin.

He tapped at it with his left hand, saw the blood and grinned as it healed over. "Do better, lover."

"Fine." She snatched a second knife from her thigh holster. One in each hand. Before he had a chance to react, she flipped the first to hold the blade, then threw it at him circus style, transferring the second to her right hand. The knife circled in the air, and struck, sinking into his shoulder a full two inches. He gasped and dropped the gun to pull out the knife. Blood poured for a moment, then receded as the flesh began to restitch. It would take a while. The pain fired him further.

"Now we're even," she said.

"We were never even. I have a soul. You, don't even have your own mind."

She frowned. "I'm in total control." She circled to her left. He did likewise. She was almost at the steps.

"Yeah? You don't know, Anastasia. You're so lost now. So confused." He shook his head, adding as much sympathy to his voice as he could, all the while stepping forward, pushing her slowly back. "So lost. I bet you can't even remember your full name. Or why you killed Billy…"

"What? Billy's not dead!" She stopped and straightened. "Jegudiel said he wasn't dead—"

"Why did you kill him, Anastasia? He'd only ever loved you."

"Stop talking. He's not dead!" The kick was aimed at his knee—a disabling move. He barely twisted away in time, the force of the blow shuddering through the banister beside him.

"Of course he is. Do you see him here? Would he leave you to me after I abandoned you in Detroit? After I murdered Cuinn? If he was alive, he wouldn't leave you with me. He loved you too much to leave you with *me!*"

Hating himself, he saw a flutter of confusion in her frown and pushed further. "Have you been taking your pills? Did the Advocate give them to you?"

"No. I don't need them now, she said."

She sprang at him again, slashing with her knife this time. He blocked it. The blade sliced his forearm, healing before the blood even started to flow. The attack was strong, but sloppy. Uncontrolled. It was working. The confusion was making her reckless.

"She said you didn't need them? Really?" He shook his head. "So you don't get the attacks anymore?"

"No." She kicked out, her foot glancing off his leg as he easily dodged.

"What about the panic when you remember all those terrible things your father did to you?"

"What? He… No—" She stood still.

"Can you breathe when you think about the prison cell at the end of the Red River, Anastasia. Do you remember being trapped there?" He stepped toward her.

The words had the intended effect; he watched her bravado shatter. Her breath came in shallow pants. Her wide eyes lost focus, slipping to past horrors. Reminders of her father. It was too cruel. *So sorry.*

Chanting from the basement swelled. Could the witches feel the change in her? Were they digging in?

Anastasia's head jerked—like she was in another fight he couldn't see. *He wanted to hold her. Christ, I'm sorry!*

He forced himself on. "Really? You don't sweat and vomit and curl up in a little ball anymore? Don't talk to the walls? Didn't he chain you in that cell, lover?"

She shook her head, pressing a hand to her temple. "Stop it!"

He was in her face now. She took a step back instinctively, so she was standing on the very top step, completely unaware of the drop behind her back.

He reduced his voice to a whisper. Spoke right into her ear. "What about when you failed him, then? When I killed him, and you couldn't carry out his last wishes. Couldn't even keep your soul locked up. He knows. He'll come for you one day, and *put you back in that cell.*"

She froze.

He drew the tip of his knife in a shallow cut across her stomach like an artist would outline with a pencil. She didn't even attempt to block him, just looked down as blood, red and slick, seeped through her t-shirt. "Please, Hux… I—"

He gritted his teeth and shoved her backwards.

She lost her footing, and flailed forward to grab at him. Whispering, "Sorry," he stepped back out of reach.

With wide eyes, Anastasia fell backward down the narrow steps, knife flying. She rolled once and landed straight into Jacob's outstretched arms.

39

TAKE CARE OF MY GIRL

BILLY AND JEGUDIEL slammed into the basement of the boarding house, pulled there by the coven's magick and Billy's own raw will. The scene froze around them, like a snapshot of chaos held in amber.

Billy's gaze snapped to the bottom of the stairs. Tazia. On the floor, a blur of motion as Jacob dragged her toward the circle of witches. Above them, Hux caught mid-charge down the steps to reach her. The witches themselves were static in expressions of ecstatic singing: wide-eyed and open-mouthed, looking as though caught in the pivotal moment of a lover's embrace.

Jegudiel landed with a pained hiss. Dagger in hand, she awkwardly turned to absorb the scene behind her.

Billy's eyes turned back to her. He waited.

"What are you doing with Anastasia?" Her brow furrowed.

"She's about to deny you, Jegudiel. Very Judas-like!" He couldn't resist mocking her.

"What?"

"She's about to be given a choice."

"Don't speak in riddles, boy. Tell me!"

"Will she stay a demon or become human?" Billy stepped toward her, his dagger ready in his hand. He could feel the energy of the mobilizing angels, all heading toward the enemy. Julie would be among them. He needed to act. He wanted Jegudiel dead, not a prisoner for them to lock up. She didn't deserve even that much freedom.

"If Taz chooses to be human, we put right all the magick you and that bastard father of hers have done to her. Her soul will be pure. She'll be whole. Human. Not your puppet anymore. Not his. Her own person."

"She will never do it." Jegudiel shook her head. "She chose me before, angel. Stabbed you to please me. She is addicted to the power I have given her. She will not choose *this!*" She gestured with the knife at the witches.

"She will." The conviction settled in Billy's gut with absolute certainty. He saw the set of Hux's jaw, the fierce focus as he closed in on Tazia. Hux was in control. He'd find the right words. He had to.

Hoping to catch her off guard, Billy sprang forward, knife at her diaphragm.

She was ready for him. In an instant, she swung herself around to use the wall as support, then seized his dagger-bearing arm at the wrist with her free hand.

Digging her nails deep into his flesh, she twisted his wrist away and held it at arm's length. At the same time, she brought her knife around and held it to his chest, ready to strike.

Just in time, he grabbed her wrist, too. It was her injured arm. She winced. Then smiled.

They locked into a stalemate of muscle and will. Jegudiel snarled and pushed, the tip of her knife breaking the skin on Billy's chest. A searing hot needle. The effort to hold her back cost him his focus; the frozen moment he'd clamped on the room began to fracture, and the sound of the chanting rushed back in.

———

Soren raced down the stairs while Jacob fastened Anastasia into wooden handcuffs, then dragged her into the centre of the circle of witches. The cuffs were steeped in holy water, as were the ropes Soren used to tie her ankles. He worked quickly, ignoring her screams and the welts that circled under the ropes as the acid-like water ate into her skin.

When he was done, he sat behind her on the dirt floor in the middle of the circle. He held her close to him and whispered. "We can make it stop, Anastasia. We can make it all stop. You just have to want it. Tell me you want to be free of Jegudiel. All this pain will be over."

She trembled, but shook her head, resisting his words. She hit back, her skull against Soren's solid chest, but the magick and holy water weakened her by the second. He felt her strength fading.

"Stop fighting. Just stop fighting, please. I can make it all go away. Take away the pain. We can save you from Hell, Anastasia. You can be human! Just say yes!"

Still she fought, wrestling against his arms, trying to break through the magick that sapped her strength. The sound of the chanting grew louder and louder. He needed to find something else. Something that would appeal to any vestige of the soul that remained.

Then he had it. "You can save Billy, Tazia."

Panting hard, she hesitated. Stopped struggling.

He pressed on. "Look. Jegudiel will kill him." He turned her head with his hands towards where Billy and Jegudiel were fighting, and whispered to her urgently. "See, you can save him from her."

She stared at the two angels caught together, their knives in motion. Jegudiel's was already piercing Billy's chest. She shook her head. "No don't. Billy!"

Soren leaned in and hugged her to him, his cheek next to hers. He felt the sudden splash of her tears.

"You can save Billy, Taz. Feel your soul, again. What's it telling you?"

"I... I.."

"Look at him! If you choose to be human, she will lose, and he will live!"

"I—"

"CHOOSE!"

Anastasia twisted around and looked at Soren with deep brown eyes. Her tears still fell, but now her voice was determined. The word rang out: "YES!"

———

Only the panting of exhausted witches sounded in the cellar; the chanting had stopped when Tazia finally spoke the one word they had needed to complete the spell.

Billy heard it.

So did Jegudiel. "No!" She loosened her grip on her dagger enough for Billy to push back, thumping her hand off the stone wall until the bones crunched, and the knife tumbled from her fingers.

It was time to finish it.

As Jegudiel's attention wavered, her hold on Billy's right arm weakened too. He shrugged her off easily and brought his hand around in a sweeping movement. His dagger struck her in the soft flesh just below her ribcage.

She screamed and flailed. Swiping weakly at the dagger with both hands.

He forced the knife up, so that the curved tip reached her heart—and pushed on. "She chose life, Jegudiel. Human life. She chose her soul. You've lost her."

Her scream battered the energy in the room and shook the earth beneath them.

Holding his position, Billy took a breath. His lungs filled weakly, immediately panting out what he took in. His eyes fell on them again. Hux still held Tazia in the centre of the circle of witches, cradling her, stroking her hair, while she stared numbly into his eyes.

He had to get this over quickly, for her—for all of them. He forced another breath. This time filling his lungs. Unnatural lightning filled the room. The angels were nearly here. He called to them from his heart. *Help me finish it!*

With a surge of energy, Billy forced the knife into Jegudiel's chest still further, pushing down so the hilt itself started to penetrate her insides. He needed the black diamond to infiltrate her heart, to transfer to the organ. It was the only way she'd die.

Desperate now, he pushed again and twisted, his hand now in her rib cage, ignoring her screams and the pounding of her fists on his back and sides. *Come on, Billy, get it done!*

He shifted position. If he could use his full weight to jam the blade further in, to where the stud lay at its heel. Surely that would be enough. Blood poured from the wound, soaking both of them. With a last-ditch effort, he threw his weight onto her. Her good leg gave way, and the two of them slid down the wall. *This is it! The end!*

As they fell, a foul, sulphur stench flooded the cellar, and a darkness deeper than night swallowed everything. In a single moment, sight was wiped from his eyes. Just as quickly, it receded, leaving spots dancing in Billy's vision.

When it cleared, Jegudiel was gone. Billy was left on the ground, his hand covered in blood. She'd been ripped from his grasp.

He felt his fellow angels stop in their tracks and return to their stations.

The Advocate had escaped.

Victory gone, Billy had no breath left to scream. He covered his face with his hands and sobbed.

————

"Stop crying, dumbass." The woman Billy first took to be a witch came and sat next to him. Despite her admonishment, the tears still flowed down his cheeks, but he suppressed the gulping sobs.

"I failed, Julie. How could I fucking fail? She was right there."

"Her demon friend got to her, Billy. Nothing you could do." Julie wiped her wrinkled brow. The heat in the basement was overwhelming. A solid hour of continual magick coupled with fighting angels, a visit from an invisible demon, and the general heat in Boston had created a furnace. "Did you really think you'd win this first fight? She hasn't been on the lam for two thousand years for nothing. She knows all the tricks, honey."

Billy shook his head slowly, still not quite believing she'd escaped.

"You gave her one hell of a beating, though." Julie grinned, the ivory-coloured teeth in her wrinkled lips reflecting the light in the few candles that had managed to remain lit.

The other witches had sunk to the ground as soon as the spell was done. Soren still cradled Tazia in the centre of the circle. She watched him, the shock in her eyes slowly receding.

Hux, too, stared. He managed a smile and even a thumbs up, which Billy returned weakly.

"Are you up for round two?" Julie asked, interrupting this brief bonding moment.

"What?"

"You're fully angel now, Billy. But you still have a choice if you want it." She stretched her arms in front of her, the tanned skin gathering in loose bags over her brittle bones. He heard the joints clicking as she stretched.

"What choice?"

"I have permission to offer you your human form again. Revert back, back to Billy—the playboy, the technomancer, the poor kid made good." She pointed a long finger at Tazia. "Anastasia may need your friendship more than ever now that she's human and all."

Billy considered. Perhaps she did. She'd need to start over. She'd never lived as a human. She'd need someone to show her the ropes. What to eat. Where to live. Where to get a good haircut. Be a good example. He laughed. *Well, Billy can't do that, can he?*

Then he looked at Hux. What a beautiful god of a man! Even now, with his blond hair falling into his eyes like that, Billy wanted to cross the room and gently push it aside for him. The massive arms wrapped tightly around Tazia, showing her how safe she was, and those light blue eyes that made him want to fall in forever... *Cut the romance crap, Billy. He's got issues!*

"I think Hux is in a better position to provide all the friendship Taz needs." He stopped and whispered. "All the love. If she chooses it."

"If you think so."

"It's time to cut them loose, Julie. He loves her. Always has. I'm not sure whether she loves him, but now, as a human, she'll have a chance to find out. He'd die for her, too." He swallowed. "She's my girl, Ju, but it's time to let her go."

"So, you want to stay an angel?"

He wiped a hand across his eyes, mixing a streak of red with the tears. "Like you said. This is just round one, isn't it? While Jegudiel's alive, I need to be at my strongest. And that's an angel. Destiny and bloody duty, I suppose."

Julie stood up and offered her hand. "Go say goodbye to them, Billy. I'm going to take you home."

"Up… there?"

"Yep. I'll show you what it means to fly."

Smiling, Billy walked into the circle of exhausted witches. He hunkered down in front of Tazia and Hux. They didn't speak. He lifted Tazia's hand and kissed her fingers, grinned, and patted her playfully on the nose. Before standing, he stroked Hux's hair briefly—he just couldn't resist—and turned away.

But Hux caught his hand to prevent him from leaving. "What are you doing?"

"Fight continues, bruv." He squeezed his hand for a moment before walking back to Julie. As he reached her, he turned back. "Hey, Hux!"

"Yeah?"

"Take care of my girl!"

40

EPILOGUE

JEGUDIEL LEFT a trail of bloody footprints through the torch-lit maze of hallways. She picked the route by instinct, etched into her memory from countless prior visits, though none had ever felt this long.

She breathed in ragged gasps, blood still flowing in a shiny, sticky stream down her chest and the front of her purple dress. It collected at the hem and dripped onto the floor, revealing its crimson hue on the creamy marble slabs. Billy had missed her heart by only a fraction. She knew it was luck that had kept her alive. Nothing more.

She reached the meeting hall. A towering cavern with glacier-hewn walls, granite and sparkling black crystal. At the far end, a lower, more intimate space where a perpetual fire burned. The shuffle of her feet echoed as she approached two brown leather chairs facing the flames.

The damage was worse than she'd thought. Sensation on her right side was failing her with each step. Her vision in her one good eye also tunnelled with lack of oxygen. She would need to rest soon. But first, she had to get things in order.

She saw only his hand at first. The rest of his body was

shielded by the curved wings of the high-backed chair. He swirled blood around a tumbler haphazardly. The thick red liquid clung to the walls of the glass, showing how dangerously close it had come to spilling over the top.

Occasionally, the glass disappeared from view, and she heard him sip and swallow.

This walk from one side of the cavern to the other was long. She'd never noticed it before, but back then she'd almost skipped it, light on her feet, clipping quickly in her purple boots. Now, each step was a painful reminder of how she'd lost the fight with an angel half her age.

She pushed the hair from her face, peeling away the sections that had fallen forward and stuck to the sweat on her brow, dried blood forming twisted rat-tails in places.

Finally, she got to the fire and collapsed into the empty chair beside him.

He didn't look at her, and silence ticked on before he said, without an ounce of emotion, "You failed."

She sought to gather the breath that dragged in her chest.

"She is free now." This time, there was a catch in his voice.

She heard it with a mixture of annoyance and amusement. "Yes, free," she agreed with an equally sarcastic tone. "Why did you wait so long before helping me?"

The Abbot threw his glass violently into the fire, the remaining drops of blood transforming into tiny steam clouds before they were sucked upward and started the long journey out into the night air.

The Advocate jumped slightly, and pain tidal-waved up from her chest, into her left temple. It was getting hard to focus.

"My daughter is human, Jegudiel! After everything we did to create her."

"Everything *we* did, Stephen? I seem to remember you

signing up for the deal kicking and screaming. Why did you not come?"

He glared, but she couldn't bring herself to care. There was too much pain.

"I pulled you out, Jegudiel. Besides, I had other things to do. This was your failure, not mine."

That was it. Dismissed. It took all she had to remain calm and penitent. He had power over her now. She was so weak he could destroy her if he wanted to. But it wouldn't always be that way.

"Plan B, then." She just got the words out before the cough she'd been trying to suppress caught up with her. Blood shot from her mouth onto the floor in front of her chair. Another hacking cough. She managed to get her hand in place this time. The blood gathered warm and wet in the centre of her palm.

For the first time, he looked at her with interest. He stood, leaned over and gathered the liquid from her palm with his tongue, and swallowed hard. Then he sucked each digit clean. She shuddered, and not from pain this time.

He retained hold of her hand for a moment. "The necromancer did not cooperate. I put him back for you to play with. Perhaps you can convince him. You can be so... persuasive." He smiled slightly.

"And the other?"

He shrugged. Letting go of her hand, he jerked his head toward the back of the hall to indicate she should follow him, then briskly walked away, paying no heed to her disabled state.

Jegudiel quietly seethed.

She pushed herself to a standing, swayed, and stumbled after him. Now completely useless, her right leg dragged, her boot catching in places on the edges of the huge marble tiles so that, now and then, she had to pause to unhook it. It would be just moments before she collapsed completely.

The cell was chiselled from the rock; one of many stretching down the corridor, all silent. There was no key. The Abbot waved his hand in front of the thick wooden door; it clicked and fell open. He stepped inside just as Jegudiel caught up. She remained in the doorway, leaning her whole body against the door frame for support.

The prisoner sat against the far wall. Arms stretched above his head, secured at the wrists by manacles pounded into the rock. A wide iron collar encircled his neck and forced his head into an upright position. It cut into his skin, and in places had pierced through to his jawbone. His feet were tied with spiked wires that had been there so long the flesh had started to grow around them.

"Are you ready to earn your freedom?" The Abbot asked and shifted to one side so the torches around the doorway lit the space inside.

The prisoner squinted at the two intruders for several seconds, his eyes changing in an instant from a beautiful sea-green hue to ice blue.

Conn O'Cuinn nodded his assent.

AUTHOR'S NOTE

The *Dark Urban Rising* trilogy was my first published work in 2017, then slightly updated in 2019. I had several novels hidden in desk drawers (or more realistically, stashed on old laptops,) but had never felt my stories were ready for an audience until *Fighting Spirit* was born.

In 2025 I decided to review and improve the trilogy. My writing skills had improved and I felt that finally I could represent the stories in the way I first envisaged. The rewrites were an act of indulgence, but I'm glad I took the time. I hope you are too.

— S M Henley, January 2026

Here is the original Author's Note from 2017:

Thank you for reading *Hero Worship*.

I had no clue Billy was going to be an angel before I started writing. My first draft had him most definitely human, and more into the technological espionage side of things. In fact, there was a whole section I removed that had him hunting

Joshua down in the middle of a steel and glass HQ of a pharmaceutical giant in Germany.

Maybe I'll use that one day…

When I started writing him though, he had other ideas, and suddenly I had to rewrite the Epilogue of *Fighting Spirit* to hint at his upcoming transformation. In fact, both the angelic characters in *Dark Urban Rising*—Billy and Jegudiel—weren't supposed to be there. But there's always that moment as an author when you've got to stop fighting, and let the characters have their heads.

Billy also went from being a teenager in the first draft to a middle-aged playboy, to a vampiric/angelic hybrid, before I finally settled on the twenty-six year old angel he ended up being.

[Kudos if you noticed he had a birthday between Book 1 and 3. Have a gold star!]

Anyway, I hope you enjoyed *Hero Worship*. If you did, please consider leaving a review on the ebook platform of your choice. Your feedback really makes a difference not just to sales but also to me. As an author, it helps to know your words are being read and enjoyed.

This second published novel marked a change in me. I stopped agonizing about every word and scene and let the story unfold itself. My style relaxed a little too. And apart from Billy, the process was smoother than *Fighting Spirit* which my paranoia forced me to rewrite too many times to count.

Next up Soren Huxford is centre-stage. It's a hard-fought tale for him, and one in which both Tazia and Billy have an active role, as well as a certain Irish demon. We tie up all the loose ends of the story with an action-packed ending.

Well, most of the loose ends, anyway. We need some for a new character to unravel… You'll meet her in a cameo role in Book 3 (so keep an eye out for her) ready to launch her own series soon.

To read Chapter One of *Raw Deal*, the final book in the *Dark Urban Rising* trilogy, turn the page, tap, or click. We open with Hux trying to take his mind off Tazia, and thinking of puppies, yes, really!

Always in darkishness,

S M Henley

PS If you're ready to buy *Raw Deal* straight-away, you can find a link to your favourite ebook store here: https://book s2read.com/rawdeal.

EXCERPT FROM RAW DEAL
1. TAKING CARE OF BUSINESS

The dog yapped up a storm trying to gain the attention of passing strangers. Through the rifle sights, Soren tracked the source. A handbag dog. A tiny white fur ball with a pink tongue and scrappy hair tied up over its paper-thin skull with a bow. Trapped in the car, it raced between the seats and desperately licked at the little fresh air that floated through the sliver of an open window. It would die in this heat.

Soren growled lightly in the back of his throat and caressed the trigger of his gun; he would do it a favour—

A movement in the car parked in front yanked him back. His target.

Although under cover, the sun was just at the right angle to bounce off the guy's bald head as he leaned forward and peered into the side mirror to check his teeth. He'd been eating a burrito packed with sloppy meat, chopped lettuce, and a nice thick layer of bright orange cheese. Soren's mouth watered for the food; his usual lean breakfast had been hours ago.

Balancing Oakleys above his eyebrows, the target continued to pick at his teeth without the distraction of a dark tint. Soren clocked the teeth: ebony black and sharpened to points, studded with little jagged diamond shards that flashed in the burning sun. A Bone Cruncher. A rich one—no one could afford that tooth job without great dental.

Despite the easy shot, he waited. If he fired now, Bald Guy would end up slumped out the window, blood spraying the perfectly white paintwork of his Dodge truck. Too messy. He wanted a clean job. Besides, it was a rental. Why should a low-paid high school kid have to clean up blood and brains? Not fair. He'd wait longer.

Still motionless, lying flat on his stomach, Soren eased out a breath. It tickled the feather, which had landed on his stretched out forearm thirty minutes ago, making it shimmy a fraction then settle again. It was down, a fluff feather used to keep the bird warm, not to help it fly. The magpie, the most probable owner, watched him from the stainless steel railing of the balcony with a beady look Soren sporadically returned. It eyed his wristwatch. Was it figuring out the time, or just attracted by the slight reflection on the black surface? Most probably the former. These days, birds weren't stupid.

He'd picked the apartment block on purpose. Only two stories high, but right in the centre of town, it was unusual for Las Vegas. It sheltered behind one of the huge, flashy hotel complexes right on the Strip. A holiday let. Cheap because of the mall car park he stared into. No view of a swimming pool or fountains moving in time to the *Star Wars* theme tune, just concrete, and row upon row of bland rental vehicles with the occasional celebrity dick-mobile thrown in for good measure. Even the rich and famous need mall stuff. Or else wanted their egos stroked for being seen out among Regular Joes.

Fame was pointless. Soren couldn't have told Miley Cyrus from Kim Kardashian. They were just faces, and fame just noise.

Bald Guy settled back in his seat, slurping a Coke directly

from the can—his fourth that day. The opportunity for the shot had passed.

Soren blinked and flexed his fingers. He'd wait all day if he had to.

Four jobs deep this month, Vegas crawled with demons. Some had always been here; others escaped the Risings elsewhere. It was a place where they could make some fast cash. Gambling, sex shops, gun sales. Everything in plain sight, the way the city had always done it. No change on the surface, but he knew better. He'd seen Detroit, the first city to fall. Five long, painful years from the first demon to the destruction of the last human. Stealthy. The underground taking control. And now, places were falling every day. The biggest surprise was Texas just last week; it had been all over the demon network. The decision-makers just handed over the keys. *Done and dusted in a month.*

Soren grunted. The whole damn state. *How the hell does that happen? Resistance was strong in the South.*

As though in response, the magpie hopped along the railing toward him, its head cocked, eyes staring. When its persistence forced brief eye-contact, it shook its wings to release a second feather. This one was for flight, a beautiful midnight blue. It floated down past the sights of the rifle. *Still no wind to factor—*

Movement pulled him back. Bald Guy was on his phone, getting pretty animated, too. Lots of hand-waving and shoulder-shrugs. His car was side-on to Soren's view, right by the walkway. People were passing by the demon all the time. Children dragged by the hand behind a parent or pushed in front in a buggy, everyone laden with bags and balloons, even now. Holiday towns! Another reason not to shoot yet; he didn't want to be responsible for some poor kid's PTSD.

The walkway emptied at the same time as Bald Guy put down his phone and stared out of the side window. *Perfect.*

Soren got ready. His breath continued to flow gently. No drama. This job had been textbook: a three-day stakeout, and now, the shot. Job done. Money in hand.

Just taking care of business like always.

Soren needed the work. The money was nice, but the distraction was better. Kept his mind off her. Mostly.

There was never any likelihood Anastasia would fall into his arms, not after Boston. But he'd thought she might at least throw him a small bone. Some kind word, or a promise to talk in the future. Just talk. Christ, was that too much to ask? But turning human hadn't sat well with her. She was having problems adjusting. And that vicious tongue!

Soren growled again, deeper this time. Long and low. That special sound he kept just for her. After Boston, she hadn't even given him a chance. But then, did he deserve one?

He'd tried to explain. The words had come out wrong, too clinical, he knew, but what else could he say? *We used you. Trapped you.* His apology—*so fucking sorry*—had met a wall of silence. Nothing. He could still see her face, the flicker of disgust in her eyes before they went blank.

He'd offered to go wherever she wanted. He would just run alongside, keeping her safe. No strings. But she wouldn't even give him that. He'd known she wouldn't let him; she could take care of herself. Still, her last words before she left to go walkabout were unnecessary: *I'll cut your fucking heart out if you follow me.*

Soren breathed out slightly more heavily, with a conscious effort this time.

Box it up, soldier!

Still, he struggled. She stalked his thoughts, sometimes dancing on the periphery, smiling and teasing him. At other times, she came clearly into view, glaring, and flipping that damn knife from hand to hand.

He didn't know this new Anastasia. Human now, was she

as capable a killer as the demon she'd once been? She hadn't even wanted Billy with her. That *was* a little satisfying, the fact she seemed to blame Billy as much as him, but only a little. Billy was the good guy in all this. He was flying with the angels, making plans to save the world, and would probably lead the charge against the demons when the time was right.

He'd told Soren to relax: *Give her a break, bruv. Let her twist her knickers for a while.*

Well, she'd been twisting them for six weeks, and the waiting was killing him.

Soren did the last checks and prepared to squeeze the trigger.

For now, he worked. He took the contracts and killed the targets in this sweatbox of a city that both intrigued and repelled him. It was as good a place as any to wait for Heaven to make its plans, and to tell him what his role would be in the coming battle.

And for his own avenging angel to return.

The musical fountain surged to its crescendo. He braced and fired.

The loud crack shocked the magpie up into the air, but it soon settled again a couple of feet away. They don't give up ground that easily, little bastards. In the parking garage, no one seemed to notice.

Bald Guy's head snapped back against the neck rest, bouncing once. His body went limp in the seat. His head tilted to the side. He blinked once, then his eyes stuck wide and staring. A dark blue trickle of blood flowed from the wound between his eyes and followed gravity over the bridge of his nose and across the top of his cheek. One drop fell from him into the darkness of the car and then stopped. Coagulation was quick for this sort of demon.

Soren nodded, clean enough.

A pathetic whimper drifted to the balcony. The dog. A

desperate plea for help. Still lying in the same position, Soren shot again, this time at the SUV where the dog sheltered. The front side window exploded.

Without checking the result, he broke up the rifle and put the pieces back into its padded carrier. He took a few photographs through the spotting-scope then packed that away too. As he stood up, he replaced his sunglasses and briefly bared his teeth at the magpie, who squawked in mild alarm, then turned its back.

Soren casually walked through the living room, leaving the balcony doors wide open. Behind him, the dog yapped loudly as it breathed cooler air at last. He smiled. No doubt it would soon be in the arms of a puppy-loving Good Samaritan.

As he left the apartment, he gave a satisfied grunt: it was time to collect his payment.

———

Raw Deal is available from all good ebook sellers and in paperback. Go to https://books2read.com/rawdeal/ to link to your favourite.

THE SPOIL HEAP

The Spoil Heap is not a newsletter. It's an introduction to the things you missed. A round-up of what I've already dragged to the surface of **The Midden**, along with a look at what's still buried.

It's there for those with the sense to ask. Just give me an email worth using.

—Digger

https://darkishfiction.com/sign-up

New subscribers receive *Bleeding Ebony* by return. Consider it a first round, on me.

ACKNOWLEDGEMENTS

My gratitude goes to:

My editors, Megan Harris for being gentle with a newbie, and Mary Matthews for her commitment to pickiness; to Kieran Clynes for impeccable beta reading and for living with the characters this long; to www.derangeddoctordesign.com for a kickarse cover; and, finally, to Rick Gualtieri for his words of blurb.

And, of course, thank you to my readers. I appreciate each one of you!

ABOUT THE AUTHOR

S M Henley was brought up in an English seaside town singing to Echo and the Bunnymen and worshipping Siouxsie Sioux. She now lives in rural Alberta, Canada, with more pets than people, where everyone is friendly, winters are long, cheese is bright orange, and the occasional moose wanders through her yard.

Her writing spans Urban Fantasy through Horror. The UF is darker than average. It dips a toe into Dystopia and splashes blood freely. The Horror is a little darker and is written under the pen name, Ellis Marsh. Still paranormally themed, characters run from flawed to freaky, blood is optional.

ABOUT DIGGER

Digger introduced himself after the first trilogy was written. He now tends bar and watches the signs.

He knows more than the Author, but not too much more. He writes **The Midden** and curates **The Spoil Heap**.

Learn about the author and Digger on the website: https://darkishfiction.com

ALSO BY S M HENLEY

Available now in digital and paperback versions, the complete *Dark Urban Rising* trilogy:

Book 1 - Fighting Spirit

Book 2 - Hero Worship

Book 3 - Raw Deal

The Dark Urban Rising Box Set (the Complete Trilogy) (ebook only)

And the prequel novella (ebook): *Bleeding Ebony*. The story of Tazia's time at Her Majesty's Pleasure in 1995. Only available with newsletter sign up.

———

And from the continuation series set in the *Dark Urban Rising* world just after the Tipping Point, *Skye Quest*:

Skye Wolf (a prequel novella) (ebook only)

Book 1 - Dead Playboy (coming soon in ebook and paperback)

———

For synopses and purchasing information and to keep track of new releases, visit: https://darkishfiction.com

www.ingramcontent.com/pod-product-compliance
Lightning Source LLC
Chambersburg PA
CBHW061609190726
48288CB00007B/2248